THE SOUL OF AN OWL

Trisha St. Andrews

This is a work of fiction. Names, characters, places, and incidents either are the product of the author's imagination or are used fictitiously. Any resemblance to actual persons, living or dead, events, or locales is entirely coincidental.

629Publications.com
www.TrishaStAndrews.com

Dedicated to the memory of my kind and gentle mother, Joan Patricia Hurlburt Weatherhead, 1930-2016, who read to me as a child, loved to write poetry, and engendered in me a passion for poetic prose.

CHAPTER ONE

"It's no use going back to yesterday, because I was a different person then."— Lewis Carroll

Excerpt from psychiatric consultation: April 6, 2016

"**W**hat is your earliest recollection?"

Luca stared at her as if she'd asked him if he were a crocodile. He lowered his smoldering deep-brown Italian eyes, and squinted in forced concentration, attempting to access the early childhood he'd somehow carelessly erased. His lips tightened and his mouth downturned into a scowl that resisted responding, as if it were none of her business.

But Luca Gherardini, age seventeen, preparing to graduate from the Swiss Conservatory for Boys in Lucerne, was most definitely her business. Luca, heir to the Gherardini fortune, would be entitled to his legacy and estate within the year, and his emotional stability and state of mind needed to be determined before that portentous day arrived. His future depended on it and he knew it. Her professional integrity depended on it and she knew it.

She persisted. "Let's try it again, Luca. Close your eyes. Relax. There's no time pressure. Your earliest memory."

Luca closed his eyes.

"The sound of a bird...an owl."

She leaned forward.

"Good. How about a face, a voice, a smell?"

His eyes opened, fixed on nothing in particular.

1

"Jasmine," he whispered. "The scent of jasmine."

Greta Landis tried not to reveal her gratification. He'd cooperated and accessed two memories, after how many attempts? *Was he being honest or manipulating her?* She took a deep breath and pursued the train of thought.

"Jasmine...perhaps outside your nursery window?" She paused. "Your mother's cologne?"

"How should I know?" Luca answered abruptly, leaving the zone. "They dumped me here when I was three years old. You know that. I don't remember my mother. You know that too. You've read my files. You know everything about me. Why does this matter? Tell me why I'm here. It's a waste of time. I'm not going to remember anything else."

"You remembered the sound of an owl and the scent of jasmine, Luca."

Luca shrugged his shoulders and glared at her.

"So? I remembered a bird and a flower. What's the point?"

"Let's take another approach. Tell me about your friends, say, Damien Scardina or Gabriel Germond."

Luca's right leg pumped against the floor as he stared at the psychiatrist without blinking.

"They're friends, that's all. What's there to tell? Damien is unpredictable, which I like. He's funny, sometimes outrageous, thinks outside the box, very smart. He likes word games, rhymes, and he quotes Bible verses but I can't hold that against him. His mother is uber-religious. Gabriel's a contrarian, a philosopher, and I like that because he keeps me on my toes. A straight shooter. They're both important to me because I trust them. They didn't choose to be my friends because I'm going to be very rich someday. Our fathers were friends so we share a history. May I go now?"

"Not quite yet."

Luca sighed and started beating drum rhythms on his legs.

"Let's examine one other thing you said earlier, Luca. You used the words 'dumped here.' Tell me what that means."

Greta saw anger, a reptilian coldness in his eyes. A shiver of fear tremored in her chest and through her upper extremities. *Had she reason to fear him?* Maybe she was just sensing his frustration and annoyance. She should have been be able to read him better. She was educated and paid to read students like Luca.

He stopped his drum cadence with a final slap to his knees. With both hands, he forked his fingers through his thick dark hair.

"All right. If I need to say it again, I will. I have suffered from a rejection originating in my early childhood. I was abandoned by my mother and dropped here by my half-brother, which translates as being abandoned twice by the age of three. Because I had no family, I didn't have a sense of worth, and my grief and rage caused me to act inappropriately in my formative years. But I have come to terms with my issues. I have matured, moved on. I am not a danger or a threat to anyone. I just want to get on with my life."

He had delivered his perfunctory statement as if he were a prisoner making a case for parole, and in a sense he was.

"May I go now?" he asked.

"Yes. Our hour is over," she responded.

She watched the tall, handsome, smart, about-to-be wealthy young man walk to the door without so much as a good-bye or thank you, and she shivered once again.

Excerpt from psychiatric consultation: April 12, 2016

Emily Walker surveyed the psychiatrist's office. Wall-to-wall bookcases, filled with psychiatry journals and leather-bound tomes, lined the room's perimeter. If Emily, a professor of American literature, was at all intimidated, her equanimity didn't give her away.

"Professor Walker, I am currently serving as Luca Gherardini's psychiatrist. As you are well aware, Luca's past behavioral problems have been a concern to the staff and administration of this institution. May I be direct?"

"Please," Professor Walker said. She crossed her shapely legs, rested her arms on the chair, simultaneously raised her chin and eyebrows, and leaned back with relaxed dignity.

"According to my file, the incident dating back to 2010 regarding the death of Luca's classmate was never ruled a murder, although suspicions ran rampant at the time that Luca was involved in the tragedy. It is my responsibility to determine whether or not Luca is of sound mind. Professor, you have apparently been a stabilizing force in his life, and according to other staff members, possibly a mother substitute for him. I admit that in the past few years, I've not been aware of any behavioral aberrations and find him to be a well-adjusted young man, despite his resistance to continuing sessions with me. However, as you are also aware, he is about to graduate, and on this eighteenth birthday, he will inherit a staggering fortune. I have been asked by a regent of our institution, who will remain unnamed, to observe Luca through counseling, and determine his stability and character." Greta paused.

"And how might I help you? And please call me Emily."

"All right. Emily, do you believe Luca Gherardini is a danger to anyone? And, do you believe he will be able to deal responsibly and maturely with the fortune he is about to inherit?"

Emily clasped her long-fingered hands together and placed them on the desk that separated them like a river in a canyon.

"As you know, Luca was abandoned when he was too young to remember. In some ways, this is a blessing. Had he been ripped from loving parents in a traumatic memory, he would have suffered more severely. Nevertheless, and I don't mean to depreciate the ordeal of his abandonment, but I don't believe that he came to understand his 'situation' until years later. He watched other boys leave school during the summer and winter holidays because they had families who wanted them. It was painful. It was his seclusion during the holidays that magnified his aloneness and eventually his feelings of rejection and abandonment. This recognition of his plight shattered him, leaving him isolated and wounded. When the intensity of his shame internalized, we all witnessed his behavioral rage-when he was seven to nine years old, around the time of that terrible hanging of the younger classmate. Keep in mind, he was never charged as the perpetrator of that death."

Without blinking her glacier blue eyes, Greta interrupted. "Do you honestly think that young boy killed himself?"

"It was ruled a suicide."

"Do you believe that?"

Emily's back stiffened as she leaned forward. "No, I believe it was an accident. But to the point, Luca Gherardini was not involved. I was there at the juvenile hearing. He is innocent."

"But indulge me, if you will. How can hanging by a belt in a closet be accidental?" asked Greta. She placed her hands in a prayer position, with her elbows resting on the desk, and brought her fingertips to her lips.

"I am not at liberty to talk about this," continued the professor, "but Luca Gherardini was not involved."

"How can you be sure?"

"You're going to have to take my word for it. You're asking me what I believe to be true; and that is, it would be irresponsible and outrageous to condemn a person for something of which he was accused and then acquitted of doing."

"Fair enough. Please tell me about his reconciling his past abandonment."

"Well, we both know that abandonment can lead to a lone-wolf syndrome, a solitary inability to connect to others due to lingering grief."

Greta nodded.

"Luca is well liked by his classmates and has a strong relationship with Gabriel Germond who graduated two years ago and their mutual friend Damian Scardina who has just graduated. They're a virtual triumvirate and everyone knows this."

"I am aware."

"I admit there was a time when he was disconnected from others. But those feelings of despair and hopelessness dissipated, and I believe he has overcome his sorrow to build a good life. He's smart, you know."

"Is he smart enough to mask his real feelings in order to escape judgment or possibly the withholding of his inheritance?"

Emily pushed a stack of books to the side of the desk to make clear the path of communication between them. Slowly and deliberately, enunciating each word as if she might never use them again, she spoke.

"Luca has been on an amazing journey from rejection to acceptance. He's realized that his situation says more about the adults in his early life than about him. I have never given birth to a child, but I have listened to Luca and counseled him like a son. I have watched his transformation from an injured animal to a self-reliant young adult. Please don't stand in his way."

"Thank you, Emily. You've been most helpful. I've heard all I need to hear. I appreciate your coming."

Emily stood up rigidly, nodded, offered her hand in a polite handshake, and reverted back to a more formal, less friendly tone.

"You're welcome, Dr. Landis."

Excerpt from psychiatric consultation: April 21, 2016

"Regent Germond, thank you for coming. I appreciate your making the appointment so promptly."

Greta Landis watched him cross the room with a slight but obvious limp. He was a barrel-chested man whose upper body appeared stronger than his lower extremities. His most outstanding feature was a large head with bushy eyebrows.

As she motioned him to a chair, he acknowledged her with a faint smile of crooked teeth.

"Thank you," he said. He took a seat on the opposite side of her massive Cocobolo desk.

"As you know, we are here to discuss our student Luca Gherardini," she continued. "Since joining the staff here at SCB, I have had numerous meetings with Luca, as well as having recently conferred with his professor, Emily Walker. Despite the concerns I have over this student's past behavior, I must admit we're referencing *past* behavior. I would appreciate it if you would voice your concerns and shed some light on the letter you sent me last week."

Clement Germond smoothed his goatee with his left hand a number of times, as if counting his points to be addressed. After all, he was an attorney.

"Although I needn't say this, anything we discuss remains in this office. Understood, Dr. Landis?"

"Greta." She nodded.

"I prefer keeping this professional, Dr. Landis. I have been anxious about this young man on a number of levels for almost a decade. As you know, the misdeeds and atypical behavior in his formative years were most distressing to the staff, parents, students, and administrators of this institution. Secondly, during his middle and later years with us, I have been troubled with my own son's close association with Luca, although my open discourse with and confidence in my son's judgment has somewhat mitigated that concern. But thirdly, and the specifics of this I cannot legally discuss with you, I have found myself the executor of the Gherardini estate. Luca's eighteenth birthday is approaching, and as I explained to you in my letter, it is my legal obligation to handle his sizable trust fund and estate in a responsible and equitable manner."

Clement cleared his throat as if either coughing to get closer to his next sentence or swallowing what he couldn't tell her.

"Let me say that there are pieces of the puzzle that haven't fit together as I would have hoped. This is not just a legal issue. It is, as you might surmise, an ethical issue as well. Dr. Landis, do you think that Luca Gherardini is a danger to anyone?"

The fingers of her right hand tapped the desk top as if playing a drum cadence, as she looked down at her file. She then looked at Clement for a few seconds before speaking.

"No, I find no reason to be concerned about his current state of mind, other than his impatience with me, digging into his past for resolution. I frankly find myself asking what needs to be resolved. He has not been the focus of any disturbances for years, Regent Germond. I mean…what are we looking for?"

"This is highly confidential. There is an indication that his deceased mother was a psychopath. His early behavior led us to believe that perhaps his predisposition, whether maniacal or chemical, might have been hereditary. That, coupled with the issues of having been rejected as a young child, added a risk that may have contributed to an instability that borders on dangerous. Nature and nurture are in question. A double whammy, so to speak. I need to determine whether or not he should have a guardian or conservatorship in place, despite his coming of age. You are the psychiatrist on staff. I'm hoping for your unequivocal opinion, one way or the other."

Greta inhaled a breath fringed with nervousness, detecting a faint whiff of cigar smoke that perhaps Clement had brought with him. She stared at the man before her whose brow was furrowed like two caterpillars trying to connect.

"Then, I must say that I think your young man has made the journey from desperation to equilibrium. I find no psychological reason to withhold his inheritance from him."

Clement sighed. "That's all I need to know. I thank you for your time."

He stood, shook her hand, and let himself out. The breeze from her open window slammed the door behind him, like an exclamation point.

She walked to the window to close it and froze like a statue while she watched Clement Germond get into his car and drive away. As he disappeared from her sight, she reflected on the power of her opinion and the finality of her decision. In the distance, she heard a siren. Someone was in trouble.

She shivered, just as she had in Luca's presence. Emily Walker's implication that Luca had traveled from the shores of rejection to the mainland of recovery surfaced. Greta hoped that her perception of future redemption was not a disguise for future retribution.

Dr. Greta Landis had given her opinion, and she had better be right.

CHAPTER TWO

"There is a higher court than courts of justice. It is the court of conscience which supersedes all other courts."—Gandhi

Eight years earlier, Clement had read a letter from Luca's deceased mother, Sofia, who implied that she had enemies, and were she to unexpectedly die, these enemies would be responsible for her death. Luca was to target them in an act of vengeance.

Clement found himself in a compromised position. It was a morally charged issue, because Clement had opened a sealed envelope, addressed to Luca, to be handed to him on his eighteenth birthday. But due to both Luca's aberrant behavior in school at the time and Clement's suspicion that Sofia lacked a moral compass, he had justified his preemptive opening of the letter to protect the boy from his mother, if need be. Upon reading the letter, he'd decided to withhold the envelope from Luca. Clement would not be responsible for a posthumous reprisal, endangering not only the targets of Sofia's revenge, but Luca's future.

Then there was the issue of the missing file that contained a safe deposit key and a reference to passports. Luca's executor Santino Scardino had died without indicating either the referenced articles or their location. Clement, who inherited the files and executorship, had asked Santino's wife Mariana if she would search for the missing Gherardini file in Santino's home office, but she'd come up empty-handed. So the instructions of how Sofia Gherardini wanted her son to carry out her wishes were at large, and by the grace of God, remained a mystery and omitted from Luca's estate records.

Clement Germond's moral issue of withholding information from his client became a moot point, his personal secret, leaving nothing other than the account in the Cayman Islands to bequeath to the young man. Meanwhile, Clement had the opportunity to watch the behavior of Luca Gherardini from two views in the stands. Clement was a regent at the conservatory for boys, so he was privy to any complaints about, accusations against, or misdeeds of the students. And both his son Gabriel, who had graduated from the conservatory, and Gabriel's friend Damien Scardina, Santino's only son, were friends with Luca, so Clement on occasion, observed Luca in his own home.

Regarding the missing documents, he recalled his first exasperating call to Mariana. He knew about her forlorn state on the heels of her husband's death, because she frequently spoke with Clement's wife Fiona for consolation. He was grateful that Mariana had Fiona as a sounding board for her lamentations and devout rantings, because he found them tedious and difficult to address. Women were better at consoling; at least, Fiona was better than he.

His detachment from the situation was further distorted by the knowledge that although Santino loved his wife, her fervent religious beliefs had afflicted their marriage. Her constant religious allusions morphed into an extremism Santino didn't understand, or care to. Clement knew firsthand that sending Damien to boarding school was strictly a paternal decision, protecting Damien from his mother's delusional fanaticism.

But despite his reluctance to interact with Mariana, Clement had needed her cooperation. He lived in Switzerland, and she in Italy, so he couldn't simply drop by the house and ask to search Santino's home office for the missing documents. He didn't hold out hope that she would find the lost pieces of the Gherardini puzzle, but he had tried. It was a matter of personal ethics, although deep in his heart, he knew that it would be a mystery better left unsolved. Hoping that having her son home for the holidays would put her in a receptive, generous frame of mind, he had called her at Christmastime. He remembered their interaction as if it were yesterday.

"Oh Clement, I'm so glad you called," she'd said. "I miss Santino dreadfully. I'm still in shock that he died before I did, considering my poor health which has long been my cross to bear. It's lonely, Clement, so lonely. Thanks to God that Damien is home from school this week. I have no one else. Maybe the Lord will just take pity on me and free me from this earthly body to be with Him in heaven."

Not wanting to listen to her whining harangue, he changed the subject.

"I'm sorry, Mariana. You know our sons have become friendly over the years at boarding school?"

"Yes, he's told me. I must admit that it's a comfort to know that you and Fiona are close, in case my boy needs someone. *Children are a heritage from the Lord.* Psalms 127:3."

Clement sighed as he tapped his foot against the hardwood floor. He didn't care if she could hear the evidence of his mounting impatience.

"Of course. Mariana, but I need your help. As you know, I was entrusted with some of Santino's files after he died. One of which was the Rudolpho Gherardini inheritance."

"I imagine his son will inherit a fortune soon. Money is the root of all evil, you know."

"Yes, I believe the love of money is." Clement cleared his throat. "And yes, Luca will inherit a fortune. But there are some missing pieces in this file...references to a safe deposit key, its location, and passports, letters. Are you aware of any files Santino may have kept at his home office, rather than his business office?"

Mariana took an introspective pause. "I can't imagine that he would. *God will judge the secrets of men.* Romans 16:2."

"Mariana, he was not keeping secrets in that respect. He was honoring his clients' right to privacy." Clement had tried to keep her on track, mustering his quota of patience. "All I know is that when his office was closed, I was sent some of his confidential files to handle. Santino was a dear friend of Rudolpho and his family, and I'm guessing, he was possibly in possession of information intended only for him to see, not his partners or assistants, so there may be a Gherardini file in his home office. Before he died, he entrusted me with the main file, but you remember how those last days were. He may have forgotten the details of his cases. No one thinks about work at the end of one's life."

He took a breath and sighed.

"I wouldn't ask you to search for this file if it were not critically important, Mariana. Would you do this for me?"

Clement held his breath.

"If he only intended you to have the main file, wouldn't it be evil of me to give you another if I found it?" she asked.

Clement sighed in exasperation as he stood up to pace the room. How much longer would he need to listen to her monotonous gibberish?

"No, Mariana. I'm sure he forgot about the file. He would want me to have it, for the sake of Damien's friend Luca." Clement reached deep for a Bible quote to seal the deal. "Santino was my friend, and I, his. *Greater love have no man than this… that a man lay down his life for his friends*."

"John 15:13. I know it well. You're right, Clement. Anything to help a dear friend. Give me a week or so, and I will check his home files for you."

"Thank you. *Auf Wiedersehen* and God bless you."

"God bless you, Clement."

Clement rolled his eyes in relief and ended the phone call. He walked into the living room where he could smell the aftermath of burned firewood from the night before. Fiona was untangling Christmas tree lights.

"You know what they say, dear—you can tell a lot about a person when faced with the task of unraveling a rat's nest of these lights."

"You are the most patient woman I've ever met. Mariana Scardina, on the other hand, is an extraterrestrial being. Fiona, if Mariana doesn't find anything, what do I do then?"

"You forget that you ever knew those pieces existed, and you make the remainder of the puzzle fit."

CHAPTER THREE

"To have a friend, be a friend."—Author unknown

Eight years earlier, when he was ten, Damien Scardina's mother listened to the plea for help from Mr. Germond, and because there was no one else to talk to, she had shared the mystery of the misplaced file with him.

The house had felt empty after his father's death, even though Santino had never been readily available to Damien; rather like an impenetrable vault of grown-up knowledge that Damien couldn't access. But Damien watched and quietly scrutinized in his ten-year-old capacity to do so.

Santino had served as a buffer against his mother's frenzy, the holy ghosts and religious references that occupied each conversation and each room like uninvited guests. After his father's death, there was no longer a monitor of how sane conversations generated and flowed. But Damien was used to his mother's religious flourish. He'd always felt a grain of truth in her allusions, and in retrospect, he supposed that he understood her better than his father had *ever* understood her. He'd known when to listen and when to turn her off, and how to comfort her when his father was angry. Besides, she was the keeper and administrator of the pills that calmed Damien and made him feel more secure. His father was the man who sent him away to boarding school after his uncle died.

The night of Mr. Germond's call was a night Damien would never forget. He was home from boarding school for the first time since his father's funeral. The night of the big storm. He looked out the window and watched the storm gather over the lake, the clouds begging to rain. When the storm finally hit, the rolling thunder sounded like roaring jet engines overhead. The lightning struck like gnashing teeth, and the mouth of the sky threatened to swallow them whole. His heart pounded and he held back his tears. Damien was the only man in the house for the first time. Except he wasn't a man. He was still a boy who was frightened by storms and not yet brave. His mother and he took refuge in the cellar where she rubbed her rosary beads and quoted the Bible to summon courage. It became an adventure, complete with lighted candles and rummaging through old footlockers that hadn't been opened for years.

That night, he thought about Mr. Germond's missing papers. Maybe he would play detective the following day. If he found anything, he'd be a hero. It would be fun.

The next morning, the storm had passed, and the skies over Umbria were crystal clear and silky, basted with white cumulus clouds and looking like a beautiful cake cover over the wreckage below. Large tree branches had sharded into neighboring wooden rooflines and cut power lines. He and his mother had surveyed their lot and felt blessed by only minimal damage, much unlike their neighbors' yards, strewn with branches and fallen trees, evoking the image of a giant's game of pick-up sticks. His mother asked him to kneel with her in the back yard and pray with gratitude that they had been spared. He hoped his neighbors' children hadn't seen him on his knees.

After they finished their appraisal of property damage that day, he launched his first conscious act of deceit. He asked his mother to make his favorite dish, gnocchi, knowing that it would require a trip to the market. She agreed, and as soon as he heard the door close behind her, he darted to the window to watch her car back out of the garage and onto the cobblestone road. He followed her with his eyes like a heat-seeking missile until she was out of sight. He locked the front door and ran up to his father's office.

He was a sleuth, an inspector, someone charged to make an important discovery. He loved reading his mystery chapter books at school and now was a real-life character. Luca Gherardini, a year younger than he, had been an acquaintance at school and good friends with Gabriel Germond. Damien had wished that he could be as close to Luca as Gabriel, and he saw this as his chance. Maybe if he could find what was missing from the Gherardini estate file, Luca would be told that Damien had helped him, and Luca would like him even more than Gabriel.

Electric power had not yet been restored to the house so he opened the curtains to allow the light to enter. There were piles of paper on the desk, on the floor, on top of the printer, typical of a wildly-busy attorney who although appearing to be disorganized, had probably known where everything was. For years, his mom had complained about his father's messy office. Damien recalled thinking, *Now that he's gone, I bet she wishes she hadn't nagged him about it, and I bet my father wishes he hadn't sent me away to boarding school.*

The stuffy room smelled like dust, stale pipe smoke, and rotting firewood, a smell that had compressed through the years and saturated the wood floors and dark green wallpaper. He hadn't entered the office since his father's death. He imagined it was an Egyptian mausoleum that he'd read about in his history class. Mysterious and holding secrets from the eyes of the world. *Why hadn't his mother emptied the office?* But he knew why—she had preserved it as a shrine.

He scoured the drawers, file after file. He tackled the papers on top of the desk and gave himself a nasty paper cut that stung like the devil and bled on his shirt. He sucked his index finger until the oozing blood stopped and his mouth tasted sweet. He wouldn't dare cover it with a bandage, because his mother would ask how he cut himself. Busted, that's what he was. He'd wash the stain on his shirt and dry it in his closet, hidden from the eyes of her curiosity and his guilt.

He rooted through the file cabinets that smelled gross, like a dead rat. He found nothing of consequence. His window of time was about to slam shut. His mother would be home momentarily. He moved faster, and when the grandfather clock struck three p.m., he jumped and gasped, not realizing he'd been holding his breath.

He came up empty-handed but was satisfied in discovering the places his friend's information was not. Damien leaped downstairs, three steps at a time, and tripped before the final landing. *Ashes, ashes, we all fall down.*

He was back stoking the fire in the fireplace, when his mother opened the front door and announced she was home. With a grocery bag in hand, she peeked round the corner.

"Damien, you're sweating. Don't sit so close to the fire. *The Lord will execute judgment by fire*…Isaiah 66:16.*"*

CHAPTER FOUR

"Curiosity creates possibilities and opportunities."
—Roy T. Bennett

Eight years later, Damien was once again stoking the fire in their 200-year-old fireplace, when his mother walked into the room.

"Who was that on the phone?" he asked. "You sounded so serious."

"It was Clement Germond."

"What did he want?" Damien asked as he poked a log and it popped with new life, spitting embers onto the hearth.

"Oh, apparently, it's about that file concerning the Gherardini estate. Your father entrusted Clement with it before he died, remember? There are some missing papers, so he hoped that I might find them in your father's office upstairs. I looked years ago but he wants me to look again. *One who is righteous is a guide to his neighbor.* I made veal parmigiana for dinner tonight, one of your favorites," she said. She hugged Damien and whispered in his ear, "Remember to take your medication." Then she turned and vanished into the kitchen like the Spirit of Childhood Past.

Damien was not a little boy anymore. Having graduated from the conservatory, he was home to gather some belongings and see his fitful but loving mother for the last time in a long while. He was free. Free to travel, to explore, to not come home again if he chose not to. But he knew he'd be back. As quirky as his mother was, she was the only family he had, and he'd been trained as a young child to *Honor thy Mother. Honor thy Mother* was like a brand, an imprint burned into his soul. He needed her, and she him. They were in this life together.

The mystery of the missing file had resurfaced. The fact that after so many years Clement had called again, indicated an urgency Damien hadn't sensed as a child, and now the stakes were higher. He not only had reason to find the file, but this time if he found it, he wouldn't share it with the old man, but directly with Luca.

Later that night, Damien and his mother watched old family videos. Clement Germond appeared on film, talking to his father in the upstairs office.

"I don't remember Mr. Germond being here, Mother."

"Oh yes, he came a couple times. You were very young. Your father and he were more than business associates. They were friends, like Jonathan and David in the Old Testament. I remember that day. We had a new video camera, and I followed them everywhere, because I wanted to learn how to use it."

Damien was ready to tell his mother that he needed a break when he noticed a rug on the office floor in the video. He remembered it from his sleuthing afternoon eight years before, but it hadn't looked out of place then. He observed that it was a sumptuous Persian rug that should probably have been hung on a wall. He mentioned it.

"Oh yes, your father insisted on carting that heavy rug up to the second floor. He bought it at an auction and was downright covetous of his newly acquired possession. I wanted to display it in the dining room where people could see it, but he persisted, and you know your father. He was definitely funny about that rug. I offered to have it cleaned a couple times, and he said that it was his rug, and it would never leave his office. So I never brought it up again."

"Is it still there?" asked Damien.

"Of course. It will be there until the Lord takes my soul. It's part of him. I'll never let it go." Mariana nodded her head as if it had been decreed as law.

Santino was a purebred Italian and was not an art collector, certainly not a rug collector. All of the art in the house was Italian. For God's sake, the man flew an Italian flag on their front porch.

The only one in the neighborhood. Why would his father have been attached to Persian rug? It made no sense whatsoever.

That night, after his mother went to bed, Damien paid a visit to his father's study, for the first time in eight years. Nothing appeared to have been touched since his previous visit as an amateur detective; it still smelled musty, like cigar smoke. Damien viewed the room differently however.

He turned on the green lamp on his father's large mahogany roll-top desk and walked to the Persian rug in the middle of the room. On top of the rug was a table with stacks of books, one opened to the Botticelli portrait of Dante. He closed it and tried to move the table but it was too heavy. He took the books from the table until he could drag the table off the stone-studded carpet, hoping not to damage any of the stones-or more importantly, awaken Mariana who had drunk a few glasses of Chianti before retiring for the night.

He slid the table and rolled the heavy carpet, feeling like Sisyphus pushing the stone uphill, hoping it would not roll back. Then he saw it, the envelope. He reached forward to tug on it but realized it was basted into the underside of the opposite edge. He gradually backed up and laid down the rug, found a pair of scissors in his father's desk drawer, and moved to the far edge of the rug to turn it over and clip the envelope free.

Like a child on Christmas morning, opening a card and hoping to see money, he peeled open the sealed envelope marked CONFIDENTIAL and dumped four separate envelopes and a file folder onto the floor. He could feel a key in one envelope and the others felt like they contained letters. He opened the first envelope marked PRIVATE:NON-OFFICE FILE-OPEN UPON MY DEATH ONLY, and out spilled two photocopies of passport pictures, one Canadian passport under the name of Madison Thomas, and the other, an Italian passport with the name Sofia Gherardini. Luca's mother.

He squinted his eyes as his brow furrowed, confused. The photos on both passports were of the same woman. Why would Luca's mother assume a different name? A letter accompanied the photos. He needed to read the contents of the envelope in private, behind closed doors, not in his father's office where his mother could walk in at any moment and interrogate him. *Pop goes the weasel*. He'd hit the jackpot. This was the mysterious, coveted envelope that had been missing for almost nine years. This was information he could possibly use as leverage to get what he most wanted. He quickly gathered the contents and stuffed them in the larger envelope, replaced the rug, moved the table back, and restacked the books as he had found them. He reopened the book of classic Italian paintings to the Botticelli portrait, stared at Dante, and momentarily wondered if he had found or lost paradise.

There are times in one's life that time stands still, and for the rest of one's life, the feeling that's recaptured is either memorably joyful, shocking, or terrible. Sometimes all three. This was one of those moments. Damien, in fear of waking his mother, crept past her slightly-opened bedroom door, feeling each toe grab the wooden floor like he was on a tightrope. The smell of burning firewood had wafted to the upper level of their home like his mother's freshly baked bread or her sweet marinara sauce always did. The crackling of the dying fire downstairs helped disguise the creaking of the floor beneath his carefully placed feet. His senses were animated, and he prayed that his mother's senses were not.

When he closed his bedroom door, he looked for the skeleton key. It was the only way he could lock himself in for the privacy the situation required. *Where did she keep the key?* The 200-year-old home had separate keys for each bedroom, but it had been years since he'd used this one. He checked the obvious places. He panicked as he emptied the drawers in his bureau. Then, in the bottom drawer, he heard a rattle. There it was. The key to not only his privacy, but his future as well.

He locked his door and turned around to pour the guts of the envelope onto his desktop. He took a seat at the banquet before him, ready to methodically sample and digest the mystery of Luca's mother. His mouth tasted stale, like he'd been holding his breath. It had turned dry and acidy. He felt like a voyeur, salaciously peeking in on someone else's life, pulling back the curtains to view the naked truth that no one else had seen;

forbidden even to his father, who hadn't opened the envelopes marked DO NOT OPEN ... *such an honorable man.*

Damien instinctively opened the file folder first. Financial statements. Not the juicy part. He laid it down.

He reopened the envelope with the passport photos to read the instructions that accompanied them. His heart pounded as he devoured each directive. These photos were to be used, in the event of her death, to prove that Sofia Gherardini and Madison Thomas were indeed one and the same. Santino apparently knew that Sofia was alive, but perhaps did not know that she had taken on the identity of a Madison Thomas. This was proof that her "island account" under her Italian name was the property of Madison Thomas of Canada. *But why hadn't Santino opened the envelope? Was he not aware of her death? Had she died?*

He opened the next envelope. In this instruction, Santino was authorized to be the executor and trustee of her estate, giving him power of attorney to sell homes and transfer Nico Gherardini's money into an account for Luca which his mother would oversee and administer, as previously set forth. All future liquidated assets would be funneled into this account. *Why was he the executor if she was alive? Or was no one supposed to know she was alive? And how much money was there?*

The third envelope was marked PRIVATE: NON-OFFICE FILE-OPEN UPON RECEIVING. Santino had read this one, because the seal had been broken. This was the envelope with the key to a safe deposit box only Luca would be allowed to open after he turned eighteen, and only if Sofia had not contacted him herself and was confirmed dead.

The fourth and final envelope was marked TO LUCA-UPON MY DEATH ONLY. Damien ripped it open. The statement gave the location of the safe deposit box at the Bank of Vancouver, address included, as well as the box number for the key. Inside the safe deposit box would be a letter telling Luca what to do, giving explicit instructions as to who was responsible for Sofia's death. "In my memory, you, my son, have a mission. I trust you to carry out my wishes."

Who was responsible for her death? Had someone killed her?

Damien's curiosity accelerated like a dramatic crescendo. He now held a wand of power to change Luca's life. And Luca would be grateful to him. But in the meantime, there were so many questions he needed answered. Perhaps his own mother could fill in the blanks. He stared at the photos of Sofia, Madison, whatever her name was. She was a fox. Gorgeous, if you liked that type.

CHAPTER FIVE

"The pain that you've been feeling can't compare to the joy that's coming."—Romans 8:18

Damien met his mother downstairs for breakfast. He loved their breakfast room. It was cheery, decorated with yellow and blue Italian ceramic dishware, pots and vases, and it smelled like dough and sauce and fruit.

"I heard you up late last night, dear," Mariana said, in her softest, curious voice.

"I'm sorry if I disturbed you. I wasn't tired so I walked around the house for a while. I do love being home, Mother."

"Music to my ears. Please sit down. I bought some freshly-baked baguettes at the corner this morning. They're still warm. Christ was the bread of life, you know."

"Thank you, Mother," he said as he reached to break off a piece of the baguette.

She raised her hand to stop him and proceeded to give thanks to the Lord for their bounty.

"Mother, last night you mentioned Clement Germond had called you, and I got to thinking about Luca's mother. What ever happened to her, anyway?" Damien picked up his butter knife to spread cold cream cheese and marmalade on the warm bread.

"No one knows. I do remember that she disappeared the day after her husband's funeral. I remember because you were around Luca's age, and it broke my heart to think he may have lost his mother. But we all believed she'd come back. Nico,

Rudolpho's son from his first marriage, said she was depressed and just left for a couple weeks to be by herself, with the intention of returning, of course. But she never did return. Your guess is as good as mine. It's difficult to believe a mother would walk away from, not only her only child, but a sizeable fortune. She'll pay for her misdeeds in hell."

She looked up from her oatmeal. "That was judgmental of me. God, forgive me. She may have met with an accident, or maybe foul play. It is an unsolved mystery, one we will never understand, I'm afraid."

Having seen the dates on the letters he'd read the night before gave Damien guilty knowledge to the contrary. One thing for sure was that his father knew Sofia had been alive. But why hadn't he informed the authorities? Or her only child?

Knowing that he couldn't dwell on the subject for long but wanting as much information as possible, Damien nonchalantly stared out the window and asked his next question.

"Did Mr. Germond tell you what he was specifically looking for?"

"He wasn't clear. Except he made mention of a key and passports. It's a non-issue at this point, because they are not in this house. A dead end in the mystery of Sofia Gherardini...no pun intended." Mariana smiled, amused by her unanticipated witticism. Then she clapped her hands as if finished with a conversation that could go nowhere, and stood.

"Do you think she's alive, Mother?" He repeatedly flicked the palm of his left hand with his index finger under the table.

"No. Certainly not, dear. She was declared missing, then I believe she was declared dead. What is that dreadful noise?" she asked.

"Sorry," he said, and stopped his finger thumping. "So...."

"So if she were alive, she would have resurfaced, come back for her child, and spent part of the fortune left to her and Luca. At this point, she won't rise from the dead."

"How do you know she didn't? Spend part of her fortune?"

"Because your father would have known, and he would have told me."

Mariana took her plate to the sink. "Would you like to join me for a walk this morning?"

"I didn't sleep well last night, Mother. I think I'll take it easy this morning. After all, this is my last holiday until I find a full-time job." He winked at her, realizing that he'd tell her about his upcoming trip to North America later. He needed to make a trip to British Columbia, on behalf of Luca, of course. Luca had less than a year of schooling before he left the conservatory. Graduation was a prerequisite for obtaining access to his trust fund. So time was Damien's ally.

He kissed his mother on the cheek and adjourned to his bedroom to examine the financial file that he had skipped the night before. The file contained the signed original of a power of attorney from Sofia to Santino (dated long after her disappearance), records of property sales of a place called Bellaterra and another enormous property on one of the Lipari Islands. There was a lot of money in Luca's estate. More than Damien had imagined. And these were accounts from over a decade ago. He fantasized what they were worth now. *If he hollers, let him pay fifty dollars every day.* He smiled.

He checked the attached record of deposits and withdrawals. There was one account in the Cayman Islands and another smaller account in the Cook Islands. The deposits were dated after Sofia's disappearance, and there were a few taps on the account made by Sofia herself, although no withdrawals in almost thirteen years. Damien closed the file and slipped it under his mattress with the rest of the envelope's contents. He flopped on the bed and lay on his back, staring at a faintly water-stained ceiling as if the marks were Rorschach ink blots that would illumine him.

His questions had only unwrapped more layers of questions. *Maybe she wanted to lose herself in the world. But why? Was she guilty of some crime? Or was she in trouble? What was in the safe deposit box and what was Luca's mission referenced in the personal letter written to him?* He would need to access the bank box to find out.

Eight years ago he had wanted to find the envelope, so Mr. Germond could tell Luca that Damien was the one, the hero, who had discovered it. He had merely wanted Luca as a friend. Now they were friends, good friends, and the bar had been raised. His new-found knowledge was not the key to winning Luca, but winning Luca's heart. As thrilling as that thought was, there was work to be done, a stage to be set. A safe deposit box in the city of Vancouver.

CHAPTER SIX

"One need not be a chamber to be haunted."—Emily Dickinson

Dori Shanihan had pulled off the perfect crime. More than a decade had passed since she, the mild-mannered widow from Muscatine, Iowa, had poisoned her daughter's killer, in a faraway land called Vancouver. The only soul Dori had ever told was her husband, Daniel, and that was at his gravesite. For months after the murder, she thought of little else, and at times, haunted by her deed, she thought she would go mad. But as years slipped away, the truth, by necessity, was compartmentalized, boxed up, and sent to the basement of her life; rarely exhumed, and never regretted. Her daughter, Trina, and her grandchildren, Cristin, and Elizabeth, were safe. The enemy had been destroyed.

Only once had she brought up the appalling chapter in their family's history to Trina, when she'd asked if the children were aware of the woman who had stalked them and had become a tyrannous threat to their family. They were not. They had been spared. Dori had spared them. She thought of it as a war story. Hunter Cross, under the names Cristin, Yvette, Sofia, and Madison, was as evil as Hitler. And Hitler needed to be destroyed. Dori had found a mote of courage to do what needed to be done to protect her family. She might go to hell for it, but she doubted it. A benevolent God didn't want Hunter Cross on earth so He sent Dori as His angel to make their world safer.

Her granddaughters were now grown. Cristin, twenty-two years old, was attending the University of Virginia. She was level-headed. Dori didn't worry about her. But Elizabeth was another story. She was impetuous and headstrong. She seemed to live in the shadow of her high-achieving older sister and was at times rebellious and antagonistic. Elizabeth, age twenty, was living in New York City and taking a year off before going to school, or so said Trina. Times had changed. Dori had never been to Manhattan and couldn't imagine living in such a large, scary city, alone. Hopefully, young Elizabeth would find the temptations resistible and would not take a dangerous bite out of the Big Apple.

On the last night Dori was to go to sleep, her breathing felt different. Shallow and tenuous. Like it was about to ease into the stardust from where she'd come. As she lay down and closed her eyes, she surrendered to the universal breath and smiled in the dark, knowing that she'd had the courage to do something she thought herself incapable of doing. And no one would ever know.

* * * * * * * * * * *

On the morning Dori died, Trina received a call from her mother's neighbor, Isabel Jones. Izzy had stopped by to take Dori to their monthly garden club meeting, and there'd been no answer. Knowing that Dori always left her back door open, Izzy entered the house, calling Dori's name, only to find her friend in bed; lifeless and cold.

Trina's immediate trip from Lincoln to Muscatine would clock eight hours in her little blue Crossfire convertible. She couldn't get there fast enough. Ordinarily, driving her car brought her great pleasure. On this trip, it was merely a machine to get her from point A to point B. But during those hours, she had time to reflect on losing her mother. She'd already lost her sister, her father, her Aunt Tess, and her husband. Loss was not a stranger to Trina. Loss had toughened her up. She also knew that she was a steel magnolia. She'd be strong and take care of business. Everyone would think she was a splendid foot soldier, not falling apart. She would muscle through the memorial service and question her own ability to feel deeply as it might be weeks before she'd cry. Then one day, she would collapse and crumble like the Colossus of Rhodes, and she would doubt that she'd survive.

By the time she reached Muscatine, the Iowa sun had shown its full face over the cornfields to the west of town. Trina pulled into the driveway, and Izzy appeared out of a mirage of Iowa heat. Her bony body hugged Trina and asked if there was anything she could do to help. Trina invited her into the house. As she opened the creaky front gate, she heard the buzz of dragonflies and bees, sounds from her childhood. She greedily sniffed a blend of cinnamon and coffee that strained through the wire colander of the screen door.

"Izzy. What is that delicious smell?"

"I thought you might want a snack and cup of coffee, dear, after your long journey."

Courtesy of Izzy, the kitchen was stocked with food staples, for which Trina insisted on reimbursing her. But Izzy emphatically refused. *Would that all people have such loving neighbors,* Trina thought to herself.

The ladies sat down, and Trina asked a litany of questions. Who should she contact at the church about funeral and mortuary arrangements? Who should be informed about Dori's passing? How soon did the obituary need to be submitted? Who could they ask to bring food to the house after the burial? Together they made decisions, created lists, and implemented a plan.

That evening, Trina picked up Cristin and Elizabeth at the airport. The McClaren women hadn't been together for months, so Trina privately considered it a hidden blessing of the inauspicious occasion.

They spent the next days, gathering photos and memories to share at the church service; writing the obituary, the bio for the church program, and the eulogy that Trina insisted on delivering. By the time the service was over, the women were exhausted.

The day after the service, the task at hand was preparing the house for sale.

"Why are you selling Grandma's house? Why not turn it into a rental?" Elizabeth asked as she assembled storage boxes piled flat in the corner of the living room.

"I don't want to be a landlady; it's as simple as that," Trina replied. "Unless you or your sister want to move to Muscatine." She smiled.

The girls giggled and shook their heads.

"How should we start?" Cristin asked with the enthusiasm of a puppy.

"Always the pleaser," remarked Elizabeth.

Both Cristin and Trina ignored the intentionally snide remark.

"Well, as my Realtor friend Val told me, when you prepare a house for sale, which is eventually and essentially what we're doing, you need G-U-T-S. So everything you touch, you decide to Give, Use, Toss, or Save. Make sense?"

"Perfect sense," Cristin said. She looked at her sister and continued. "So you're leaving tonight?"

"Yes. Eager to get rid of me? When are you leaving?"

"I can stay three more days. My counselor has arranged for me to make up a lab and has contacted my professors. I'm good until Friday."

"What kind of lab do you take in your line of study?" Trina laughed.

"Ghostbusters 401," Elizabeth said.

Cristin didn't laugh. "This lab investigates children who claim to have past life memory. They're between two and five years old, too young to fabricate or intentionally deceive us."

"Maybe they have overactive imaginations?" Trina asked.

"Maybe they're just weirdos," said Elizabeth.

"Neither. They've been screened. They know things they couldn't possibly know otherwise."

"Like what?" Trina asked.

"Well, last week, we had a young boy who complained about the pain of two birthmarks, a long red slash on his upper thigh and another on his forearm. But there was no pathology. They were only birthmarks. He phonetically called himself T-I-M-U and said he'd been stabbed, although he used the word 'cut.' But he violently acted out being stabbed. It was so frightening to his parents that they brought him to us. At home, he'd turn around the knives at the kitchen table so the points wouldn't hurt anyone. He'd hidden the household knives and scissors. He was unnaturally afraid at age two and a half. We searched the origin of the name that we only understood phonetically and discovered that it was Finnish, not Italian, as we'd first suspected; furthermore, we discovered a case involving a man from a rural town outside Turku, Finland, who spelled his name T-E-E-M-U, who was stabbed to death trying to defend his family seventy-five years ago."

"Oh my God," Trina said.

"Creepy," Elizabeth remarked. "Not to change the subject, but why does Grandma's house always smell different?"

"Maybe it's the plastic coverings on the sofas," Cristin said.

"No, that's not it, maybe it's just Iowa. Can a state smell?" Elizabeth chortled.

"Maybe it's traces of Grandma's cooking?" Trina asked.

"No. I never liked Grandma's cooking. I think it just smells old. Grandma was old," Elizabeth said as a matter of fact. "Pass me another box, Pris."

"My name is Cristin."

"Yeah, but you are so prissy."

"Try not to be offensive, Elizabeth," Cristin said. "Let's not get on each other's nerves. We're here for Mom. Okay? Be nice."

"I am nice," Elizabeth said with disdain. "I'm going downstairs to the basement to explore. Ta ta."

Cristin and Trina exchanged glances. Elizabeth's sibling rivalry often reared its jealous head in the guise of pettiness.

But when she later surfaced from the basement, Elizabeth had tuned into her kinder self, as if she'd decided to behave for her mother's and her grandmother's sakes. After all, she was leaving in a few hours.

Dori's grandfather clock ticked away the seconds until Elizabeth's taxi arrived to deliver her to the airport. She'd insisted not to disrupt the packing mission, saying she needed alone time, to decompress.

After dinner Trina and Cristin moved into the bedroom, the most personal room in the house. Trina felt the moistness of tears on her face a number of times, especially handling her mother's clothing—the gray cardigan sweater, her gardening hat, the dress she'd worn to Daniel's funeral, her dressing gown.

"Cristin, smell this. Grandma's gardenia cologne. You can smell it in this fabric. I have to save this shawl. The scent makes me feel so close to her."

The house felt peaceful without Elizabeth, Trina's guilty admission to herself. There wasn't much talking, just the handling of each item and making the corresponding decision. Trina had already gone through a similar packing process after her father died, but this was a bigger undertaking, because it didn't only involve personal items, it was an entire household. She wondered if Cristin projected that someday she would be doing the same for her mother. Morbid thought, but in the cycle of life, someday Cristin and Elizabeth would be sorting through her belongings with GUTS.

"Mom, now that we're alone, I need to tell you about a dream I had about Grandma Dori. Keep in mind, that sometimes dreams are just dreams, and it's possible that I dreamed about her because I'm here and thinking about her. But, this had a real quality to it."

"Tell me," Trina said.

"Well, first of all, let me tell you that she looked beautiful and peaceful, and felt so real. And this doesn't happen to me often in a dream, but she hugged me, and I said to her, 'If I only knew I could hug you, I wouldn't have felt so lost when you died.' "

Trina's eyes welled with happy tears.

"Anyway, she whispered something cryptic in my ear. She said, 'I protected you and your sister. Forgive me.'"

Trina stared at her daughter, knowing that Cristin's sixth sense was strong and shouldn't be ignored.

"Mom, what did she mean?"

"I haven't a clue."

CHAPTER SEVEN

"Truth makes many appeals, not the least of which is its power to shock."—Jules Renard

"**M**om, I didn't know Grandma had a passport."

Trina responded without looking up. "She didn't. She never went anywhere."

"Well, she had one." Cristin displayed the evidence and leafed through the empty pages. Trina walked to where her daughter was sitting on the floor and sat down beside her.

"Here's a stamp. When did Grandma go to Canada? It says...it's hard to read but it looks like June, 2006. She went to British Columbia in June, 2006...June 26th, to be precise."

"She couldn't have. That's impossible. Let me see that."

She snatched the passport and read the stamp. Her heart began to pound as she made the association of the time, place, and mysterious death of Hunter Cross, a.k.a. Madison Thomas. "No. This couldn't be."

"What couldn't be? Good for Grandma. She did something mysterious and didn't tell anyone."

"This was the trip she took after your Grandpa died with some friend from church. They went to Yellowstone and Glacier, as I recall."

Trina scanned every corner of the room, out the window, at the fireplace, as if taking inventory of her parents' home for the first time; as if her parents were people she hadn't known at all. The only thoughts that registered were a blend of questions and doubts. Trina took the passport and squinted to read the fine type.

"This border crossing, Peace Arch, is north of Bellingham, Washington, on the British Columbia border. I've been through there before. Something's not right."

"Well, as I said, good for Grandma. I hope she had a good time." Cristin delved deeper into the box. "She must have; look at this. She saved a menu from a place called The Coffee Grind in Vancouver."

Trina flashed on the name of the coffee shop where her private investigator Scott Holgate had observed Madison Thomas every morning. Dori *had gone to Vancouver to find her daughter's killer?* But more startling than that was that Madison Thomas had died within a couple weeks of that passport stamp. *Was it possible that her meek, passive, unadventurous mother…? No. Impossible. It had to be a coincidence.*

"And look, Mom, here is a travel guide to Montana and a city map of Vancouver."

"Let me see those." Trina tried not to look flummoxed. She opened the book and found a timetable titled CALL TRINA with designated time appointments and corresponding page numbers in the travel guide. There was also a work schedule from The Coffee Grind. But the dates corresponding with Yellowstone and Glacier National Park visitations were also dates on The Coffee Grind work schedule with two names, Delores and Sissy, assigned to morning and afternoon shifts. Dori's childhood nickname had been Sissy.

"No, this couldn't be," Trina exclaimed in a whisper. "She *couldn't* have been in two places at once." Trina checked the travel guide pages to find yellow outlining and notes in the margins to *Tell Trina*. As she read the highlighted remarks, she remembered her mother saying close to the exact words when describing her trip. She'd been amazed at Dori's ability to capture the scenery with poetic description and an unusually enriched vocabulary. Specifically, she remembered her mother quoting Rudyard Kipling, describing Yellowstone's volcanic history as the "uplands of Hell." And there in the travel guide was the quote, outlined in yellow marker. On the top of the page was the name Sheila Evans.

"Is there anything else in the box?" Trina asked.

Cristin pulled out a piece of paper. "It's an email from you, Mom, with some kind of report."

Trina grabbed the page and stared at the toxicity report that she'd received from her private investigator in Italy, the breakdown of poisons found in Sofia Gherardini's Italian greenhouse. A wave of nausea came over her, just like the first time she'd read the report. Holding the papers made real that the shocking contents of the box were not refutable.

Cristin looked up from the empty box and saw her mother's wide-eyed face, stunned and bloodless.

"Mom, what's wrong?" Cristin demanded.

"I can't talk about it, Cristin."

"Of course you can. I'm your daughter. You can tell me anything."

"I need time. I'm done packing for the day. I need to talk to Izzy. Keep going, honey. That's what you can do for me. I'll be back in an hour."

Trina looked at her daughter's shocked, questioning face, as she robotically picked herself off the broken foundation of her mother's memory. She walked out the door into another world, to Izzy's house.

Izzy answered, wearing an apron, blanched with flour.

"Trina? What a nice surprise. I just took two cherry pies out of the oven and was going to bring one to you this afternoon. Come in."

"Thank you, Izzy."

"Of course, dear. Please have a seat."

Trina sat on an orange-patterned velvet sofa that not only looked squishy, but was the kind one would expect to see in a small-town grandmother's home. Trina clenched one fist in her lap, and with the other hand, held on to the doilied arm as if it were her anchor.

"Izzy, do you know a woman named Sheila Evans?"

"I can't say that I do." Izzy's voice cracked from age.

"She was someone from church who my mother took a trip with, shortly after my father died, remember?"

"Well, I must admit that I am a bit short on memory these days, but I don't recall a Sheila Evans."

"Izzy, I'm positive my mother said that this Sheila belonged to one of the women's groups at church." Trina's mouth twitched as she spoke while her blinkless eyes widened.

"Well, dear. I don't remember, but I have church directories from twenty years ago in a box downstairs. I could check them. Directories don't lie."

"Oh, would you, Izzy? Could I see them? Right now?"

"If it means that much to you, dear, of course. Excuse me."

"Thank you, Izzy. Can I help you?"

"No, they're not heavy. What years are we looking for?"

"Nothing after 2006. Let's try 2000-2006," said Trina.

Five minutes, hundreds of pounding heartbeats, and four bitten fingernails later, Trina watched Izzy emerge from the basement with a stack of directories.

"You take these three, and I'll look through the others," Izzy said.

It took only two minutes to decipher that there was not a Sheila Evans in the church's census of membership. Coming up empty-handed and worse the wear, Trina asked about the garden club, to which Izzy replied, "I'm *sure* there is no Sheila Evans there. I am a past-president and it's a small group. Who is this Sheila person?"

"A friend from Muscatine my mother traveled with. Supposedly."

"I remember that trip!" Izzy said as if a light bulb had switched on. "I was worried about your mother because she'd never traveled by herself. I was with her the morning she left. I brought her a basket of warm bran muffins and a bottle of lemonade. But she didn't leave with anyone, Trina. She told me she was going to stay with you and your family in Nebraska. I remember it well now. I was happy that she had family at such a lonely time."

Trina had what she'd come for. It was time to go. Only when she clasped Izzy's hands to thank her did she realize that her own hands were shaky and sweaty. Izzy then handed her a pair of oven mittens to carry home a warm cherry pie.

As she walked out the door, the only thought on Trina's mind was what she would tell Cristin.

****

Cristin was standing at the front door waiting for her mother when Trina came down the lane. Trina's mind flashed on a French Impressionist painting that she'd seen once, an image of a lovely woman whimsically walking down a road, bordered with red poppies. She fleetingly wondered if Cristin had seen the painting too. But as she neared the door, she knew there was nothing lovely or whimsical about her own countenance or approach.

"All right, Mom. You need to tell me what's going on. I'm an adult. I'm your daughter. And I love you," Cristin said as she took the pie from her mother and walked her into the kitchen.

"You're right. But let's put on a pot of tea. I need to talk, but I promise you, this isn't going to be easy. I hope what I'm thinking is wrong, but I do need to run it by another person who loved Grandma Dori."

While the tea brewed, they pulled out the chairs at the kitchen table. It was covered with a rooster tablecloth; its centerpiece, a burned-down vanilla candle, begging for just one more chance to shine. Trina opened the window to feel the prairie breeze with a hint of wheat and flax in the air to soothe her overstrung nerves. Stalling the inevitable conversation as long as she could, she lit the candle and poured the tea.

Cristin sat impatiently, holding tension in her jaw and shoulders, with both fists clenched on the table.

"Cristin, something happened years ago that I've never told you. I never thought I would, but I guess I'm a fool to think that it wouldn't come out eventually. I just didn't imagine it would be today."

"Mom, you're scaring me."

"No, don't be scared. It appears that your Grandma Dori, my darling mother, made certain that you'd never need to be afraid of the person I'm going to tell you about." Trina took a sip of tea and struggled to inhale a deep breath. "You know that you were named after my younger sister who died in a fire on a neighboring farm."

Cristin nodded. She'd heard the story a million times.

"Aunt Cristin didn't just die. She was killed."

"Mom!" Cristin's face contorted. Her arms crossed with closed fists across her rib cage like she was trying to hold her heart inside her chest.

"We believe she was poisoned by her high school friend, Hunter Cross, who lived on that farm, and after poisoning Aunt Cristin and her own parents, set fire to the farmhouse. But no one suspected foul play. I mean, this is Muscatine. And it was in the mid-Nineties. Hunter then disappeared to start a new life as Cristin Shanihan, using my sister's identity. Years later, I read a novel that led me to believe that an author named Tess Monson Parker knew this Hunter Cross a.k.a. Cristin Shanihan."

"Aunt Tess?"

"Yes. She knew my sister's killer because Hunter Cross embedded herself in Tess's life to start a new life. We eventually discovered that she was in Vancouver, living under one of her many aliases. So we hired a private investigator to track her. We hoped she would slip up, and we could have her arrested. But she somehow figured out that we were on to her, and she started threatening our family. We had a lot of circumstantial evidence but no binding proof, and because we were terrified of this woman, then known as Madison Thomas, we bowed out, gave up, and folded our tents, to protect anyone else from being injured or worse."

"Mom, why haven't you told me this before?" Cristin asked,

"Because by the time you were old enough to hear it, Madison Thomas had died and was no longer a threat."

"But what does this have to do with Grandma? I don't understand."

Trina stood and started to pace, her hands shaking.

"Until this afternoon, I didn't know that Grandma went to Vancouver."

"So?"

"Grandma told me that she and her friend went to Yellowstone and Glacier National Parks on a trip she took after Grandpa died. Look at these notes." Trina pulled the schedules from The Coffee Grind and the fabricated CALL TRINA schedule. "I just talked to Izzy. Grandma didn't go with a friend to see the national parks, Cristin. There was no friend. She drove to Vancouver alone."

"To find the woman?"

The room filled with a volume of silence; brooding, horrid silence. A sudden wind came up from the West and slammed the back door shut. Startled, the women both jumped.

"I guess we're a little jumpy," Trina said nervously. "Cristin, The Coffee Grind is where our private investigator watched Madison Thomas every morning. According to this work schedule, Grandma worked there."

Cristin lowered her voice and timidly, reluctantly, asked the obvious question.

"When did the woman die, Mother?"

"Before my mother returned to Iowa."

Cristin's eyes wrinkled into tiny deep, dark holes of disbelief.

"Grandma killed her?"

"Maybe. Maybe Grandma killed the woman so she couldn't harm us again. We may have just unlocked your dream."

CHAPTER EIGHT

"Listen to the silence ...it has so much to say."—Rumi

At seven-thirty a.m., Clement was enjoying a cup of tea and reading the morning news on the Internet when the phone rang. He jumped, spilling his tea on a pad of paper he'd used to outline one of his client's legal needs.

"Hello!" he snapped, angry at his clumsiness.

"Hello, may I speak with Mr. Germond?" asked the somewhat familiar voice.

"This is he. Who is this, please?"

"Luca Gherardini, sir. I wondered if I might meet with you. I would like to talk to you about my parents ... in person."

Clement was stunned and aware of his cogitative pause before delivering his answer.

"Hello, Luca. I don't know how much I can tell you, but I would be happy to meet with you. How about this Tuesday at three p.m., at my home? Do you remember where we live?"

"Yes, sir," he responded. "I remember. That would be fine. I'll see you at three p.m., and thank you, sir, for taking the time to speak with me."

"You're welcome, Luca. I look forward to seeing you."

Both men disconnected.

Clement looked out the window at a brooding sky. The foggy, wet curtain that hung before his eyes made visibility merely a word, not a reality.

What was he going to say to the young Gherardini boy? That he'd once surreptitiously read a letter from his mother that had been personally addressed to Luca? No. That there was a safe deposit key to a mysterious bank location and two passports at large? No.

No. For the sake and safety of the innocent American women referred to in the letter, and because he had exercised due diligence in recovering the missing key and passports, Clement was done with it. There was no letter, not anymore. Luca would eventually inherit the fortune in the Cayman and Cook Islands accounts in its entirety. End of subject.

But there was a gray area. What did the boy want to know, and more importantly, what did he already know?

Clement briefly reflected on his Christian name to fortify his mettle. Although the fourteen popes named Clement were not all wise and pious, Clement Germond wore his name with high expectations of a noble character. This Luca Gherardini business had been a challenge.

On Tuesday, Luca arrived punctually, dressed in slacks, with a collared shirt under his coat. He was an uncommonly handsome young man which even Clement could appreciate. Clement rarely noticed physical appearance unless unusually beautiful or ugly. Luca was beautiful, and there was something fascinating about beauty, even a beautiful man. He was tall, with a strong jaw, with eyes like Omar Sharif; his dark wet hair plastered to his forehead. He smelled fresh, like the rain.

"Hello, Luca. Let me take your raincoat and umbrella." Clement hung them on the hall tree, ushered the boy into his study, and called to Fiona to alert her to the fact that their guest had arrived.

She came to the study to greet him and carried a tray of tea and biscuits.

"Luca, how lovely to see you again."

"Likewise, Mrs. Germond," he replied.

"I'm sorry Gabriel isn't back yet. He plans to attend school in Granada next semester, you know." She paused. "Of course, you know. You just visited him last weekend, didn't you? Did you have a good time?"

"Yes, as a matter of fact, I did. But four days weren't enough. I want to go back," Luca said, and smiled. "I now understand why he loves Spain as much as he does."

"I hope we don't lose him to the Iberian Peninsula for good, but I'm glad you enjoyed yourself. Well, I'll leave you two alone for a visit," she said. She wanted to escape before she was asked questions that she didn't want to address about Luca's mysterious, duplicitous mother.

The door shut behind Fiona.

"Well, Luca, tell me how I can help you," Clement said.

"Mr. Germond, I thought it was time that I met with you, not as Gabriel's father, but as the executor of my family's estate."

Clement responded with a dignified chuckle. "Yes. I had planned on calling you to discuss your estate this year, but you've beaten me to the punch. Do you wish to know the details of your estate today?"

"No, we can talk about that later."

"Good, as it's been a busy week, and I want to have the time to review the intricacies before we meet again."

Luca nodded. "However, I do want to clear the air about something. As you know, I have been to therapists since I was seven years old. I'm not proud of my behavioral history. But with years of counseling and the help of my teacher, Ms. Walker, I want you to know that I am happy. I no longer feel alone or resentful. And before you say anything, please hear me out." Luca held up his hand like a traffic cop, to forestall any interruption. "For years, I was angry, but I now realize that my 'situation' wasn't because I wasn't lovable, but because my parents were not. I don't know what I would have done without Ms. Walker. I'll always be indebted to her."

Luca stopped to drink his tea, and Clement honored his request to not be interrupted. Clement made a mental note that Luca's voice was calmer, his eyes more focused, his speech more deliberate than he had remembered.

"But that being said," Luca continued, "I know I have been in your home a few times, but I was always the younger friend of your son, and when I would visit, we were busy being boys. It never felt appropriate to ask you to discuss my parents. But I know that you knew them."

"Yes we did," Clement acknowledged with noted reticence.

"I want to know who they were and what happened to them. Until recently, I wasn't ready. It was frankly easier to think they were both terrible people, people I wouldn't have wanted to know. But I'm ready to hear whatever you have to say."

The springs in Clement's large leather chair creaked as he leaned forward and folded his hands on the desk. He looked like Father Time, wise and beneficent.

"Luca, Fiona and I knew both of your parents, although we knew your father considerably longer and better than your mother. Rudolpho was a very dear friend of mine, an astute businessman, and an adoring father. You were almost three when he died. He had been ill for a few years. A specific diagnosis was never made, but he became weaker and weaker until his heart just stopped beating. It was a most difficult time, because there was no treatment for whatever ailed him. If he had lived, I truly believe, that although you may have attended boarding school, you would have been brought back to Bellaterra, your home in Italy, for the holidays and summer breaks. He was a good man, Luca. I miss him. I miss his friendship."

"And my mother?" asked Luca, with a sober brow and pursed mouth.

Clement sat up and coughed, as if he needed to expel a black cloud.

"Your mother?" Clement sighed. "Simply said, there was nothing simple about her. She was rather an enigma. A beautiful woman, long thick dark hair, gorgeous eyes. It was no wonder your father fell in love with her at first sight. I introduced them, you know. At that time, your mother was an artist by the name of Yvette Vandal. She attended a party at our home where she met your father."

"Yvette Vandal? I didn't know she had another name. Was she French?" asked Luca.

"Swiss, I believe," Clement replied. He was careful not to mention her ties to America. "Anyway, we were celebrating something so we threw a party. One must always have something to celebrate, right?" Clement chuckled and reached into his desk drawer. "I found a photograph of her with your father that night. Would you like to have it?"

"May I?" Luca took the picture and stared at it intently.

"Your mother married Rudolpho and settled in Italy, where she changed her name to Sofia Gherardini. You were born a year later, if my memory serves me correctly."

"But whatever became of her? I ask because I have no memory of ever seeing the woman in this photograph, and I've wondered why she never came to see me. My counselors at school said they thought she died, which was horrible news, but at least it explained why she didn't visit me. Is it true? Did she die?"

"I presume so," said Clement.

"But when did she disappear? My father surely told you something."

"Your father had already died, Luca. As a matter of fact, I saw your mother the night before she disappeared. At Rudolpho's funeral. She was devastated, losing him. She left suddenly, the day after the funeral, for a hiatus. That was the last we ever heard of her."

Clement felt a wave of guilt. She'd been alive at least for a few years after her disappearance and maybe still was. He honestly didn't know.

He continued. "From what I understand, she was declared missing within a couple weeks, and five years later, declared dead. I'm sorry."

"I have so many questions. Is there anyone else I could talk to about her? Anyone at all? And was Bellaterra sold or is it still in the family estate?"

"The estate was sold and the net proceeds added to your mother's account, your account. To clarify, Luca, after your half-brother Nico died, all funds were in Sofia's name, and you are her only heir. So as regards her money, the estate is definitive. However her personal life is less conclusive. Perhaps the new owners of Bellaterra retained some of your father's employees who might remember her. You might start there," he suggested. "Luca, I'm sorry you've had to go it alone for so many years. It couldn't have been easy."

"It was hell at times, pardon my expression. But no other concept fits. But the hardest part is over. I'm ready to face the reality of my past and put it behind me, no matter what the truth is. And as they say, scar tissue is stronger than original skin, right?"

Clement nodded and smiled.

Luca stood. "You've been kind to speak with me this afternoon, Mr. Germond. Thank you for the photograph. Please thank Mrs. Germond for the tea. I won't take any more of your time."

Clement stood to shake Luca's hand, then walked him to the door and helped him on with his coat. "I wish I could tell you more," Clement said. It was true, albeit withholding.

When the door closed behind him, Fiona appeared in the entryway.

"So?" she asked.

"He appears to be thoughtful and even-tempered, just as Gabriel has told us, just as we have witnessed in recent years."

Clement adjourned to the study and sat in his ample leather chair, in the silence of his home, in the silence of his mind. Yes, Luca had appeared to be a well-adjusted young man. But was Luca as good at hiding his nature as his mother apparently had been?

The rain began to fall. He heard it first on the roof. Then he watched it hit the window and splatter the window sill, obscuring his vision. Nothing was clear.

CHAPTER NINE

"Will you come travel with me? Shall we stick by each other as long as we live?"—Walt Whitman

On the evening of the new moon, after returning from Italy, Damien paid a visit to Luca's dormitory. He rather fancied a quick in-and-out procedure to extract Luca's passport, so there would be no chance of Luca discovering it missing and associating it with Damien's unanticipated visit. Nothing at this point could seem abnormal, nothing out of place.

They had lived together, off and on, so he knew Luca kept important documents in the bottom drawer of his desk. He first checked the hallway, then knocked on the door. No answer. Luca was not in his room, so Damien seized his opportunity. He entered the room and closed the door behind him. He opened the bottom desk drawer. It wasn't there. It had always been there. He checked the next drawer. The next. *Where was the fucking passport?*

He stopped and took a labored breath. His eyes rifled the room for a target that made sense. He opened one bureau to discover that it belonged to Luca's roommate. He opened the other bureau and rummaged through Luca's clothes, hoping to find the documents. Nothing. Then he remembered ... there were built-in drawers on the side of the small closet. He walked to the closet and opened the top drawer. Yes! His personal papers. Luca's birth certificate, some legal documents, and at the bottom of the stack, the elusive, coveted passport. He grabbed the passport and birth certificate, put them in his inside jacket pocket, slammed the drawer shut, and quickly walked to the door. As he pulled it open, he felt the simultaneous push of someone on the other side of the door handle. In a fraction of a second, Luca's roommate stood in front of him.

"Who are you?" Damien preemptively asked.

"I'm Hans Koefler. Who the hell are you? And what are you doing in my room?"

"It's good to meet you, Hans," Damien said as he shook the young boy's hand. "Luca has told me about you. I was Luca's roommate last year. I've graduated. You must be new or I'd recognize you. Welcome to SCB. I'm here to see him."

Damien realized his short barrage of verbal artillery would be too much information for most newcomers to process, and he needed to get out the door before any more questions were asked.

"Do you know where I can find him?"

Hans looked perplexed. "Ah yes, he's in the basement study. I'll tell him you were here. Who did you say you are?"

"No need, I'll tell him myself. Good to meet you." In his hurried exit, Damien bumped into the boy on purpose, catching a whiff of body odor, evocative of week-old cheese left in a cheap hotel.

Trying to avoid any further run-ins with students who might recognize him, Damien took the service stairway to the basement. Speaking to young Hans now necessitated talking to Luca. And what the hell? Hans had already seen him, so why was he sleuthing down the service stairway? Not as smooth as he had hoped. So much for Lady Luck.

He could feel his adrenaline pumping and was glad he'd made the decision to go off his meds. They evened him out too much. He needed to feel the spike of sharp thinking and exhilaration. He could control his mania. If he tanked and depression set in, he'd take the nasty little monsters again.

He found Luca in the basement study, a dismal, cool, gray room with not one poster, picture, or even a clock on the walls-

guaranteed to not provide distractions to a serious student. It smelled musty, but an upgrade from Han's Koefler's stench, although he *did* miss the smell of men from his dormitory days.

Damien greeted him loudly. "They told me I could find you down here."

"Shhh," the students in the room responded in unison.

He theatrically cowered as he smiled his "I am irresistible" smile and sat down next to Luca.

"What are you doing here?" Luca whispered, happy to see his friend.

"I hadn't seen you for a while and thought I'd stop by before I left for the other side of the pond."

"You lucky bastard. A few more months, and I'm taking off and may never come back. I envy you. Where are you going?"

"America, Canada, maybe Mexico, but first the States. I'm taking some time off. My dad left me some money so I'm ready for some fun. Maybe we'll travel together someday soon," suggested Damien, aware as soon as he'd spoken that perhaps he shouldn't have been so bold. He continued, "I've always wanted to cruise around the United States, maybe see the Canadian Rocky Mountains, although let's face it … they probably don't hold a candle to our Alps, right?" He smiled broadly.

"When did you decide to go to the U.S.? Does Gabriel know? I talked to him last night and he didn't mention it," Luca said.

"I don't know if I told him." Damien knew that he *had* told Gabriel and was instantly irked at him for not thinking it was worthwhile enough to mention. "I didn't know Gabriel was back. Did he have a good time in Spain?"

"Actually, he's not back yet. I went down there too, because it was the last trip I could take before exam week, but I came back ahead of him."

Damien didn't reply, hoping that his sudden rush of jealousy didn't translate in his face.

"We would have asked you to come too, but you were in Italy visiting your mother. It was a last-minute decision. Next time, okay?"

"You're on," Damien said. "Did you see any bullfights?"

"No. Not my thing. Aren't they outlawed now? Animal rights, and all?"

"Oh, I think they've cracked down, but it's part of their culture. They can't do away with it completely. That would be like outlawing yodeling in Switzerland. Ha! You know, they eat the bull after it's been killed so the animal's death is not in vain. And I've read that a good bullfighter kills efficiently so the bull doesn't really suffer," Damien said.

"I wouldn't know. I'm not a bull. It just appears that he's abused before the kill. As I said, not my thing."

"What would Hemingway say if he were alive?"

Luca stared at him without an answer.

"Ole'! That's what he'd say." He laughed out loud until shushed into remembering where he was. "Study hard. And by the way, I went to your room, thinking I'd find you there, and bumped into your new roommate. Hans? Anyway, he seems like a good guy. Tell him to take a shower."

Luca laughed. "I'll be thinking of you having your way with easy, willing, beautiful American women."

Damien's smile disappeared. He uncomfortably uttered "Ha," then continued. "I'm sure you'll miss me. And Gabriel? Now that he's going away to school in Spain, what are you going to do without us, buddy?"

"Maybe I'll join you in America and visit the stomping grounds of some of my favorite writers. You aren't planning to go to New England or South Carolina are you? That would kill me. Wait for me to go to South Carolina."

"I promise. No South Carolina without you." Damien put his hand on Luca's arm that felt harder and more sinewy than he had imagined. "As yes. So stand up to say good-bye, my friend, and wish me luck. The next time we meet, our fortunes will change for the better."

Luca stood and Damien hugged him. Long and hard.

CHAPTER TEN

"A sister is both your mirror and your opposite."
—Elizabeth Fishel

On the day she flew home from her trip to her Grandma Dori's house, Elizabeth arrived at Kennedy Airport by five p.m. Her boyfriend Shane, who reminded her of Johnny Depp from the first moment she'd laid eyes on him, picked her up and asked her where she wanted to go for dinner. His treat.

"Something exotic, please! Something I couldn't find in Iowa. How about Indian? Natraj!"

Shane nodded approval and made a U-turn in the direction of the restaurant.

The hostess wore a maroon and gold sari and welcomed them into a gold room with low-hanging maroon glass lamps. Paintings of gods and goddesses, some with multiple heads or arms, were encased in and protected by richly ornate frames. On the far side of the room, there was a mural of the tree of life, with a preening peacock sitting on a branch with his head tilted upwards as if sniffing the curry, onions, lentils, and hummus that hung in the air.

They ordered lamb curry and shrimp tandoori with sides of naan and saffron rice, and Shane popped the sensitive question.

"So how was it seeing your sister again?"

"About the same. She's Cristin. And as much as my mother would like to believe that we're best friends, we're too different

51

to be best friends. She says potato and I say potahto. You know what I mean?"

"So what's she like, your sister?"

"She's huki-buki. She got the curly, thick auburn hair and green eyes. And dimples. I got the straight mousy brown hair and nondescript dark eyes. No dimples. Do I need to say more?"

"Are you kidding me? You look like Emma Samms. You're beautiful."

"You never told me that I look like Emma Samms."

"Well, you do. Now back to your sister. I now know her coloring. What is she like?"

"She's nice. Not Miss Personality like me, but nice." Lizzie playfully stuck out her tongue. "I mean, she's not mean, she's just different."

"What bugs you about her?"

"You don't want to know. I'm not in the mood."

"No, seriously, what's the problem? It's fresh in your mind, and you're never in the mood to talk about it. So spill and get it over with."

"Okay. In a nutshell, she was named after my mother's sister who died when she was a teenager, and my mom loved her sister, so what does she do? Names her first child after her dead sister."

"Okay? What's wrong with that?"

"Nothing on the surface. But my Mom reveres her. It's nauseating. I was so glad to get out of the house. No more 'your sister did this, your sister did that. Your sister wouldn't do that...why do you insist on being so belligerent?' "

"Are you? Belligerent? "

She raised her voice, irritated, but smiling. "Whose side are you on anyway, Shanemeister?"

"I didn't know there were sides. I'm just trying to understand," he replied. "What's the huki-buki part?"

"Oh. She's studying ghosts at UVA."

"Vermont?"

"No. Virginia, dumbass."

"Thank you for that. How was I to know, dumbass?"

"Sorry. I'm still re-entering our world. I'm out of sorts."

"Apparently. So what's the department? Ancient history?"

"No. Parapsychology."

"That's news to me. I didn't know universities had parapsychology departments. What's the draw?"

"She has ESP. She's gifted in that way. She's not only the living embodiment of my mother's dead sister, but she's uncommonly attuned to the dead." She wiggled her fingers and wobbled her voice, imitating her impression of a ghost.

"Whoa. That's wicked."

"It's too weird for me. And to wrap it up with an awkward bow, I'm not only not gifted, but I'm not going to college. Mom isn't amused. She basically cut me off financially until I change my mind. But I told her not to hold her breath. This girl is free and not Cristin's clone. I've been thinking of changing my name, by the way."

"That was an abrupt left turn. To what?"

"Something not so formal. Maybe Maggie or Lizzie. What do you think?"

"Lizzie would be easier to get used to."

"Then Lizzie it is. Let's try Lizzie for a week and see how it feels. I can always change it again."

"You're crazy, girl." Shane laughed. "Since we're talking about making changes, while you were gone, I received a job offer that I'm considering taking. But I'd want you to come with me...Lizzie." He peered over the top of his Johnny Depp glasses and took a sip of his Darjeeling tea.

"What job? Where is it?"

"I would be in the accountancy department at an industrial equipment office. Not real sexy but the pay is good, real good."

"And where pray-tell is this job? Brooklyn? The Bronx?" she questioned with obvious reserve, folding one arm over the other like a scolding mother.

"Beaufort, South Carolina."

Then came the expected silence and the equally expected response. "No way! I don't want to live in the South. It's buggy and snaky and humid. Why would you even consider this?"

"Because I've been there. It's beautiful. Pampas grasses, Spanish moss, angel trees, live oaks. Canals connecting waterways with reeds, bearded grass, egrets, Virginia rails, Carolina wrens ...."

"Since when did you become a travelogue writer?" She paused while the first plate was served. "... and a botanist?" The second plate was delivered. "... and an ornithologist?" She leaned over the second plate and said, "Hmm. Smell that curry."

"Don't change the subject. I'm serious. Just take a short trip with me to check it out before you say no. Please? Lizzie?" He looked at her intently and had used her new name twice already, to soften her up, and she knew it.

"Well. I can't imagine changing my mind, but I'm in the mood for a road trip, so what the hell. Let's do it. No promises though. It's just a scouting expedition, right?"

"Right."

Within a week, Lizzie and Shane drove to Beaufort, stopping in Richmond, Virginia, for a night. They ate at a charming Irish pub on Cary Street where they tried a signature drink called the Cary Street Crush, blended from freshly squeezed orange juice, vodka, triple sec and Sprite, and they shared a plate of beef brisket tacos and a bag of salt and vinegar potato chips.

After dinner, they walked along the James River and promised each other that someday, they would return to this charming city that boasted a rich cultural heritage, and was close to Jamestown and Williamsburg, to boot. History no longer seemed boring. It was alive in Richmond, Virginia, to be sure.

By late afternoon the following day, they arrived in Beaufort. Shane drove directly to the heart of Old Pointe, where horse-drawn carriages carried visitors down narrow historic streets, canopied with antediluvian trees, dripping with Spanish moss. It was the definition of charming.

Shane booked their first night at the Rhett House Inn. Much to Lizzie's surprise, he hadn't overpainted the town. In the morning, they borrowed two bicycles provided by the inn, and pedaled under enormous magnolia trees that shaded a clear blue southern sky. Gnarled oaks trees bordered the property lines of antebellum mansions, and they rode past a graveyard commemorating the Confederate dead.

Later, they went for a leisurely walk.

"Shane, this feels like a place where you visit, not live. I mean, look at these channels and peninsulas and islands, and marshes, and lagoons. Look at that blue heron! Last night at the inn, I read an article that explained why even the beaches sparkle. The sand is a combination of granite, feldspar, quartz, and mica, I think, that flows through the river system from the Appalachian Mountains. Now if that isn't right out of a fairy-tale, I don't know what is. And not only that, when you look on the map, check out how close we are to Charleston and Savannah. If you worked here, neither of us would get anything done because there's so much to do."

Shane laughed. "That sounds like something Yogi Berra might have said."

"Who's Yogi Berra?"

"Doesn't matter. But what does matter to me is that you like it, don't you?"

"I kinda do. Knock me over with a feather...a Carolina wren feather, of course," she said in her most seductive southern belle voice, laced with a titter.

"Seriously, Shane, I do like this place. If we moved here and found out we didn't like it, we could go back, right? I mean, nothing is set in cement, right?"

Before he could respond, she continued. "We need to try shrimp burgers at the Shrimp Shack tomorrow. I mean, I may actually faint if I have to look at one more cup of catfish chowder or okra gumbo. Where is my fan?" She struck a pose from a Scarlett O'Hara parlor tableau.

"What are you looking at?" she asked.

"Look at that tree," he whispered. "It's filled with white egrets. Have you ever seen anything more beautiful, against those sunset colors over the marsh?"

She stared at the tree and saw the magic.

"Let's do it. Take the job. Let's move here."

"Are you sure?" he asked. "It's a land of alligators...."

"And loggerhead turtles," she countered.

"And bugs...."

"And doe-eyed deer."

"And snakes."

"And oystercatchers, and painted buntings, and anhingas."

"What are anhingas?"

"They're amazing water birds that hang their wings out to dry in the breeze, like Bela Lugosi."

"Where do you learn this shit?" Shane asked.

"My dad was a naturalist, remember? He made a living, taking photos and writing stories about wildlife, particularly birds. So I come by it naturally."

"So you think you could live down here for a while?"

"Mmm? Yes." She smiled and kissed him.

Shane took her around the waist to deepen the kiss.

"I come by *this* naturally."

CHAPTER ELEVEN

"The ease of my burdens, the staff of my life..."
—Miguel de Cervantes Saavedra

In Lucerne, Switzerland, night descended like a heavy theater curtain upon Act One of his life. Gabriel Germond had been home from Spain for only two weeks and was already packed to leave for the University of Granada, an internationally oriented institution with an outstanding department in political science, the main draw. Entrance was easy because his grades were stellar, and it was an EU university, having reciprocity with Switzerland. If all went as planned, his minor would be history. Spain had a rich political history, because the country had remained relatively isolated for centuries by the precipitous barrier of the Pyrenees and surrounding seas. Spanish history and culture, and Moorish architecture, had fascinated him since he was introduced to it in Grade Three at SCB, and the haunting call to Spain was too compelling to ignore.

His trip with Luca had been terrific. Too short, but terrific. They'd scoped out the campus and visited Alhambra, the palatial fortress and gardens established by the Moors in the eleventh century and captured by Queen Isabella and Ferdinand in the late fifteenth century. He had imagined walking the grounds of the Alhambra since he was ten years old, and the experience was more moving than he'd expected. History was alive and deep and rich and thrilling in Spain. Not everyone felt the rush. But he did and it was *his* life.

In school, Gabriel always played the part of the contrarian. When someone took one side of an argument, Gabriel, whether he believed it or not, posed the contrary position for the sheer delight of instigating a lively conversation. Clement had seen this as a vital and all-too-rare talent for a crackerjack defense attorney, and had encouraged his son to consider law as a field of endeavor.

How often had he heard his father tell the story about the time when Gabriel, as a fifteen year old, had walked into a cigar smoke-filled room and overheard adults talking about the death penalty? While Gabriel, impressionable and thoughtful, listened, the adults concurred that there had to be a legal, punitive difference between kidnapping someone and killing someone. Otherwise, kidnappers would naturally kill their victims so they couldn't be identified. Therefore, the death penalty was just.

Out of nowhere, Gabriel's adolescent voice had offered a contrary opinion, or at least a worthy opinion that gave the men pause to reconsider and rebut. He said that what they concluded made logical sense, and he couldn't argue with them in principle. But were kidnappers ergo murderers? And had it been proven that the consequence of capital punishment was a deterrent to criminals? Because if not, if legal execution did not protect the community, then it was barbaric. The gentlemen had stood and applauded young Gabriel, and as Clement told the story, he had never been more proud.

Gabriel was interested in politics. He wanted to make an active difference in people's lives. He was likeable, trustworthy, and conscientious, more than he could say about most politicians he'd read about in history or present day. In his mind, no matter how evolved the culture of a country, if the politics were evil, the culture would die. Nothing else mattered if the politics were not altruistic and noble. If artists weren't free to express themselves, to compose, draw, dance, sing, write, build, design; if scientists were not provided funding to advance technology to find medical cures and protect the planet, then man could not be creative and advance civilization. All it took was one evil empire, manned by a power-hungry, selfish, paranoid monster, to destroy all that was courageous within the human spirit. Proven point. Nazi Germany, Mao's Cultural Revolution, Stalinist Russia and its maniacal, murdering minions in Cambodia, North Korea and Cuba, to name a few. He could go on and on as he often did. Politics mattered because without the decency of good politics, nothing else did matter.

His father commended his idealism, but asked him to at least contemplate law as a back door through which he might someday walk. Gabriel remembered nodding his head in deference to his father's wishes. He suspected that Clement had chosen a safe, steady road in estate law, but secretly wished he'd chosen a branch of law that was more challenging, perhaps more exciting. But Gabriel knew where he himself was headed. His passion would prevail.

That particular night was the last night of his childhood, the last night of his warm-up years before he entered the realm of manhood. It was an artificial conception that he'd self-imposed. However, it was his life to conceive and manage. Now there was only one obstacle to hurdle before he boarded the plane to Madrid en route to Granada.

Clement had fallen asleep in his overstuffed easy chair in front of the fireplace. His feet were propped up on the ottoman, and the fire was burning low, just barely crackling with hot white embers beneath the grate still heating the room. Fiona had retired for the night.

His father looked peaceful, snoring lightly. His eyebrows had grown unruly, and his chin sagged beneath his goatee. His hands were folded and rested on his protruding stomach. Gabriel didn't want to disturb him. But his unrevealed truth was not going to accompany him like unwanted baggage, to Granada. It would be unloaded and buried in Lucerne that night, along with the dying embers in the fireplace.

"Dad," he said, as he lightly shook his father. "Dad," he said louder as he shook him a bit harder.

Clement snorted and jumped.

"What's the matter? Are you all right?"

"I'm fine, Dad. This is my last night in the house for a long while, and I just want to speak with you about something before I leave in the morning."

Clement sat up, taking his feet off the ottoman. He opened his eyes widely a couple times, scrubbed his face as if washing himself awake, and assumed the posture of an attentive father.

"Dad, I want to talk about what happened back in 2009, when Harold Brockmeyer hanged himself."

"Why on earth are you bringing that up?"

"Because I need to get this off my conscience before I go away tomorrow. I want to tell you what I think happened."

"I'm listening," said Clement, who was now wide awake and leaning forward with his hands opened wide and gripping his knees.

"There was a game that we played at school called the choking game, the fainting game. I know you knew about it because it came out at the inquiry. But I never told you my part in it. Now that I look back, it makes me sick. The older boys had told us there was no danger. You'd just feel high and have the benefit of an altered state of consciousness without taking drugs. Back then, we couldn't articulate it that well, but you get the gist of it. I witnessed other guys doing it. I helped a few down before they strangled. It was a high watching them, and a high saving them. It was so stupid, so dangerous. But what can I say, we were kids."

Clement interceded. "Did you ever do it?"

"I did it once. So did Damien. But it scared us so bad, we never did it again. I mean, the peer pressure was awful. You were considered a chicken if you didn't do it once. The older guys talked about an even more intense high of ejaculating while hanging but that was too weird. And we were really young. Where it went wrong, was in bragging to the younger kids. We told them never to try it alone. They had to be older. But Harold Brockmeyer must have tried it in his closet, thinking that he could cut himself loose, then talk big to the older boys. But he didn't make it."

"So his death was not a suicide," stated Clement.

"No, and he didn't kill himself because Luca was bullying him, like people believed. People believe what they want to believe. It was a terrible accident."

"And why didn't you come forward with this before now, Gabriel?"

"I never told you because I was ashamed, and I didn't want to be expelled. I was just a kid. I know that's not a legitimate excuse. But after it was over, we all made a pact to never play the game again and never tell the details to anyone. And then time passed and no one talked about it anymore."

Clement was visibly shaken. "My question stands. Why have you come to me now?"

"Because I'm the one who told Harold about it. Damien and I, acting like tough guys, told him how it worked. Specifically, Damien told him, and I warned him not to try it until he was older, with the caveat that he had to be with someone he trusted. Harold didn't wait. He tried it by himself, and he killed himself. It was a horrible accident, Dad. Damien and I felt responsible for his death. It definitely wasn't Luca. Luca never even tried it. He had too much sense...and was scared, for good reason."

"I guess I'm not going to wake up in the morning and realize I've had a nightmare about young Brockmeyer, am I?"

"No, Dad. And honestly, there was a time that I thought I'd never tell anyone. I felt ashamed and guilty. But Luca's inheritance is around the corner, and I know that you've been concerned about his behavior through the years. You don't need to be. He's one of the good guys. I just want you to know that. "

Clement didn't respond.

Gabriel stood. "I'll see you in the morning. I hope you don't think less of me. But if the truth be known, it was important, right now, that you think more of Luca."

Gabriel closed the door behind him. The room now suffocated Clement, and the usual suspects of Regret, Shame, and Guilt took their turns. Why hadn't his son confided the truth to him years ago? How could he have been unaware that Gabriel had carried such a burden of shame for so long? Surely, there had been signs of his son's unhappiness that went undetected. And all along, Clement was guilty in wrongly suspecting Luca's involvement in young Brockmeyer's death.

For a man of conscience and justice, he had failed in understanding, but during the next hours of contemplation, he succeeded in gaining humility. The world didn't change that night, but Clement's private world was shaken. The following morning, Fiona would find him asleep in his chair, as if nothing of consequence had occurred.

CHAPTER TWELVE

"The sun loved me again when it saw that the stars would not abandon me."—Jenim Dibie

On an extended weekend in October, Luca boarded a plane to Florence, Italy, the country of his birth, where he had not visited since his enrollment at SCB. He'd seen photos and read about Italy in history and geography classes, but he wasn't prepared for how different, how beautifully different the countryside was. Traveling by car from Florence to Castiglione, he'd felt he was on a slow-moving roller-coaster over a landscape of olive groves, vineyards, and sunflowers. His time was restricted, so there would be no sightseeing. He took a room in the town of Castiglione for two nights, with the explicit purpose of exhuming history about his family at Bellaterra.

On the first morning, he drove past the bronze-filigreed Bellaterra gates, but he lost courage and didn't stop, because of course, the people who lived there would not have known his family. Minutes later, he reconsidered his decision and made a U-turn. His rented red Fiat slithered down the country road like a snake in Eden, back to where it all began. Maybe they *had* retained employees as Clement had conjectured. He pulled into the entrance, and an older man stepped out of the gate shack.

"May I help you?"

"I know this is a long shot, but I used to live here, and I wondered if you know if there's anyone who was employed by the Gherardini family who might still work here."

"And who might you be?"

"Luca Gherardini."

"Signore Rudolpho's son?" The man clapped his weathered hands together.

"Si."

"You're a young man. I haven't seen you since you were two years old. Yes, I see the resemblance. Your father was a great man, Luca." The gatekeeper's eyes teared up. "My name is Jonas. I have worked here for thirty years, and I knew your father. And loved him."

"And my mother?" Luca asked.

"Yes, and your mother. Signora Sofia," he replied.

"Could I talk to you about my parents, Jonas? I have so many questions."

Jonas agreed, although Luca noticed his pause to consider before answering.

"I don't get off work until six-thirty tonight but I can meet you at Taverna Vingiano in town, if it pleases you?"

"Thank you, Jonas. I would be grateful."

The afternoon dragged like sludge through a pipe. Since his meeting with Clement, Luca had researched his parents and found out what the world knew about them. But he wanted more. He wanted to know what the world *didn't* know about them; the mysterious, personal side; the side that made no sense; the side that might explain why a mother would abandon her child, without looking back. Had she met with foul play and actually been a loving mother who wanted to be with him but was cheated of the chance? That's what he wanted to believe.

Luca arrived at the tavern punctually at six-thirty. He blew in with a gust of cool Italian air, ushering a flurry of leaves through the door. Inside, he could practically taste the garlic in the air.

A woman in her late thirties named Pia directed him to a table. He asked for a glass of water and said that he'd place an order when the man he was meeting arrived. Pia looked at him curiously and asked if he was visiting, as she thought she'd recognize him if he were a local.

"Yes, although I lived here when I was very young," he said with an engaging smile that disarmed her subsequent questioning. She smiled and blushed, in return.

The tavern was busy due to the time of day, but despite the activity, Luca felt alone. Loneliness was a familiar state, one that had been thrust upon him, not sought after. He remembered back to his early schoolboy years, that when the other boys returned refreshed and loved from their holidays, he was withdrawn and hurt. The boys thought he was mean because he didn't interact with them. And when confronted, he wouldn't back down, which was in fact, his need to appear strong because no one had his back. Eventually watching the others leave for holidays became bittersweet, but tolerable. He was alone, but in being alone, he could listen to the owl outside his window; he could cry without anyone hearing him; he could strategize without interruption; he could expose himself to himself. He reflected upon the hours that he'd talk to himself in the mirror like talking to a friend, pumping up his friend in the looking glass to help him find his worth. He often wondered from whom he had inherited his survival instincts, his father or his mother?

Then suddenly, the exclamation "Jonas!"

"Olympia, how is my girl?" Jonas retorted, giving the waitress an affectionate, full-bodied hug. "How's business?"

"So-so, but why are you here? We don't see much of you anymore."

"Since my wife died, I don't get out much. I'm here to meet someone."

"Could it be that handsome hunk of a stranger in the corner?" she asked, pointing to Luca, and turning her head to stick out a lascivious tongue.

He laughed. "It is indeed. Don't let Vinnie see that look in your eyes."

Pia pursed her lips and made a loud kissing sound, just to tease him.

"Pia, look at me, and don't overreact, don't look surprised. I will introduce you to him, but I want you to be prepared. It's Luca Gherardini, Rudolpho and Sofia's son."

Pia glared at Jonas in shocked disbelief, the exact look he hadn't wanted Luca to see. He turned toward Luca and walked to the table.

"Luca, I must admit, I am astonished to meet you as a grown man. I knew you only as a little boy," he restated as he took a seat.

"Thank you for meeting me, Jonas. I feel like I'm walking through a dream. I don't remember my parents, but this is why I'm here. I'm searching for some answers about my past. I can hardly believe I found someone who knew them, on my first day back. It must be a good sign."

"We were so worried about you when you disappeared from Bellaterra, my boy. You're safe. That's more than a good sign. It's a gift from heaven."

Luca stared at Jonas as if looking at a grandfather he'd never known. *Someone had cared for him and had worried about him.*

"Disappeared? What do you mean?" Luca asked.

"How much *do* you know about your past, Luca?"

"Not much. I know my father died, and my mother disappeared the morning following his funeral, and she never returned or contacted me. She was presumed missing, then dead. That's all I know. Did she take me with her?"

Pia appeared and handed them menus to which Luca responded, "I'm not hungry. Just a Prosecco, please."

"I'd like a Bellini, Pia, and bring a *cucina caprese*. Luca here has not tasted your *caprese*. And Pia, may I introduce you to Luca Gherardini. I believe you knew him as a boy, no?"

Pia nodded. "I did."

"Did you know my mother?"

"I was her personal maid. I'm so happy to see you are safe, Luca." Pia's eyes watered with tears. "We were so worried about you when you disappeared. Where have you been all these years?"

"At the Swiss Conservatory for Boys in Lucerne, since I was three," he replied.

"Wait until I tell Auriane. She will burst into tears of joy when she hears you're safe."

"Who's Auriane?"

"Your nanny. When Nico took you away...you've heard of Nico? Rudolpho's son from his first marriage?"

"Yes, I've been told of him."

"Good. Well, when Nico took you away, Auriane was despondent. She loved you very much. Let me bring your drinks and the *caprese*. On the house! I'll be right back." She made an about-face as if a soldier on a mission.

"What's her job here? Waiting tables?" Luca asked.

"No, she's just filling in for someone. She married the owner about five years ago. Vinnie Vingiano. He used to be a private investigator, but when his father died, and his brother Dominic married an American girl and moved to the States, Vinnie inherited the place. They serve the best gnocchi in town. Good, honest folks," Jonas said. "So what do you want to know, Luca?"

"Pia just answered one of my questions. Nico took me away. But where? And tell me about my mother, please. Why didn't she take me with her?"

"Do you want me to be straight?"

"Of course. I can take it. I lived my whole life thinking no one loved me, and I've already discovered in less than a day that three people—you, Pia, and a woman named Auriane—were worried about my safety. I've never felt so loved. Lay it on me."

He smiled broadly.

"All right. After Sofia didn't return, Nico took you away one night. So he knew where you were, but unfortunately, no one else did. One rumor was that he took you to his Cousin Mia's home in Capri, but by the time we heard that, you were no longer there. When we heard that Sofia was pronounced legally dead, we presumed you were with her and possibly had died with her. But glory be to God, that isn't true. You were in boarding school in a different country. Ha ha! But if she had been with you, you'd probably have some memory of her."

"Which I don't. Can you think of anything else?"

Jonas paused thoughtfully.

"There was a private investigation concerning a suspicion of foul play about your father's death, which was compounded after learning that your half-brother died prematurely."

"Foul play? What happened?"

"There was reason to believe that your mother and Nico were romantically involved."

"After my father's death?"

A long pause ensued.

"No, before his death," Jonas answered.

Luca felt the blood from his head drain to his solar plexus. "So what are you implying?"

"I think you should speak to Pia's husband."

"Why?"

"Because he was the private investigator on the case."

Luca stood up and walked into the kitchen of Taverna Vingiano and returned three minutes later to shake Jonas' hand and thank him for his time.

"What just happened? Why did you go into the kitchen?" Jonas asked.

"I told Pia that I must speak to her husband ... I'll be back later this evening. Thank you, Jonas. I will never be able to repay you for your kindness. Please know, that my father and I are eternally grateful."

As quickly as Luca had blown in the door, he disappeared. Again. But this time, he was coming back. Jonas smiled, and under his breath, he uttered, "Glory be to God."

CHAPTER THIRTEEN

"Why hold on to the very thing which keeps you from hope and love?"—Leo Buscaglia

Hearing from Pia about the dramatic re-emergence of Luca Gherardini, Vinnie had mixed feelings about meeting him. Vinnie was curious, of course, but reluctant to tell the boy the details of his investigation into the life of his maniacal mother. One thing was certain-he would not share the names or whereabouts of the women who'd employed him or why. He would not give Luca a reason to retaliate on his mother's behalf. Vinnie Vingiano would have no blood on his hands.

He arrived at the tavern at eight-thirty p.m. through the back entrance. The kitchen smelled of rising yeast and tomatoes. Pia kissed him and warned him to be careful and discreet. Vinnie waved her off.

"Vinnie, listen to me, baby. You don't know how much of his mother is in his blood."

"Pia, settle down. I've thought it through. I'm not going to give him details. I'll just let him know that Sofia died. That's all. He deserves to know that his mother is dead."

"Okay," said Pia. "And here's his *caprese* from this afternoon. I wrapped it to go. He's sitting at table four."

He kissed her and confidently walked into the dining area toward Luca's table.

"Luca, Vinnie Vingiano. Good to meet you. Glad to see you're alive and well, and the mystery of your disappearance is solved."

"Thank you for coming. I hope you can help me by answering some questions, Mr. Vingiano."

"Please call me Vinnie. I'll do my best. And here's your *caprese*. On the house."

"Thanks, Vinnie. Did you ever find my mother?"

"Yes. Not personally, but through other contacts, I learned of your mother's death in 2006. It was confirmed."

"Where? How?" Luca pressed.

"In Vancouver. In the home she rented there. Heart attack." His delivery sounded brusque so he added, "My condolences."

"It's all right. I didn't know her anyway. I had hoped that if she'd died shortly after leaving me, it would explain why she never came for me. But it sounds like she moved away for a good year and a half without coming for me, so she didn't want to see me."

"I never met her, Luca, but some women aren't maternal. I think she was one of them."

"It's difficult to imagine, isn't it?" Luca sipped his tea. "But I've accepted it. I've spent years in therapy, discussing my unknown mother, my abandonment, and the shame, rejection, and betrayal associated with it. I could give a week-long seminar on dealing with abandonment. But that's not interesting to anyone who hasn't experienced it."

"No actually, it's impressive to hear you talk so openly. You had to be really angry. I would have been furious," Vinnie said.

"Anger was only part of it. I went through years of being shattered, lonely and withdrawn, before the rage set in. How could life be so unfair? Why didn't I have parents who loved me? Why did my parents dump me and never look back?"

"Your father was a decent and good man who had the respect of everyone in this community, Luca."

"I know that now. My father was a good man. But no one talks about my mother. *She* is the culprit. *She* is the reason I grew up alone. *She* is the cause of the emptiness and sadness of my childhood. I was recently told that she left after my father died because her heart was broken, but I don't believe that anymore.

I'm not sure she had a heart. Just today Jonas told me that she was suspected of having an affair with my half-brother, so maybe she was planning a life with him, and that's why she left. Why else would she leave?"

Vinnie's sense of decency wanted to tell Luca that his mother was evil; that she was run out of town by a family of American women whom his mother had persecuted; that she was suspected of a series of stolen identifications and murders by poison. But to what end? And although it couldn't be proved, her sudden death had seemed suspicious as well.

Luca shook his head. "Wasn't she young to die of a heart attack?"

"Yes, she was. But we don't know her personal history. Perhaps she had a congenital defect. Perhaps she abused her body with drugs. On a personal note, if there is any hereditary factor, you best be aware of it. It wouldn't hurt to check it out, because I agree, she was young."

Luca stared blankly at his Prosecco as if perplexed as to what it was and what he should do with it. Suddenly, as if the spell was broken, he stood to leave and extended his hand to Vinnie.

"You've been very kind to me, Mr. Vingiano. I appreciate your answering my questions so candidly. One more thing, if you don't mind."

"Not at all. What is it?"

"A friend of mine told me that my mother changed her name when she married my father. When she died in Vancouver, was she still Sofia Gherardini?"

Vinnie thought it through in an instant, and seeing no harm in giving him a direct answer, he said, "No, her name was Madison Thomas."

****

Luca drove back to his hotel and decided to sit in the interior palazzo to digest what he'd learned that day. The air was cool and moist, the night sky so clear that the Milky Way was visible to the naked eye, like a swath of ice on a window to another world.

Maybe if he looked deeply enough, answers from a celestial sphere would be shared with him that night.

When reality grabbed him by the throat, he jolted with a gasp. He had left the tavern without processing his feelings well enough to know what the next questions should have been. Now they stacked unevenly and teetered upon the foundation of his new knowledge. *What about Auriane, his nanny? Did he want to meet her? Maybe someday. What about Bellaterra? Would it be presumptuous to ask Jonas if he could see the grounds, request permission to see the home that his father built? Was Nico's Cousin Mia, his cousin too?...or only related to Nico from Rudolpho's first marriage? Would Vinnie share his investigation file on Sofia with him? Who had hired him to investigate her and why? Was she really suspected of poisoning his father and brother? Had they proof that she and Nico were having an affair? Who had been little Luca's advocate? Nico? His mother's lover and possibly co-conspirator of his father's death? If they were lovers, Nico had to have known she was the orchestrator. Had they killed him for money? Had she killed Nico for more money?*

He remembered Ms. Walker telling him repeatedly that a wound was a place the light can enter. He held on to that. He remembered a William James quote: "The greatest weapon against stress is our ability to choose one thought over another." He held onto that too.

So he chose another thought. The best part of his day was discovering that his disappearance, his kidnapping, had alarmed and concerned so many people. He *had* been wanted. He *had* been loved. And throughout his entire life, he hadn't known it.

He sipped his absinthe, then rubbed his index finger on the rim of his glass, round and round, creating music from nothing, but music, nevertheless. He told himself that he was satisfied with what he'd learned that day ... at least for a while. There was no reason for him to stay in Castiglione. His life was before him. Within a few months, he would graduate from SCB and his inheritance would open a world of opportunity and adventure.

Perhaps he'd travel to America and visit the libraries of his favorite American authors. Perhaps he'd visit Vancouver.

He had come to Italy to discover more about his mother, and he had. She was a beautiful, selfish woman without maternal instincts, who may have had an affair with her husband's first son. She was suspected of conspiring to kill both of them. She had a year and a half to come for Luca, but she hadn't. She had hidden from the world for some reason and had died prematurely at the age of thirty-one in a foreign country, with a different name, alone. What else was there to know?

He heard an owl; it was close. It was the sound he'd remembered when Dr. Landis had asked him to access his childhood. It was the same owl, the same sound. He'd always loved owls. He'd only seen one, outside his dormitory window. The owl was the bird that could see in the dark, with a neck that allowed it to observe in all directions, obtaining a wisdom of its surroundings, like no other animal could. The owl could seize its opportunity to swoop in silence to apprehend its prey, without any others being the wiser. As a boy, when he'd communed with his owl and thought of his mother, the owl would say, "Who? Who?" The owl understood his confusion and discontent.

Ms. Walker had once quoted someone who had written...*The owl stays awake when the rest of the world sleeps. What does he see and what does he know that the rest of the world is missing?* Luca would stay awake all night to listen to the owl. It had lessons to teach him. He wanted more than anything in the world, to take on the mantle of the owl. To assume its soul.

CHAPTER FOURTEEN

"Even if you are a minority of one, the truth is the truth."
—Gandhi

Autumn in Virginia was breathtaking, on par with New England and the upper Midwest; painted in resplendent colors that defied description. Autumn in Virginia inspired crunchy, aromatic walks, the wearing of sweaters, and paintbrushes bristling to orgasmic attention to capture the brilliance. The air smelled of chimney smoke and crushed leaves.

But when Cristin returned from Iowa, she didn't see its glory. She was a different person, tarnished by the knowledge that her beloved grandmother had committed a murder. A murder that could have remained a secret forever, if Cristin hadn't opened Pandora's Box. When she thought of her discovery, she could actually smell the dank scent of the cardboard container that resided under her grandmother's bed. The only two people on the planet who knew this secret were she and her mother. Their communal weather vane now pointed in the direction of sharing their new-found knowledge with her sister only. It wasn't necessary to tell the extended family.

Unlike her sister, Cristin preferred talking to people in person, so she needed to figure out a time she and Elizabeth could meet, face to face. She was so social media deficient that Elizabeth had shamed her into setting up a Facebook page and an Instagram account, a compliance Cristin considered an olive branch.

"You'll be an outcast among your friends, Cris, if you don't jump on board," Elizabeth had warned.

Since she'd left Iowa, Cristin hadn't checked either her Facebook or Instagram account. After all, she'd seen Elizabeth only a little over a week ago. *How much could have happened?*

But as soon as she logged on, Cristin realized how wrong she'd been. There, big as life, was a photo of Elizabeth and Shane in Beaufort, South Carolina. Her sister hadn't said anything about taking a trip. Cristin picked up the phone and called her.

"What are you doing in South Carolina?"

"Oh, hi Cris. Shane and I are checking out the haunted houses in Beaufort," she replied.

"You are not! You didn't mention anything about a trip when I saw you," Cristin said, as she mindlessly unraveled a thread on her afghan.

"I know. Shane has a job offer down here, so since I don't have a job right now—don't tell that to Mom—I joined him on a scouting expedition. A recon mission, sort of. "

"Do you think he'll take the job? Will you go too, if he does?" Cristin asked.

"I think so. There's really nothing tying me to NYC, other than the fact that it is the most happening city on the planet. And to tell the truth, I thought I'd end up seeing Grandma Katie in Boston and Aunt Tia in D.C. more often, because it's not *that* far to either city, but it's just far enough. There's really no reason to stay. Besides, I like it down here. You should see the birds. I've even looked into a naturalist program through Clemson. Go Tigers! It might not give me a degree but I'd be accredited. Mom would be happy if I went back to school, especially if I studied something I loved, right?"

"Yes, she would. I'm just rather stunned, that's all. Good for you."

"And I'm serious, Cris, Beaufort would be heaven for you. All kinds of haunted places. There's a haunted church, mysterious lights off Land's End, a haunted castle, and even a lighthouse. Surely a lighthouse has stories and should be haunted. And of course, add the spooky Spanish moss hanging from the trees at night, it's a virtual ghost's paradise."

"You're hilarious, Elizabeth. That's not what I do, remember? You're talking about folklore. I deal with the paranormal in a very real way." She laughed. "Did I just say that? But seriously, I'd like to see you soon."

"I just saw you," Elizabeth wisecracked. "No offense."

"I know but this can't wait. Something's come up. Could you meet me halfway?"

"No. Tell me now."

"That's not going to happen. I want to see you," Cristin said.

"Okay. Be that way. Shane and I are driving home to make arrangements for our move, so could you meet us, let's say, in Fairfax or Arlington?"

"That would be awesome. But I'll need to talk to you for about an hour, privately."

"No problem. Shane can get lost at some local pub. We'll be ready for a car break. This sounds mysterious. Are you pregnant? Oh my God, is Mom okay?"

"Nothing like that but we do need to talk, so figure out a date, time, and place, and I'll be there."

"Okay. And by the way, you can call me Lizzie now. I'm trying it on for size. Elizabeth is just too formal for me. You used to call me Lizzie the Lizard, remember? May the ghosts be with you," Lizzie said in her spookiest voice. "Boo!" Then she hung up.

Her sister was never serious. After the call, Cristin felt unusually alone and tired. She heard a mourning dove in the distance...or was it an owl?

When Lizzie heard the news about Grandma Dori, she'd be serious. Cristin imagined her sister's face when she was told. Horror-stricken, as she was sure her own face had been. Lizzie liked drama. When she couldn't find drama, she created drama. But what Lizzie couldn't see coming was their real-life drama that their Grandma Dori had killed someone to protect them. Try that on for size, little sister.

She was glad she'd see Lizzie soon, because their mother would be back from Vancouver before long, to verify what she suspected to be true. Cristin listened to her thoughts. *Did people just believe what they thought was true, without proof? Did she?* She was putting the cart before the horse, as her Grandpa Daniel would have said. The proof was in the pudding, as Grandma Dori would have said.

The good news was that Lizzie was looking into going back to school. That was a step in the right direction. She'd attended NYU, thinking she wanted to be an architect, but it became a pipe dream when she realized how much math was involved. In Cristin's not-so-humble opinion, Lizzie could have integrated her naturalist inclinations and become a landscape designer, but because that suggestion came from Cristin, it had been unequivocally rejected.

After two years, rather than transfer to a different major, Lizzie did the unthinkable. She dropped out of school. It didn't help matters that Cristin had graduated from the University of Virginia *summa cum laude*, and gone directly into the Division of Perceptual Studies for her master's degree. But what was she to do? Slow down, not excel, not follow her dream, so her sister didn't feel inferior? In the meantime, Cristin endured Lizzie's sarcastic remarks.

Cristin had an undergraduate degree in English with an emphasis on American literature which unless she was going to be a writer or a teacher, was relatively useless in the job market. It may have been naïve on her part, but she actually thought she could get away with studying something she loved because she would probably fall in love, get married, and figure out the income issue later. After all, her mother hadn't worked in a field related to her college degree, and she had a very comfortable life. So when Cristin didn't fall in love, in spite of two significant relationships in her undergraduate years, she not only didn't have a degree that was financially promising, she had stumbled into another income- deficient future by continuing her education in a field that she loved even more—parapsychology.

But Cristin had talent and she hoped she could help others, which was the altruistic aspect of her study. However, the most compelling reason was that it was fascinating. It preoccupied her mind, night and day. She went to bed, eager to dream; she awakened, ready to be used as a conduit to link this world with the unknown worlds of the past and future.

She had dreams that manifested. She saw auras. She'd had a near death experience during her sophomore year at UVA, after a ski accident in Vermont; and dreams foretelling events that later occurred in real time. These were not the kinds of things she could speak openly about because people tended to think she was peculiar. Or worse, that she was fabricating to attract attention. So her inner life was solitary, seldom shared for fear of being shunned. She was happiest at school, in class with others who shared her interest and sometimes, her talents. But outside the classroom, she was basically alone, except for the company of her nerdy but beautiful Persian friend, Flora.

Keeping things to herself had become a lifestyle. She'd not felt well for a long time. She was constantly tired, no matter how much she slept. Her legs and back ached for no plausible reason, and even on warm days, she would get chilled. But she was a stressed twenty-two-year-old university student, and she'd overheard others talking about similar maladies. It would pass just like everything else.

She walked to a full-length mirror in her apartment and looked at herself. She looked Irish. Irish and tired. Her auburn hair was duller than it used to be. Her green eyes were not dancing like they once did. The sprinkling of freckles across her nose that appeared every summer had faded. Why didn't she have a steady boyfriend? Most of her friends were engaged to be married, and some were already married with a child. How would she meet someone when she stayed in her apartment to channel spirits? What was wrong with her? She needed to get out more. She needed to make herself available to life's cornucopia of opportunities. If she was truly connected to the universe, she could open herself to meeting a compatible, loving partner. She had an inner power. She just needed to channel it.

CHAPTER FIFTEEN

"The reality is that you will grieve forever. You will not 'get over' the loss of a loved one; you will learn to live with it. You will heal and you will rebuild yourself around the loss you have suffered. You will be whole again but you will never be the same. Nor should you be the same, nor would you want to."
–Elisabeth Kübler-Ross

It was time to connect with Cristin. Trina's heart thumped as she picked up the phone, then put it down. She lit a cigarette and took a few drags to relax. Never had she felt less like herself. Bruised, hardened, and angry, like her underbelly had been punched. And furthermore, she was battling a beast of a cold. She coughed, took a shallow breath, and made the call.

Trina spilled what she'd learned in Vancouver. The work records at the coffee shop had been destroyed when the ownership changed, and no one working there knew Sissy a.k.a. Dori.

"I asked about the name Delores on Grandma's work schedule from 2006. One of the older waitresses knew her and told me where to find her. And I met her."

"Oh, Mom, what was she like?"

"She was Grandma Dori's age but not well-kept, not well-groomed, not well-anything. Very sad. Her apartment smelled of body odor and a cat litter box that hadn't been emptied in at least a week. I nearly gagged, Cristin. There were flies on her peanut-butter toast from that morning, or the week before. Hard to tell.

"I told her that Sissy was my mother and that she'd died recently. I watched the smile fade from Delores' face like a Dorian Gray painting. I asked her what she remembered, hoping that she could hang with me until a few questions were answered. It was evident that her short-term memory was poor.

"She repeatedly mumbled that Sissy was dead, but other than that, I wasn't learning anything new, so I asked when Grandma left the coffee shop. She told me it was right after one of the regulars had suddenly died, found dead in her house. The next day, Grandma was gone."

"Mom, just what you suspected," Cristin said, biting her nails.

"Yes, regrettably. I *did* tell Delores that Sissy had spoken of her, just to perk up her spirits. God forgives little white lies, when they're spoken to appease a saddened heart. Then I asked if she remembered the lady's name, the one who had died. And she did, at least the first name. She said that it was easy to remember because the lady looked like a Madison Avenue type, right out of a magazine. Her name was Madison.

"I had what I'd come for, confirmation of your Grandma's wrong-doing, even if only circumstantial. Delores asked to keep the photograph of Sissy, and I couldn't refuse her. I thanked her and quickly left her apartment, her building, and her country, as fast as I could."

"So, Mom, without grasping at straws, your conclusion?"

"Listen to me. I shared with Grandma a toxicity report regarding plants that could be used to poison people. And when we were in Iowa, I logged on to Grandma's computer, and in her Internet history, I found inquiries into poisons that she could grow in her own garden. It's circumstantial but enough evidence for this jury of one."

Cristin gasped, then sighed.

"But that's not fair, Mom. You can't judge people by their Internet searches. Writers look up bizarre information all of the time. Just because you want to know how to build a bomb doesn't imply that *you're* a terrorist, even if your character is."

"Grandma wasn't researching a character, Cristin. She was researching a way to eliminate someone who was not above killing any one of us. And keep in mind, in her mind, she had nothing to lose. Grandpa was gone. We were all she had. And she travelled to a foreign country to meet her daughter's killer. I put myself in her place, Cristin, and so help me, if someone murdered you, I'd kill the fucker."

"Mom!"

"Don't Mom me, Cristin! Someday when you have a child of your own, you will understand. Being a mother is like no other role or position on God's green earth. Believe me, when I say, I would have done the same. What haunts me, and I've had plenty of time to think about this, is that if I hadn't told my mother the whereabouts of Hunter Cross or Madison Thomas, or whatever her name was, Grandma Dori would not have killed her."

Trina coughed, then continued. "But open another sliding door. If Grandma hadn't stopped her, maybe the monster could have killed one of us. Madison Thomas was incensed that we had ruined her plans. We'd tracked her down like the animal she was. With one false move, we could have exposed her as the murderer she was. We became her focus, the problem she needed to resolve, the problem she needed to eliminate. Don't think for one minute, that Grandma Dori wasn't just one step ahead of her. What the evil one didn't know is that we had discovered where she was. Timing was everything, and Grandma Dori knew it."

"Mom, you don't sound like yourself. I've never heard you talk this way. You're scaring me. And do you have a cold?"

Trina couldn't disguise the wheezing sound at the back of her throat when she spoke.

"I'm fine. I'm just telling you the truth, Cristin. And sometimes the truth is hard to hear, and sometimes, even harder to accept. But it's over, in the past. And I'll make no apologies for my mother."

Trina sensed Cristin's uneasiness.

"I'll let you go. Call me after you talk with Lizzie. Are you okay?"

"Yes."

"Then, good night for now. I love you."

"I love you, Mom."

Trina hung up and walked to her recliner in the sun porch where she collapsed into its plush embrace. There were moments like this that she truly missed her husband. Telling Cristin what she'd learned wasn't easy, but necessary. She plowed through it to get through it. Her delivery had been matter-of-fact and uncompromising. She knew she sounded harsh, but that's how she felt. Harsh. And angry. Angry that her mother had put her in this position; angry that she hadn't been alone when she discovered the box; angry that Bryan had died and left her to deal with this mess on her own; angry that perhaps Cristin thought less of her for the things she'd said.

Who was she anyway? Who was Trina Shanihan McClaren? Obviously more than a kind mother of two who belonged to a book club and enjoyed photography. She was damaged, angry, and harsh. That's who she was. As difficult as it was to accept, she knew she was stronger for it. Inside her head, like she'd said to Cristin earlier, the truth was hard to hear, and sometimes, even harder to accept.

CHAPTER SIXTEEN

"Would you believe what you believe if you were the only person who believed it?"–Kanye West

Three days after her phone call with Trina, Cristin met her sister at a park near Arlington National Cemetery.

"It's cold out here, Cristin," was Lizzie's greeting, as she texted someone else on her cell phone. She didn't make eye contact. "You had to choose an outdoor rendezvous point? Near a graveyard?"

"It's more private than a restaurant or a hotel lobby. You'll understand why we need privacy." Cristin noticed that her sister was wearing a heavy warm sweater, hat and gloves; in other words, she was plenty warm. She was just being her irritable self.

"This better be good, big sister. The urgency of having to meet you has kept me awake at night." Lizzie paused, smirked, and added, "Not really."

They chose a bench under a large oak tree that had shed most of its leaves. The sun filtered through a skeleton of branches.

"Don't you wonder where the birds go when they don't have leaves for protection and camouflage?" Cristin asked. She watched disbelief flood Lizzie's eyes like a crashing wave arriving on a shore.

"What?" Lizzie asked "Are we in the vicinity of a point? I didn't come here to talk about where the birds live when the leaves fall, Cristin. I only have an hour. I told Shane I'd pick him up at four, when the game ends. It's the Giants versus the Redskins ... big rivalry. And I don't want to be late, so let's get on with it."

"Then put your phone away. I need to you to listen." Cristin spoke in almost a whisper as if any remaining birds above might be listening. She felt the warmth of her fleece gloves as she rubbed her hands together.

Lizzie tucked her phone in her sweater pocket, folded her hands, and stared into her sister's face with deliberate, strained attention.

"After you left Muscatine, Mom and I discovered something that you need to know. Not because you can do anything about it, but because it wouldn't be right if we kept it from you."

Lizzie shook her head and moaned in exasperation, looking away from Cristin, staring straightforward.

Cristin's mouth sucked at her words. "Okay. Okay," she finally said. "You want it straight? Here it is: Our Aunt Cristin was murdered."

"What?"

Lizzie's face registered the shock that Cristin had anticipated. Cristin filled her in on everything she knew; the murders and details leading up their grandmother's revenge.

"You're implying that Grandma Dori killed Aunt Cristin's murderer?"

"Looks like it."

"You're lying. Grandma Dori didn't have a malicious bone in her skinny little body."

"Lizzie, listen to me. Mom took a trip last week and verified that Grandma was in Vancouver at the time the woman died. It's circumstantial, I know, but too coincidental to ignore."

"I don't believe it. It couldn't be true."

"I'm afraid it is, little sister."

Cristin told her about the woman stalking them at school in Lincoln. She shared the existence of the poison report, "Sissy's" work schedule, the map of Vancouver with circles drawn around the locations of The Coffee Grind and Madison Thomas' rental home.

Cristin dropped her head between her knees.

"What are you doing? What's going on?" Lizzie whispered.

"Nothing. This has nothing to do with the story. I've had some dizzy spells lately. I just need to catch my breath and get oxygen to my brain. Probably lack of sleep."

Lizzie put a hand on her sister's back and patted her until Cristin righted herself. She then rested her head on Cristin's shoulder. Cristin took Lizzie's hand in hers, and they both stared into the park as if they were looking at a Pissarro painting, not blinking, not seeing people walking by, not hearing the birdsong from the birds who had lost their summer homes. After what seemed like an endless amount of time, Lizzie's teary eyes met Cristin's.

"What are we going to do?" she asked.

"Absolutely nothing," Cristin responded.

Later that afternoon, while Cristin drove home, she developed a cramp in her left leg which she attributed to stress. She had to make a pit stop. She locked the car and perambulated through the parking lot a few times to stretch her legs. The sound of the brittle piles of dead leaves under her feet brought her comfort, like the sound of a friend. She wasn't alone.

She'd been surprised that Lizzie had been so calm and reasonable about keeping their family discovery quiet. Their grandmother was dead, and there had been no public link between her and the deceased. Dori had committed the perfect crime, and it was no one else's business. The world was a better place without the Madison Thomas monster, and that's where the story ended.

She'd mentioned to Lizzie that Grandma Dori had come to her in a dream asking for forgiveness and saying that she had done it to protect them. Cristin rarely shared her dreams with her sister because Lizzie didn't believe her. But this time, Lizzie listened. Cristin's gift was complicated. Even she herself didn't understand it. She didn't ask for her glimpses beyond the veil, she just saw things, heard things, sometimes burdensome, sometimes enlightening, sometimes both. This was one of those times.

Her leg pain lessened. She unlocked her car door and continued her trek home. Only another forty-five minutes to go. Within minutes, the wind was blowing and the rain pelting her car like an angry god with a water hose. She defrosted her steamy windshield and watched the haze evaporate like scolded ghosts.

She felt fatigued. She often did lately. She didn't like to drive when tired. She especially didn't like the feeling of opening her eyes while driving, which indicated she had closed them, even if only for a second. The metronomic pulse of the windshield wipers had a hypnotizing effect on her, intensifying her fatigue. Not good. But it was often in this state of relaxation that she was receptive to "happenings."

Staring out the windshield, Cristin suddenly saw a woman's face, like a slide flashing on a screen. Cristin heard the words, *It's your turn.* Then poof, it was gone. She stiffened her arms against the steering wheel and gasped. It had happened again...a visitation, unpredictable in timing from an unrecognized soul. Her heart thumped wildly, and she realized that her *turn* was approaching. She steered to the right to exit the freeway. *Why did this happen to her?* She didn't ask for it, and it was always unnerving. This time the face had been distinct. Young, long dark hair, high cheekbones, large eyes, beautiful; and the message, clear. But it had felt more like a warning than a reminder.

Her heart continued to pound as the storm escalated. The trees on the boulevards conducted a raging chorus of Mussorgsky's *Night on Bald Mountain*, their branches waved wildly to encourage the percussion of the riotous wind and the brass of the assaulting rain to a final climax.

She was so relieved to park her car in front of her apartment, she would have kissed the ground, had the weather not been such a bully. Gales of wind and rain pushed her toward her front door and the sanctuary within. She didn't bother to use the umbrella in her back seat. This was the kind of storm that inverted and flew them to a coat room for missing umbrellas in the sky.

She no sooner shed her wet sweater and dropped her purse when her cell phone rang. It was her mother calling, undoubtedly to find out how the conversation had gone with Lizzie.

"Hi, Mom, I just walked in the door. We're having an angry storm, and I'm relieved to be inside," she said, as she walked to the teapot to turn it on.

"How did it go? I've been thinking about you two all afternoon."

"It went well. Lizzie will probably be calling you when she gets back to New York. She was stunned but agreed that we'll keep this to ourselves. There are a lot of unanswered questions though. I know we're reeling with this discovery of Grandma's involvement, but maybe someday, you can tell us more?"

"Someday. I truly thought we'd never speak of that monster, and frankly, had I been alone at Grandma's house that day, I probably would never have mentioned it to anyone."

"One more thing." Cristin kicked off her shoes and shook her feet. "This will sound weird, maybe unreasonable, but do you have a photo of that Thomas woman?" Cristin asked.

"Why on earth...?"

"If you do, would you email it to me? Trust me. I just need to know what she looked like, okay? If she shows up in a dream, I want to recognize her."

"In a nightmare, you mean. Okay, I have one that Katie sent me. I'll send it to you, but please don't dwell on this. It's water under the bridge. It's over."

"Mom, I'm really tired. I need to get some sleep. Do you mind if we talk later this week?"

"Not at all."

"Thank you. I love you, Mom."

"I love you too, honey."

Cristin hung up the phone and took her boots off, which seemed to become tighter throughout the day. The teakettle whistled, so in Pavlovian style, she headed to the kitchen to pour a cup of hot pomegranate tea to soothe her soul and counterbalance the cold, windy rain that pummeled her roof.

She sat at her computer and stripped off her socks to curl her toes into the shaggy fleece rug she'd splurged on with her birthday gift cards. She glanced at her feet and noticed that her ankles were badly swollen, like she'd just taken a trans-Atlantic flight. That was weird. Maybe the boots had been too tight. She'd look again in the morning

She checked her emails and saw that her mother had already sent her an attachment. She opened it to discover a photo of the face she'd seen in her windshield only minutes ago. Chills cascaded through the latitudes of her body like a scanning X-ray machine, slowly, invasively, until she gasped for a life-restoring breath. It was the same face. The face of Madison Thomas had visited her to tell her to take the turn off the freeway. No. What had she said exactly? *It's your turn.* That's what she'd said. Why would this horrible phantom of a person, the murderer of her aunt, warn her to take an exit off the freeway? Or maybe that had merely been an interpretation. What else could *It's your turn* mean?

CHAPTER SEVENTEEN

"Let us do evil that good may come."—Romans 3:8

Damien arrived in Vancouver during Indian summer, a phrase he wasn't familiar with until he overheard a restaurant waiter mention it. Vancouver was colorfully picturesque, as stunning a season as he'd ever experienced. The trees splashed riotous, vibrant hues against the cloudless blue sky and placid blue water; the air was warm and breezy, fragrant with pine and evergreen. Any thinking person understood the imminence of cooler months, but when living through the splendor of Indian summer, winter was merely a myth.

He sat by the water's edge and observed a young man pass him, with a walk he recognized. It was similar to Luca's walk. Damien had memorized Luca's gait, the way he held his hands as if lightly grasping small birds; the slightly out-turned step of his right foot; his shoulders modestly curled forward. He'd studied Luca since he was young boy, not really knowing why, but fascinated, nonetheless.

Fascinated, agitated, vindicated, copulated.

Enough of Luca. *Focus, focus. Hocus pocus.*

As he stared at the water, Damien refocused and contemplated his task at hand; specifically his own talents and skills that now appeared to be part of his destiny. Who was the kid at school who had learned to forge hall passes? He was. Who was the kid who was the master of disguise when pulling pranks?

He was. Who was the kid who kept the others amused with voices of famous people and imitations of teachers' idiosyncrasies? He was. And now, now after years of practice and not knowing why, he would call upon his talents as servants who always appeared when called upon, and who meticulously obeyed their master.

Mariana frequently quoted the verse, "Watch ye therefore. For ye do not know when the master cometh." But he did know. *He* was the master. His mother would be proud.

Surely whatever was hidden in that safe deposit box would be something he could use to help Luca and further his own selfish cause. Or was it selfish? To want to be happy? In the meantime, while he was working and designing their future together, Luca would live in the cellar of his heart. But in Damien's cellar where he couldn't escape. Yes, yes. He saw things so much more clearly when he was off his meds.

****

During the previous week, he had gone to the bank to open his own savings account as blond, blue-eyed Damien Scardina, using his own passport. He had purchased a safe deposit box so that he could learn the inside system. It had gone smoothly, without a hitch. Security cameras surveyed the bank lobby, but there didn't appear to be any cameras in the safe deposit room. Still, there was no room for error, and he only had one shot. He decided it would be best to be in full disguise as Luca Gherardini on the day of reckoning. Although no one at the bank had ever met Luca, when Damien went to open the Gherardini box #26310, he didn't want the assisting guard to recognize him from the previous week, and realize that he was opening a different box under a different name. He also resolved that late afternoon, when the bank was busy, was the best time to strike.

He had dreamed for a month what it would be like to walk into the Bank of Vancouver to earn his prize. The afternoon had finally arrived. For a short half-hour, he would become Luca Gherardini. The day before, he had dyed his hair dark brown, inserted tinted brown contacts, and could pass for the younger man in the passport picture. He felt like he imagined Luca felt—confident, composed, and rich. He liked it. He dabbed Luca's favorite cologne, Joop, behind his ears and under his nose. Now he even smelled like Luca.

He strode into the bank around four-thirty when the bank was bustling. He stood in a queue and talked to people with his charming Italian accent. When it was almost his turn, he realized that he would be speaking to a man behind the counter, and he'd prefer to deal with a woman. So Damien turned to a young girl behind him who'd been complaining about being late to her next appointment and let her go ahead of him, in order to be in queue for the next female teller. The girl accepted his gallant gesture and walked to the counter.

Now it was his turn. He regarded the young female teller with a seductive smile and a tilt of his head as if he were attracted to her. He then told her he needed to open a safe deposit box left to him by his mother. She blushed, smiled, and called her manager to the counter.

The manager was male, stoic looking. Not the female he thought he might manipulate if need be. His heart raced, angry. He bit his lower lip, tasting his own blood.

"My name is Forrest Campbell. May I help you, sir?"

"Yes, thank you. My name is Luca Gherardini. My mother left a safe deposit key for me to use when I came to B.C. Here is the letter from our attorney authorizing me to open the box."

"Do you have your key and identification, Mr. Gherardini?"

"Yes, of course. My passport and birth certificate."

Mr. Campbell officiously looked at the documents, and read the letter on Damien's father's legal stationary.

"Let me check our records to see whose names are listed to access this box, sir. Will you step aside so we can help the next customer? I'll be back in a few minutes."

Campbell disappeared behind a door, and Damien stood in No Man's Land. Impersonating someone's voice was different than impersonating a personage. His heart thumped as he tried to appear self-assured, wondering what kind of roadblock he might come up against. *Why wasn't his mother there? Should he say she was dead? No. They might want a death certificate. And although she'd been legally declared dead, he didn't have a death certificate.* He was in a foreign country and suddenly felt vulnerable to a system he might not understand.

Campbell reappeared and motioned Damien to the safe deposit room.

"Yes, we have on record that you are a signatory on this box, Mr. Gherardini, even though you were very young and unable to sign, at, let's see, four years old?" Campbell laughed jauntily and Damien's relief broke through his wall of anxiety.

"Your mother was certainly thinking ahead, young man. She leased this box for fifteen years. I don't think I've ever run across this before. Anyway, sign here please." Campbell pointed his stubby, dirty, unmanicured finger to the line on which Damien was to sign. They walked into the familiar room, and together used the keys to remove the box.

"I can either stand here with you, Mr. Gherardini, or you can go into the side room for some privacy," said Campbell. Once again, he pointed his nasty finger, this time to the private room.

"Thank you, sir. If you don't mind?"

Campbell nodded.

Damien picked up the box, walked to the private chamber, and closed the door behind him. The room was small, the walls close, and he immediately felt them closing in on him. Expecting to see only a letter, he opened the box and gawked at a tremendous amount of cash. *Good Lord.* His adrenaline, already in high gear, ratcheted up a notch. He rifled through one stack, then another, emptying the box as fast as he could. There was in excess of a million dollars, perhaps more, in U.S. currency. The box was a large rectangular shape and seemed bottomless. *Where was the letter?* He panicked. Without the directive from Sofia, he had no leverage, no proof that he was willing to go to the limit to help Luca. He reached under the remaining stacks and felt an envelope. He pulled it out and ripped it open, his hands shaking.

Dearest Luca,

I am your mother, Sofia. If you're reading this, I am dead. You've not known me, and I'm sorry that I wasn't a mother to you in the truest sense of the word. But that doesn't change the fact that you are my son, my only child.

You were born into a wealthy Italian family, and by now, you are probably eighteen, and Santino has given you the envelope that led you to this box. You're about to inherit an immense fortune. But first I have something to ask of you.

If I had survived, I would be telling you this in person. I am thirty-one years old and living in Vancouver. I plan on leaving here soon and moving to the South Seas, far away from anyone who has ever known me, even, regrettably from you. I've always been a cautious person, Luca, and I'm hoping that by the time you turn eighteen, I will have come back into your life, and you will have never read this letter. But evidently, that didn't happen.

Life is capricious, and sometimes dangerous. I want you to know that the reason I left you was that I was being hunted down by a family from the United States—an old friend of mine who turned her three sisters against me. Their claims that I had done them wrong were ill-founded and would have hurt the Gherardini name, so immediately after your dear father died, I fled, leaving you in the charge of your half-brother Nico's cousin and her husband. Shortly thereafter, you were enrolled at SCB, and within a year, Nico died from a severe allergic reaction. So if I am gone, you are alone.

I need to enlist your help, Luca. I'm asking you to avenge my death. Blood is thick and you are my son, so I know you can do this. On the attached sheet of paper, I have listed the women who are responsible for our estrangement, and ultimately, my death. But I don't want you to be caught in any wrong-doing, so you must be wary.

Family is critically important to these people, so the death of one of their own will be the most passionate revenge. The sisters will be older. They're not my concern. But my oldest friend, Trina, has two daughters, one named Cristin McClaren. She would be the *greatest loss to all of them, because she, in name, signifies another person who died years ago. Concentrate on her, my son. Stay invisible to these people, but find a way for that family, particularly Trina Shanihan McClaren, to know that her daughter Cristin's death is payback. They ruined my life.*

Peace be with you. I'm truly sorry we didn't know one another. I have never asked anything of you but I trust you will do this one thing for me, Luca. Make them pay. Please.

Love,
Your mother, Sofia

Damien turned the page, to find a list of six women: Tess Parker (Minnetonka, Minnesota); Katie Shepard (Boston, Massachusetts); Tia Monson (Washington D.C.); and Trina McClaren (Lincoln, Nebraska) with two daughters, Cristin and Elizabeth. Addresses were complete, at least as of ten years ago. He put the letter along with the addresses back in the envelope and stuffed it in his left inside pocket. His shirt was wet with perspiration. His heart pounded in his chest, his temples, and his wrists. *Oh, Luca. We hit the jackpot.*

Then he looked at the money. He'd never seen so much money in one place. He restacked it, trying to get a notion of how much was there. There had to be over a million dollars. He grabbed four packets of $100 bills and stuffed them in the inside pockets of his suit jacket. *Highway robbery.*

He closed the box and walked into the room where Forrest Campbell was waiting.

"Did you find what you needed?" Campbell asked, looking antsy to leave.

"Yes, thank you, sir. I may need to come back tomorrow to add some papers. I appreciate your help," Damien said to the minion.

They locked the box with both keys without saying anything more, and Damien exited the bank, feeling wiser...and richer.

CHAPTER EIGHTEEN

"The righteous will rejoice when he sees the vengeance."
—Psalms 58:10

Damien didn't sleep much that night, which wasn't good since he hadn't slept the night before. But he had a lot of thinking to do. He now knew what the request was, the specific target of Sofia's revenge. He now had to set it up for Luca to carry out. Luca would thank him for this someday. He smiled to himself, thinking that Luca had no idea what a loyal friend he had in Damien. More loyal than Gabriel would ever be.

But something else had gone down that afternoon that he hadn't anticipated. The money. He needed to think it through. When he eventually handed Luca the letter, Luca would see the reference to a box, not a safe deposit box or its location. Sofia had mentioned contents, but she hadn't mentioned money. Luca would read the letter, but he didn't have to know that it had come from a safe deposit box in Vancouver. Damien could just say that he found an envelope referencing Gherardini in his father's office drawer that included a key and location of a small box that contained a letter. *The* letter. No one ever needed to know about his "borrowing" the passport *or* his trip to Vancouver. Couldn't he, Damien Scardina, take the money without anyone ever knowing?

He'd sleep on it, but Damien was leaning towards returning to the bank in the morning with a backpack, or more, and taking it. *Yes sir, yes sir. Three bags full.* No, one bag would be enough. He would stash the loot in a new safe deposit box and supplement their lifestyle together, as if he had significant means of his own. *This was ingenious.* Or perhaps, he would need the money if Luca was not receptive to his eventual advances. Even though that thought was dark and couldn't be, wouldn't be entertained, everyone needed a backup plan. He'd already established subconsciously that he was capable of stealing the money, because he'd told the teller with the dirty fingernails that he was planning on returning the next day to "add some papers." But until that night, he hadn't acknowledged to himself that he was a thief. *Rich man, poor man, beggar man, thief.*

The night was long and torturous. He woke around three a.m. with a disturbing thought—Luca was still seventeen. The letter said that Luca was to have access to the box when he turned eighteen. The clerk at the bank hadn't looked at the birthdate on the passport. Damien looked older than his age, so it hadn't been questioned. But what if there were a different clerk, and he or she *did* look at the passport birthdate? If he wasn't allowed in the room again, he had lost his chance to get the money.

He felt hot. He cracked open a window to feel the cool breeze evaporate his sweat. But he didn't go back to sleep. He prayed, not to God, but to his mother. He needed to access what he affectionately called the Mariana trench. Mariana was powerful and he needed her energy.

The morning was stubborn in coming and dismally rainy. No surprise. An emerald city like Vancouver had to be a rainy one. He first stopped at Walmart to make a purchase. Then, wearing a freshly-pressed raincoat and shined black shoes, he walked into the Bank of Vancouver. His new Walmart backpack matched the color of his raincoat, and he carried the empty envelope he'd supposedly place in the box.

Campbell was in the safe deposit area. Damien approached him and was recognized and welcomed. He went through the familiar drill, and Campbell didn't ask to see his passport. Mariana had protected him.

Alone in the private chamber, Damien quickly transferred the packages of $100 bills into his large backpack, returned the emptied box, and walked out of the bank in less than fifteen minutes, over one million dollars richer. No one questioned the heavy pack he carried in his left hand to his car. Oh Canada... glorious and free...free...where no one checked your bag leaving a bank or any other public building.

He drove like a maniac, back to his hotel. When he arrived at his suite, he hung the Do Not Disturb sign on his door. He felt exhilarated, energized like he could run a Marathon. But he couldn't tell anyone. In a frenzy, he poured a mountain of money onto the bed until it spilled onto the floor and covered his feet. He let out a primal scream and took a flying leap into the bills, mimicking the breast stroke through waves of his new-found wealth. He was rich. He had means. He wouldn't be a kept man. Money was power.

He counted the packets to the tune of 1.4 million dollars, more than he'd originally estimated. He called the front desk and asked that his backpack be secured in the hotel safe. After all, he *was* paying for a suite which made him a valued customer. He couldn't fit it in his room safe and couldn't very well walk around town with an excess of a million dollars on his back.

That evening, he took a few hundred dollars, placed a lock on his pack and met an elegant manager at the front desk. He exchanged some money to Canadian currency, then insisted on personally watching the manager lock his prize in the hotel safe. Damien tipped him handsomely, but not before inquiring where he could go for the evening. The manager suggested a club and smiled at him, adding, "I work until two a.m., sir." Damien nodded and smiled.

He left his car in the hotel parking structure and took a taxi to the suggested upscale club in the heart of downtown Vancouver. He'd just had his nineteenth birthday so was of legal drinking age in B.C. *Ninety-nine bottles of beer on the wall. Ninety nine bottles of beer.*

The bar was located on the sky-top level of a high-rise building. He entered a room, with a panoramic view of the city from every window. The floor was malachite, with pulsing lights in the seams of malachite-green tiles, set on a diagonal. The columns at the back of the bar and the bar itself, including the footings, looked warm with fluid green light, dramatic against the walls and ceiling of cherry wood.

He took a seat at the bar and ordered a local Canadian IPA. A few minutes later, a statuesque blonde appeared and in a honeyed voice, she asked his name. He stumbled through a bizarre pause, deciding who he was that night, and finally said, "Damien, Damien Scardina. And yours?"

"Carmen, like the opera," she replied.

"Do you like opera?"

"Not really, but my parents do. Where are you from? I like your accent."

"Italy. Where are you from?"

"Here. Not too exciting. But Italy! Wow! Would you like to join me and my friends?"

She pointed to a nearby table where three women smiled, signaling approval, and where three guys were absorbed in a heated conversation.

"We just saw you sitting alone and thought maybe you'd like some company."

"Sure. Why not?" He grabbed his IPA and stood. It was then he realized that she was a good inch taller than he was. *Take me to your ladder and I'll meet your leader later.*

He had long heard that Canadians were friendly folk, and this group fit the putative definition. Carmen and her girlfriends hung on his every word while the guys politely nodded their heads and talked hockey.

Hockey was a big deal in Canada, and the season was underway. Midst the female badinage, he heard snippets about the Sedin brothers possibly retiring; one of the men was fixated on past trades that had released Kesler and Bieksa? Bieska? To the Anaheim Ducks.

"Get over it, Cam," joked the only guy who wasn't wearing a plaid flannel shirt. "Or let's dig up some ancient history like when the Oilers lost Gretzky to L.A. in eighty-eight, while you're at it!"

"Shut up!" retorted the whiner.

Damien liberally bought his new Canadian acquaintances rounds of beer, tequila shots, and various whiskeys and ryes. At one point, he excused himself, distancing from Carmen and her hockey matadors. He walked down a long hallway on his way to what the Canadians called the washroom.

Standing outside the washroom door was a well-built, well-groomed man, who bore a slight resemblance to Luca. He stuck out his foot in front of Damien and said, "What took you so long?"

Damien felt a furious rush of adrenaline. He gripped the man by the arm and pulled him into the washroom, locking the door behind them. He pushed him up against the wall, and like a feral animal on the kill, he let out a loud, primal cry that pulsated through his orgasm. He turned the man around, aggressively kissed him, then shot out the door.

He labored at catching his breath and asked the first person he saw, "What time is it?"

"One-thirty," said the phantom figure.

The clock struck one and down he run. Hickory dickory dock.

Damien stormed through the club, not making eye contact with anyone along the way, and hailed a taxi back to the hotel. On his way through the hotel lobby, he caught the manager's eye, gave him an invitational nod, and returned to his room. Damien was sufficiently inebriated, or "over-served", as his friend Gabriel Germond euphemistically labeled being drunk. It felt great. He was drunk. He was rich. He was powerful. He was a new man.

A few minutes later, there was a knock at the door, and Damien had company for the night.

The following morning, he woke early. His mouth tasted sour and gritty, like the bottom of a birdcage. The naked stranger lying next to him smelled of stale alcohol and sex. The sun slanted through his twelfth-story window like a search light and lit the glistening stickiness of the stranger's body that revived the memory of the erotic night before.

Damien took a shower, dressed, and packed his bag. His head pounded with the unforgiving pain of a hangover. Before he left the room, he looked, one last time, at the stranger sleeping in his bed. He *wasn't* Luca. And Damien didn't want strangers, not in the long run. He wanted Luca.

He had wrestled with the idea of actually becoming Luca Gherardini. But he knew he'd eventually be caught; and to become Luca, he'd have to eliminate him. As tempting as the entire fortune was, his world was a better place with Luca in it.

He checked out at the front desk, retrieved his backpack, and sat in the lobby for a few minutes to email Luca and Gabriel about the exotic vacation he was enjoying on the beaches of the Sunshine State of Florida.

He drove to a hair salon to have his hair dyed back to its natural color, and he lost the dark contact lenses before he headed to the border. He was Damien Scardina once more. A richer, more powerful Damien Scardina.

Next mission: He needed to return the passport and birth certificate before Luca discovered they were missing. He hadn't been overly concerned about taking the birth certificate. After all, how many times in a lifetime did one need proof of one's birth? His taking the passport was riskier. Travel was easy between the countries of the European Union, and most of the time, it wasn't even necessary to show a passport at the border within the Schengen area. However, there were airports which could impose identity checks that included passports. Fortunately, Luca was in school. He wouldn't be traveling, so the documents would go unmissed.

But before his trip to Switzerland, he would drive to Lincoln, Nebraska; an inconvenience, but necessity. It would take him two days of hard driving. But he couldn't risk taking the money through security at the airports or checking a bag with that much cash. If he'd asked for a cashier's check, there would have been red tape, tax consequences, and an investigation as to how a nineteen-year-old man had come across that amount of money. No, he had to keep the fortune with him and open a safe deposit box under his name in an American bank. Driving was the only transportation that safeguarded his future. And Lincoln,

Nebraska, was the city to which he would return; the home of his first American bank, the home of Trina McLaren, the mother of a woman named Cristin, who was a critical link to his destiny.

CHAPTER NINETEEN

"I never considered a difference of opinion in politics, in religion, in philosophy, as cause for withdrawing from a friend."
—Thomas Jefferson

After his conversation regarding his role in the death of Harold Brockmeyer, Gabriel didn't talk to his father for three weeks. He knew that his admission of associative guilt was disappointing to Clement, but he'd felt compelled to explain, almost as a rite of passage. His honesty could have bred his father's distrust, but more importantly, because Clement was circumspect of Luca's emotional stability, Gabriel's admission would exonerate his friend on that count. A victory.

When Gabriel called home, he spoke to his mother. Her voice was soft and chirpy, like a parakeet. Fiona was always delighted to take his call, share news of his sister's family in Vienna, and talk about her flower garden or Swiss politics. Gabriel didn't sense that Clement had shared the exhumed Harold Brockmeyer story with her. Either that, or Fiona was so forgiving, that she wouldn't bring it up during limited phone time with her son. A mother overestimated her child's integrity. Even if his father had confided in her, she would not chance throwing a dirty rock into the tranquil pool of her maternal relationship.

After the call, he checked his emails. Ding. A message from Luca. He'd taken a trip to Italy and uncovered information about his mother; the mysteries of which had been the topic of conversation in boarding school for years. Luca's abandonment had colored his early youth black. Luca's mother, Sofia, had been an empty name, a faceless fable, an infernal enigma, a black hole whose energy had been sucked into a powerful emptiness that couldn't be accessed by anyone, not even her son.

Luca needed to get out of his head. Gabriel dialed his cell phone.

"Hey. It's Gabe. I just read your email."

"What's going on? Any notable senoritas to report?"

"I haven't had time, man. But I have a long weekend coming up. What are the chances you could fly down? We'll go to Ronda. There's a place we can stay that overlooks a 400 foot gorge, really cool. And you'd love it because it's where some American novelists expatriated and hung out. Ernest Hemingway and Orson Wells, whoever he was."

"*War of the Worlds? Citizen Cain?*"

"Okay. If you say so. So do you think you could come down next weekend on Thursday night? You could be back to class Monday morning."

"Let me check with my profs. One missed day shouldn't be a problem. I can hardly wait until graduation. Then I can leave whenever I want. Hallelujah. I had a message from Damien. It sounds like he likes it over there but he's coming home for a short trip, because his mother isn't well. Have you heard anything from him?"

"Yeah, that's basically what he told me too. Get back to me about next weekend, and if it's a go, I'll check accommodations on that gorge. We can talk about Italy then, if you want to."

"Sounds good. Thanks for the call."

Gabriel hung up and checked his Facebook page, which he did at least once a month, without fail. He wasn't a believer in time spent on social media, because he recognized his compulsive behavior. Checking every day would swallow up time that he couldn't recapture, and frankly, couldn't afford to lose. *But just this once*, he thought. The last message had been from Damien who was in Florida checking out bronze-bodied beauties in Miami Beach. For the heck of it, in hope of seeing photos of some bikini-clad specimens, he prompted Damien's personal page and found a tagged photo from a gorgeous blonde named Carmen sitting on a man's lap in a bar in Vancouver, British Columbia. He looked at the man closely. It looked exactly like Damien with dark hair and dark eyes.

Gabriel posted a reply. "Busted! I thought you were in Miami. What's with the dark disguise? Let me know what's going on. "

He closed Facebook and cracked open his favorite German beer before resuming his studies. He formulated thoughts about the plight of the Spanish Jew in preparation for a paper he would write for his history class. The next thing he knew, he woke up. The room was cold, and outside his window, stars peppered the blackened sky like grains of salt. He closed his eyes, and when he opened them again, he watched the light of sun seep through the crack of night and spill into day. It was astonishing to witness. He wondered why he didn't watch nature's daily spectacle every morning. Simple answer-"I'm a bum," he muttered to himself.

Before he left for class, he checked Damien's Facebook page. It had vanished. The sudden cancellation was as curious as his instinct to check it. Gabriel questioned his own sanity. Had he really seen Damien in the tagged photo? Yes, he had. Perhaps he'd seen something that Damien hadn't wanted anyone to see. In that case, it would have been enough to hide the photo from viewing, but to cancel the page? A bit drastic, even for Damien. And why would Damien go to Vancouver when he'd told everyone he was partying on the beaches in Florida? Why would he disguise himself? How did someone have access to his FB page to tag him in a photo? The dots of this constellation did not connect.

He rechecked his emails. A message from Luca. He had permission from his teachers to miss classes the following Friday. That was expected and good news. But Luca had also discovered that his passport was missing.

CHAPTER TWENTY

"There is no end. There is no beginning. There is only the passion of life."—Federico Fellini

The missing passport was problematic. Luca always kept it in the same place. He spent an hour tearing his place apart in search of it, to no avail. He knew he had it in his possession when he returned from Italy a few weeks before. Was it possible that he lost it between the security line in Firenze and his arrival in Lucerne? That was the only explanation that made any sense. He would have to apply for a new one. His picture was outdated anyway. He researched the airlines and found one that only required a driver's license to travel to Spain. The flight required an extra stop but would get him there, so he made the travel arrangements and waited out the week.

****

Gabriel was there to greet him at the baggage claim area. "*Bienvenido, Senor.*"

They high-fived and began a familiar banter about the flight, the attractive females in view, the frivolity of such a quick trip, and the fun they were about to have.

"You fit right into the scene down here, Luca. You could pass for Spanish, Italian, Greek...definitely Mediterranean. The women are going to love you. You're eighteen, right?" asked Gabriel.

"In two more months."

"That's okay, we'll make it work. Drinking age is eighteen, except in Asturias. It's still sixteen there. You just have to know the bartenders. They don't give a shit. We'll be fine."

The roar of a jet engine overhead drowned out Gabriel's comment, but Luca didn't ask him to repeat it.

They crossed the street to the car park, past billboards for an upcoming boxing match and advertisements for visiting the famous Alhambra. For Luca, a curtain had been raised, and he had walked into a scene of his upcoming life of freedom. Two G.Q.-looking Spaniards walked by. One of them greeted Luca with a seductive smile, followed by a whistle and a solicitous clicking sound.

Gabriel started laughing. "*Chihuahua*. You're not only a hit with the senoritas, Gherardini."

Luca sneered, uncomfortably.

Gabriel's apartment was Spanish in décor. Beige and ochre walls, brick and wood accents, wrought iron light fixtures, and colorful tiles. Luca dropped his bag next to the pullout sofa where he would be sleeping that night.

"This apartment smells like a gymnasium. You ever air it out?"

Gabriel laughed and banged two beers on the counter. "Take your pick. There's more where these came from. Spain isn't exactly known for beer, although you'll be trying *Cruz Campo* by tomorrow. But tonight? A taste of home, right?"

"Love it!" Luca grabbed a beer and drank from the bottle.

"So what did you think about finding out that my mother was having an affair with my half-brother before my father died?" he asked.

Gabriel swallowed hard and shook his head.

Luca continued. "It's not the kind of thing I was happy to hear. But the people in Italy were convinced it had happened. It makes it easier to hear about it secondhand, without having ever met the players." He turned his head and looked out the window at the plane tree branch that was knocking on the pane.

"I don't think I would have liked my mother. Then again, I don't have all the facts, and it looks like I never will. It *was* confirmed that she died, which I now know for a fact, so I won't expect her to walk through the door with open arms someday, right?"

"I agree with that. Sometimes memories or longing for memories can hold you hostage, not allow you to move on. Like being a prisoner of your own perceptions, while the door of your cell is unlocked," said Gabriel.

"Well said. Maybe you're the writer. Anyway, I think I would have liked my father. Everyone seemed to love him. Maybe later next year, I'll go back to learn more about him, maybe meet my nanny. She was apparently devastated when my brother removed me from Bellaterra, and there was a reference to cousins who took care of me before I was sent away to Switzerland. I think I'd like to meet them too. Someday. It's all too raw right now."

Luca took a long swig of beer and sighed.

"Do you know how lucky you are? To have a mother like Fiona and a father like Clement?"

"And a friend like you? *Saluti!*" said Gabriel.

"Of course, a friend like me. But seriously, Gabe, your family is the closest to a family I have, and I'm grateful. *Saluti.*" They clinked their bottles.

"*Para la familia,*" Gabriel retorted.

"Well, enough about my dysfunctional beginnings, tell me something interesting. What are you writing your paper on?" asked Luca.

"Ah, you don't want to hear about that."

"Yes, I do. Anything to change the subject." He laughed.

"Okay. I'm writing a paper about the eviction of the Jews from Spain in the late sixteenth century. Fourteen-ninety-two, to be precise. An expulsion ordered by Queen Isabella when the Catholics conquered Alhambra, right here in Granada. The Christians, Muslims, and Jews lived peacefully in this city for eight fucking centuries, Luca, until Isabella, Ferdinand and the Inquisition came to town. The Jews have survived destruction and exile how many times? I haven't counted but it's staggering, and they always survive. Their culture miraculously survived the

Holocaust, and they now live in fear and with courage, I might add, in the state of Israel. Meanwhile, they are being decimated around the world by low fertility and constant intermarriage. This great people face annihilation. Our great-great grandchildren may someday hear about them as a story, a myth. I could go on and on. I bet you wished you hadn't asked."

"No, it's interesting. But why the Jews? It's like you're personally invested."

"Yeah, my Grandma Leah was Jewish. I've always been fascinated ... and invested."

"You really love this stuff, don't you?"

"Actively trying to understand the world is my mission. When I'm on my death bed, I don't want to look back and think I wasted my chance at life by walking through it, conforming to it, and never asking the questions that could break through the walls of conventional wrong thinking. That would be a tragedy. I want to catch glimpses of insight. I want to learn and think and feel and honor my life."

"Whew, let me catch my breath. You need to take that show on the road, my friend," said Luca. "You're a natural. An Elmer Gantry, without the deceit, of course."

"Yeah, I get a little carried away when I talk about the subjects that really matter to me. By the way, my father always said, the best talks that you have with your guests occur during the first night of the visit. He may be right."

Luca laughed. "Maybe so."

Gabriel continued "So what about you? What's turning you on these days? Still those American writers? What are your plans after you graduate?"

"Nothing in cement. I know I should go to school, but I really want to travel before life gets too serious. I was thinking of going to America, to the South. South Carolina. One of Ernest Hemingway's homes is in Florida. And I'd have to make it to California to visit the stomping grounds of John Steinbeck, Jack London, and Robert Louis Stevenson. I mean, I couldn't take more than a few months, but I could seriously spend years studying over there, walking the forests of John Muir and the southern avenues of F. Scott Fitzgerald's hometown."

"Look who else has passion. Do you seriously think you want to be a writer?" asked Gabriel.

"Maybe. I certainly have a pool of experience to drawn from. My life does seem to be filled with surprises. And you know, they say you should write about what you know. Whoever *they* are."

"Speaking of surprises, before I forget, I must tell you, you're not the only one who happened upon something puzzling. It's bothered me all week, off and on. Have you heard back from Damien?"

Luca sat back in his chair and shook his head. "Not since last week when he told me he'd be back because his mother was ill. Have you?"

"Not exactly. But after you and I talked last week, I went on my Facebook page and transferred over to his. Some blonde named Carmen had tagged his page, which he probably hadn't seen yet. But the weird part was that he was in disguise-dark hair, dark eyes. And in Canada, not Florida. I mean, he wasn't hanging out with the beach babes like he told us. He was in fuckin' Canada. The girl was ten points, don't get me wrong, but still. I left a message in the reply box, but when I checked again, because it was such a mystery, not only the photo but the entire page was gone. Cancelled. I'm really curious what the story is."

"There's got to be an explanation. Do you know when he's coming home?"

"I have no idea. He's incommunicado with me."

"What do you say we score a few points of our own? The senoritas *are* beautiful." Luca smiled and nodded his head once to punctuate his enthusiasm.

"It's been my experience that two guys traveling together don't tend to get lucky at the same time. You know what I mean?"

"Maybe we'll need to split up," Luca said.

Gabriel started laughing. "You *are* ready to graduate, my man."

CHAPTER TWENTY-ONE

"Jealousy is nothing more than the fear of abandonment."
—Arab proverb

Most people, when returning to the country they know best, feel good to be home again. Not Damien. He was there to replace Luca's documents, then fly back to the U.S., as soon as possible. The trip to Canada had gone well, with the exception of the night he'd spent worrying about the passport birthdate potentially denying him access to Luca's money; and the photo on his Facebook page which he hadn't discovered before Gabriel had seen it, the price he'd paid for getting drunk and accepting the beautiful Carmen's Facebook invitation. Oh, but it had been a night to remember. Carmen was the lie, his cover. The strangers were his truth.

His newly acquired wealth was secure in a bank in Nebraska. He hadn't really stolen the money. He was keeping it for his life with Luca, a justification that left open the possibility he was a decent human being. No harm, no foul.

Regarding Gabriel's imminent questions about the Facebook photo, Damien would have credible answers. Gabriel liked him and wasn't looking for a reason not to trust him. And Gabriel was in school in Spain, away from Luca.

After his plane landed in Lucerne, he took a taxi to the school and walked into the dormitory that had been his home for seven years. The halls still smelled like books and sweat and rules. The memory of this building would never leave him, like the memory of Christmas and his mother's cooking.

The dorm doors were never locked. He just had to time it right, during classes. He walked to the second floor via the side stairwell, usually used by janitors or boys sneaking from floor to floor at night. He encountered no one. His modus operandi was to be inconspicuous, which was counter-intuitive to his past persona within the hallowed halls of SCB. He'd always been Mr. Personality, bigger than life. Sneaking around, without being seen, was novel behavior, foreign to him, but considering the stakes, necessary. He stole his way to room Two Seventeen and knocked. There was no answer.

Imploring the gods of legerdemain and the protection of Mariana, he slipped into the room to the drawer in the closet to return the documents. On his way out, he impulsively grabbed a bottle of French cologne, *Joop,* on the windowsill next to Luca's bed. He stuffed it in his pocket and exited the room. Mission accomplished. Almost.

On the first floor, he encountered a group of freshman, or so they looked. Young, naïve, immature. They were laughing at a photo in a magazine and not aware of Damien coming toward them. Just as he turned the corner, one of the boys asked, "Hey, what are you doing here?"

Damien turned. "Well, hail, hail, the gang's all here. Not that it's any of your business, but I used to live here. I was looking for a friend of mine, but he didn't answer his door so he must be in class."

"You're looking for Luca, aren't you?" the boy persisted.

Damien looked more attentively and realized it was Luca's roommate who had recognized him.

"Young Hans. Yes, I'm passing through so thought I'd catch him. Do you know where he is?"

"He's visiting his friend in Spain for the weekend. He'll be back tonight."

"Gabriel Germond?"

"I think so. I'll tell him you came by."

"Don't bother. I'll call him myself."

The exchange, which had taken place in less than a minute fueled Damien's belly with fire. He turned from the cadre of boys, but not before hearing one of them say, "He's weird."

Damien looked back and yelled, "But I'm rich. And Mr. Koefler, take a shower. You stink."

He thrust open the entrance door of the dormitory with Herculean force, propelling himself into the gnashing teeth of the green-eyed monster.

Luca with Gabriel? Luca was supposed to be at school, studying, preparing to graduate, so he could inherit his fortune, and they could be together.

He, not Gabriel, had knowledge of what Luca's mother intended for him to do; he, not Gabriel, would soon be traipsing across the world to find the girl whom Sofia wanted Luca to avenge; he, not Gabriel, was a surrogate son of Sofia, who had the power to help Luca fulfill his destiny: he, not Gabriel, was willing to personally discharge Sofia's request; and he, not Gabriel, loved Luca and would protect him for the rest of his life. Damien, not Gabriel. Fuck Gabriel.

Luca had been the only person he'd entrusted with his own past. And somehow, knowing that Luca was damaged too made him a safe keeper of secrets, made them fellow commiserates. Luca was the only person capable of understanding Damien's childhood pain, and in sharing his pain, Luca had become his partner, his gatekeeper, his confidant.

He hailed a taxi. The radio was playing an old Nineties' song, *Fremd Im Eigenen Land*, translated as *Stranger in My Own Country*.

"Please turn off the radio. I'll pay you to turn off the radio." He flung some Euros into the front seat. The driver checked him out in the rearview mirror and complied.

Damien obsessed about Luca and Gabriel together. By the time he reached the bar, he was Othello, convinced that his love was cheating on him. When he paid the driver, he stiffed him the tip and flipped him off.

He'd been to the same bar a year before with Luca. Switzerland was a rational country with legal drinking age of sixteen for beer and wine. He would have to use a false I.D. in the States, which was insane. Guys could risk their lives in the military at eighteen but couldn't legally drink there. At least B.C. had the sense to strike a balance at nineteen.

The mirror behind the bar was enormous, reflecting the room and making it appear larger than it was. Waiting to be served, he listened to the lead singer from an American band called Green Day sing "Boulevard of Broken Dreams." Billie Joe? I think that's his name, he thought to himself. He loved that song.

He ordered a Kronbacher and caught sight of himself in the mirror. He saw the semblance of his father who had taught him to keep his friends close but his enemies closer. Ironically, Gabriel had been his first friend at the conservatory many years ago. Now they had taken an abrupt U-turn and Gabriel had become his enemy. Now there wasn't room for Gabriel.

He also saw an aspect of his mother, around his mouth. His mother, who had taught him to *Honor thy father and mother, so that you may live long in the land of the Lord your God is giving you*-Exodus 20:12."

He saw the man he was becoming, obsessed with another man and undeterrably set to do whatever it took to be with him. He picked up his cell phone and prompted the number.

Gabriel answered on the third ring.

"Hey, Damien, where the hell are you?" he asked.

"Hi Gabe. I'm on my way to see my mother. She hasn't been feeling well so I'm home for a couple weeks, then back to the U.S."

"Sorry to hear about Mariana. Anything serious?" Gabriel asked.

"I don't think so but I'll know more tonight," he replied.

"So, buddy, I've been curious as hell about something. You know that photo of you that posted on your Facebook page? What was that all about?"

Damien was prepared to field the looming question, so without missing a beat, he answered.

"Someone hacked my page. As soon as I saw it, I took it down. I don't use social media much anyway."

"Yeah but it looked just like you with dark hair, dark eyes."

"Some joker must have photo shopped my face. I don't know how that works, but I wasn't even in Canada. I was in Florida. Really strange, right?"

"But why would someone single you out and go to the time and inconvenience of hacking your page? Are you in trouble?"

"I'm fine. It was random. How are you? What've you been up to?"

"Are you taking your meds?" asked Gabriel.

"Don't mother me. I already have a mother," he replied.

"Sorry." Gabriel paused and continued. "I've just been studying a lot. Luca came down for a few days to visit. We went to Ronda. If you'd been around, you could have come too. You would have loved it. Next time."

"How's Luca?"

"He's good, flying back to school as we speak. But he did go to Italy to investigate his background, his mom and dad, his half-brother. Turns out they're all dead, but he found some people who knew them, so it put some closure on the story. Say listen, I'm on my way out to meet some friends, but please say hi to your mother for me and don't be a stranger, buddy."

"Will do." Damien hung up. He stared into the mirror behind the bar. The lines in his forehead had softened, less angry. Gabriel was cool, maybe not a threat. At least, he believed his Facebook story. And Luca had finally gone to Italy. He'd talked about it for years but hadn't been ready to confront his mysterious, absent past, until now. Like Damien's father had always said, *if you don't want to hear the answer, don't ask the question.*

It was ironic that all Luca had ever wanted was a key to his mother's heart, and all she'd left him was a key to a safe deposit box.

Trisha St. Andrews

CHAPTER TWENTY-TWO

"All are lunatics. But he who can analyze delusion is called a philosopher."—Ambrose Bierce

"So what about that girl you're seeing? Making any headway, Luca, King of Light, Slayer of Dragons, Master of Women?"

Gabriel adjusted his computer screen so he could check his emails while talking.

"You've been playing too many video games, my friend. She's good," Luca answered.

"I don't know what she sees in you." Gabriel laughed.

"It would be weird if you did. Change the subject," said Luca.

"Okay. I don't know if I told you, but Damien called a few days ago. He was in Lucerne, passing through after seeing Mariana, because she was ill. It was on the day you left Spain, but you weren't home yet. Have you heard from him?"

"Yeah, he called me last night from Nebraska, of all places. We talked for quite a while, but he didn't mention his mom so she must be fine," said Luca.

"Well, that's just it. I called my father because my parents are close to his mother, or should I say, they keep tabs on her. I thought they should know she hadn't been well. My mother called her, and not only was she fine, but she hadn't seen Damien in over a month."

"Well, maybe he intended to go and found out she was feeling better, so he changed his mind. He always keeps his options open."

"Could be. Sometimes I think he fabricates drama to make his life more interesting. Don't get me wrong. I love being with Damien. Never a dull moment. But sometimes he muddies his life and falls victim to his stories. Like he's taken a drug, and his myths hold him captive and alter his perceptions."

"Or maybe he hasn't taken his drugs and his reality holds him captive, etc."

"Scary thought. But ever since we've known him, if he's not in the thick of things, he places himself there. He likes to be in the eye of a cyclone, watching the storm around him but only as an observer. He somehow remains unscarred by its destruction," Luca said.

"So you *have* declared creative writing as your major." Gabriel laughed at the attempt to metamorphose Damien. He stared as his computer screen and noticed a cyclone off the coast of Japan. Weird, he thought to himself, but didn't say anything.

"Hey, remember Brock? You know as well as I do--that tragedy was a direct result of Damien introducing the game," Luca said.

"Yes, but I've never blamed him personally for what happened. Funny you should bring it up though. I recently told my father about it."

"Why now? Why did you tell him so many years later?"

"I did it for you. I wanted to prove to him that you were not personally responsible for Brock's death. And with your inheritance on the horizon, and he being your executor, he needed to know."

"Thank you for doing that. Thanks for telling me. Speaking of your dad, he emailed me. He needed a copy of my birth certificate for his file. I went to where I keep my papers, and my passport was there. Remember when I couldn't find it? Well, like magic, it reappeared."

"Maybe you overlooked it?"

"No way. It wasn't there."

"Well then, someone took it and brought it back. That's the only logical explanation," said Gabriel, as he quivered his pen between two fingers and launched it across the room.

"But why? It's not any good to anyone else, although I was so young in the photo, it probably wouldn't be hard for someone else to use. Anyway, it's back. I was actually going with a poltergeist explanation. A lot more imaginative, right?"

"You sound like Damien," said Gabriel. "Ha! And by the way, I asked Damien about that phantom photo on his Facebook page. I guess someone hacked it so he took it down."

"He told me the same story. You don't believe him?"

"I wish you'd seen the picture. It was right out of the Theater of the Absurd. Although I must admit, he did look good as a darker version of himself. Kinda like you."

"That's weird. The next thing I know, you'll be telling me that he woke up as an insect. I'm sure there's nothing to it." Luca laughed and scratched where he imagined a bug crawling up his leg.

"I remember that story. Ultra-weird. But seriously, did he seem hyper or depressed when you spoke to him? You know how he gets when he goes off his meds."

"Hard to tell without actually seeing him. I hope he's okay."

"Well, he always lands on his feet. Listen, I need to get back to studying. Let's talk next week, okay? "

"Got it. Bye."

Gabriel went back to writing his paper on the undermining of modern statesmen by their reliance on the teleprompter. His position was that when politicians rely on speech writers, they don't speak spontaneously and honestly, making them glorified actors with power. *Frightening*. The teleprompter allowed the public to be deceived, or more critically, the public allowed themselves to be deceived. Gabriel found his own political skepticism mutating into a cynicism that was unsettling.

He turned off his computer and stared out the window.

From his chair, he watched a man reach into a waste bin on the street and extract something. Had the man accidentally dropped something of value while disposing his trash? Absent-minded? Was he retrieving something that was planted for him to recover? A spy? Had he stolen something earlier and needed to stash it until he could return? A thief? Or was he hungry and salvaging something to eat? Homeless? Gabriel's judgment without the facts was a delusion.

So how could one tell when a friend had the wisdom to navigate his or her life without delusion? That was a sticky wicket, as his English buddy would say. Were his concerns about Damien well-founded or was he himself becoming cynical about people's motivations, perhaps taking life too seriously? Distrusting the innocent, suspicious of the irregular? Did it all really matter? Probably not.

As he fell asleep that night, his last thought was to ask Luca to check his passport for entry stamps, to know if someone had actually used it for travel. If so, it had been stolen. If not, the poltergeist theory would be the way to go.

CHAPTER TWENTY-THREE

"He seemed for dignity compos'd and high exploit; But all was false and hollow."—John Milton

Damien's conversation with Luca had been the salve that soothed his jealous heart. Luca sounded happy to hear from him. He openly shared what he'd learned in Italy about his mother, and what he and Gabriel had done on their trip to Ronda. Damien didn't need to ask him. Luca wanted to share his life. The only uncomfortable question broached by Luca was why Damien had gone to Nebraska. The answer of course, was to follow a girl he'd met in Miami. A half-truth. He *was* there to track a girl.

He felt strange talking about women to Luca, but he reasoned that Luca had to finish school and leave the country to be with him, before he could discover their future together. It was safer that way, and by then, Cristin would surface, Damien would share the letter from Sofia, and Luca would understand what had to be done. It was a connection that would bind them forever. He'd say that he'd found the letter at the Scardinas' home among his father's papers; and rather than turn it over to Clement, he'd guarded Luca's privacy. That reserved him the chance to facilitate Sofia's retribution. If he hadn't protected Luca in this manner, Clement would have known about the Americans, particularly Cristin McClaren, and Luca's mission would have been foiled.

No mention would be made of the safe deposit box and its contents, nor Damien's trip to Vancouver. That information was extraneous, unnecessary, and complicating. But Damien's jumpstarting the search in America for the chosen one was the ultimate sacrifice. Luca had been spared the search aspect of the search-and-destroy mission but would be an intricate part of the destruction phase. Luca would show his gratitude and become Damien's lover. It was already mapped out.

Damien realized that there were some jagged edges in his conspicuously seamless plan, to say nothing of the perceived immorality and illegality of the reprisal. But in the context of what one would do for love, Damien's intentions were pure. The creation of a love affair didn't happen overnight. Not without collateral damage. Like the unfolding of history, there would be unanticipated turns in the labyrinth of their relationship. But sooner or later, there would be an exit that opened into the well-executed dream.

After he'd cancelled his personal Facebook page in Vancouver, he'd created another page under a false name in order to search for the McClaren girls. He couldn't get to Cristin directly, so he attempted to ferret out her younger sister Elizabeth. That came to no avail. He resorted to the address of the mother. Trina was her name. That's where he would start.

He drove to her residence in his rental car and confirmed the name McLaren on the mailbox. He initially parked down the block to observe her home. Trina lived in a suburb of Lincoln, with gorgeous, full-splendored trees, dressed in autumnal colors that had only just begun to shed their skirts of leaves on the wide boulevards below. On the first morning, he watched a woman with sunglasses whom he presumed to be Trina, leave the house with her dog for a morning walk. He kept his distance but followed them in his car to a park, three blocks away. He watched them circumnavigate the small lake twice, then head for home.

Trina McClaren appeared to be a patient person, allowing her dog to sniff mushrooms, scents of other dogs, critters on tree bark, and nasty trash containers. From a distance, she looked attractive, long auburn air, slender. She dressed in black, like a cat burglar, reminiscent of photos he'd seen of Audrey Hepburn or Jackie Onassis. She was gone for approximately forty-five minutes, then didn't leave the house for the remainder of the day. There was no sign of a man, coming or going.

Damien watched the routine for two days. Rather boring, but his down hours afforded him time to finely tune the conversation he'd eventually have with Luca regarding the discharging of Sofia's request. One thought he kept buried was the possibility that Luca would not be complicit with his mother's wishes. What would he do then? Damien would just have to help him understand that one must *Honor thy mother.*

Both mornings, Damien noticed Trina stop along the path to take photos with her phone. She obviously liked nature photography. Also evident, was the fact that no one joined her on her walks—no girlfriends, no running buddies. Just her and the pooch. On the second day of his reconnaissance, when she returned home, she put the dog on a leash in the front yard and called him by name before entering the house. His name was Puccini.

When she was out of sight, he took a photo of Puccini from his car window and headed for the dog pound. It opened within minutes of his arrival, and he showed a volunteer named Chloe the picture of Puccini and asked what breed of dog he was.

"A schnauzer, I think. Are you looking for a schnauzer?" she asked with an accent.

"Where are you from?" he asked.

"From West Virginia, home of the Mountaineers." She beamed a broad smile, suggestive of the Cheshire Cat.

"Where are you from? Not from around here, that's for sure."

"No, I'm from Switzerland, home of Alpine skiing." He smiled to be polite, but not to encourage her.

"Why did you come here? If I came from Switzerland, I'd never leave. I want to go there someday. Maybe I could visit you."

Damien squirmed, uncomfortable with her flirting. "Now, tell me, what would be a compatible dog with a schnauzer that's available for me to buy this morning?"

"Well, there are no guarantees, but we have a cute little poodle mix that came in two days ago that no one's claimed. Let me show you."

They rounded the corner past breeds and mixes that Damien had never seen. Switzerland was fond of Doberman pinschers and boxers. The minute he laid eyes on the poodle mix, he said, "Sold. I'll take it."

"It's a boy, is that all right?"

"Fine. How old do you think he is? I don't want to train a puppy."

"No, he's about five years old. What are you going to call him?"

"Wolfgang," he replied.

The following morning was golden with color when Damien and well-fed Wolfie set out for a walk with a brand new leash with a musical staff pattern on it. He heard an Egyptian goose honk as it glided in the water across the lake. It reminded him of one of his favorite palindromes, "Do geese see God?" On a glorious morning like this one, there was no doubt.

When Damien and Trina finally met, they greeted one another with a *good morning.* The dogs sniffed each other.

"You have a cute dog. What's his name?"

"Wolfgang," Damien replied. "I'm Italian but I was raised in Switzerland and I love Mozart."

Trina laughed. "That's wonderful. I had an Aunt Tess who passed away last year, and she loved Mozart. Coincidentally, my dog is Puccini. We're both obviously music lovers." She pushed her thick auburn hair from her face, her sunglasses shading her eyes from his sight. "What are you doing so far from home?"

"Business. I am doing an internship for Mutual of Omaha so they sent me to Lincoln. Go figure. The dogs certainly like each other," he remarked.

"Aren't they cute? Well, we had better be on our way. Perhaps we'll see you if you walk your dog very often."

"We'll probably bump into you again. My name is Mario, by the way."

"I'm Trina."

"*Guten Morgen,* Trina."

Trina smiled and stepped up her walk to set distance between them.

Two days later, Damien and Wolfie waited for Trina and Puccini to set out around the lake. They exited his rental car and proceeded to catch up to them.

"Do you mind if we keep you company for a lap?" Damien asked.

"Not at all," she responded. "I'd enjoy the company. We don't meet many Europeans here in the heartland. What's Switzerland like?"

"It's colder than here. Mountainous. Quaint."

"Do you have a family?" she asked.

"My parents. I have one older brother Tony, and two sisters, Christine and Elizabeth."

"That's amazing," said Trina. "I have two daughters, Cristin and Elizabeth."

"Really? Are they still in school here or off seeking their fortunes?"

"Lizzie, is moving to South Carolina and hopefully going to school at Clemson. She wants to be naturalist. She takes after her father, my late husband. Cristin is at the University of Virginia, studying of all things, parapsychology."

"They have a degree for that?"

"Well, I think it's under the auspices of a Division of Perceptual Studies."

"That's awesome. Well, I better speed up or I'll be late for work. It's been a pleasure to see you, Trina. Wolfie, say goodbye to Puccini. *Auf Wiedersehen.*"

"*Auf Wiedersehen,*" Trina said through a giggle. She waved and he was on his way.

Two hours later, Damien savored his own cunning by sending an email to Luca.

My dear friend,

You're going to love traveling in this part of the world. There's so much to see. I'm headed for Virginia this week and will take copious notes so that when you're free, I can be your tour guide. I think you mentioned wanting to visit South Carolina? Is there any chance you could come to the States before you graduate? Think about it. More to follow. Damien.

He was proud of his scheme to get Trina alone and extract her daughters' whereabouts. Now what to do with Wolfie?

"Come here, boy," he commanded. Wolfie jumped into his lap and licked his face. His tongue was soft and slobbery, unlike the rough, sandpaper tongue of Damien's childhood cat, Felix.

"We're going for a ride, boy."

Damien rolled down the passenger window as a gesture of good will so Wolfie could stick his head into the cool air during their final drive together. His ears flapped in the breeze and his tongue panted with doggie enthusiasm.

When they arrived at the pound, the gate was locked. Damien climbed the fence, and dropped the dog on the pavement on the other side.

Wolfie yelped. Damien drove away.

His last stop before leaving Nebraska was the bank. One more transfer. The money would go with him to Virginia, where it would stay until he and Luca had accomplished their mission.

CHAPTER TWENTY-FOUR

"I'm not afraid of storms, for I'm learning to sail my ship."
—Aeschylus

It is a well-known fact that turning eighteen is a milestone in anyone's life. Luca Gherardini was no exception. For most young men, it was the legalization of drinking hard liquor in public places, a forthcoming graduation from compulsory schooling, and liberation from parents. But for Luca, beer was legal at sixteen years of age, his school was the only home he'd ever known, and he had no parents, no siblings, or anyone to whom he needed to be accountable. He instead would be an independently wealthy young man with no ties. And that was dangerous. With no accountability, he could become a loose cannon, living a worthless, albeit wealthy life. Or not.

His teacher, Emily Walker, had talked to him about the temptations of his situation. There would be a tendency to squander money; to overspend, overindulge, and overserve himself with whatever sated his desires. He could become a playboy, a race car driver like his brother Nico. He could ski the steepest mountains, own polo horses, or scuba dive in the Red Sea. Money would never be a deterrent or concern. He could own mansions, villas, beach homes, penthouses, and castles all over the world. But then what? Would there ever be enough things and thrills to make him happy? *Beware of alcohol and drugs,* she'd warned him.

Ms. Walker had brought to his attention that he wasn't the only one in the school who'd experienced loss or abandonment. Throughout the years, other boys had lost parents to illnesses or accidents. Torger Omdahl had lost both of his parents in an airplane crash; Tryg Pederson had been orphaned when he was five; and then there was Brock who had died at age nine in his closet, alone, and terrified. Luca wasn't alone.

He sometimes wondered if the reason he was drawn to American literature was because he loved the teacher who taught him the subject. She had reinforced her belief in him that he was strong and wise enough to make sound decisions, to find his passions, and give a gift back to the world; to find his value and aspire to become valuable, to leave the world a better place by virtue of his mind and compassion, rather than his trappings. He was accountable to her.

Luca also felt accountable to his friends, Gabe and Damien. They were his brothers, and he'd never let them down. His only father figure was Gabe's father, Clement. And Luca felt answerable to the Italian people who had been concerned about his whereabouts and well-being for all of those years he'd been at school. All those years he'd agonized over no one caring for him. The world had dealt him a challenging set of cards that he needed to turn into a winning hand. His eighteenth birthday offered a change in fortune. In the turning of a calendar page, at the stroke of midnight, his new life would begin.

Luca's birthday arrived on a blustery Saturday. The windy day brought intermittent blasts of cold rain, not quite sleet, and short of wet snow.

Clement Germond was waiting in the office of his home when Fiona answered the door.

"Luca, how lovely to see you. Please come in and let me take your coat and scarf. Clement is in his office."

"Hello, Mrs. Germond. Thank you." He slipped out of his wool coat and unwrapped the scarf from his neck.

"Happy birthday, Luca. I'll bring you both a cup of hot tea, if you'd like?"

"Thank you. Yes, please."

Fiona smiled and directed Luca to the office with her dainty, blue-veined, fragile hand.

"Come in, Luca. It's a big day for you. Happy birthday," said Clement. "Please, sit down."

Luca noticed Clement's more casual manner and friendlier tone. He flashed on the fact that Gabe had recently exonerated him from the Brock tragedy. Clement had always reminded Luca of a barn owl, with a round face, wise, deep-set eyes, and a white goatee. He also walked with a slight limp, which according to Gabriel, was an injury from a train accident years ago. Luca watched him take a seat behind his large oak desk, and Luca anticipated a serious discussion because Clement was a serious man. According to his son, Clement was a conscientious attorney with a vested interest in Luca's well-being and future.

"Before we begin, how does it feel to be inheriting an immense fortune?" Clement asked with a jovial grin.

"It feels great! I've never really lacked for anything monetarily, but I've also not been responsible for a great sum of money. I'm excited. Gabriel and Damien and I have some adventures to look forward to. I plan on being generous with my friends."

"It's most fortuitous, isn't it, that your two best friends happen to be the sons of your late father's dear friends? Rudolpho was a great man, and I know that I can speak on behalf of both your father and Damien's, that we are proud of you, Luca, proud of how you worked past what I'm certain felt like insurmountable odds at times."

"It's true. There were times when anger was the only emotion that made me feel alive. But those days are over."

"I have remorse about those years myself, Luca. I could have been a stronger part of your life, a mentor, a role model. I have no excuse but to say that my work consumed me, and I justified my discretionary time in caring for my own family. I regret that I may have disappointed my friend Rudolpho *and* you. I am sorry I was not more available to you."

"Mr. Germond. That has never crossed my mind. Please don't apologize."

"Thank you for being gracious. But it doesn't change how I feel. I can say that I would be honored to be a support for you in the future. If you ever need a father to talk to, I will be there for you, I promise."

"Thank you, Mr. Germond. You have no idea what that means to me." Lucas swallowed a lump lodged in his throat. Tears appeared before he could wipe them away.

"After our last talk, I took your advice. I flew to Italy to find someone, anyone, who knew my parents at Bellaterra. I learned that I probably would have loved my father and would not have liked either my mother or half-brother."

"It sounds like you've achieved some closure on the subject. I'm happy for you, son. Well now, let's get down to business."

He proceeded to open a folder and explain the ladder of disbursements and the size of the Gherardini fortune. There were pots of money that would not be disturbed for years, and funds available to Luca immediately, when he graduated from college, and every year thereafter, until his thirtieth birthday. At that time, he would have access to his entire fortune, if the executor deemed him of sound and responsible mind.

"So at this point, I'm opening an account for you at the Bank of Lucerne with this amount." He wrote a number on a paper and passed it across the desk. "Upon your graduation, in two months, this amount will be added." He passed another number across the desk. "At that time, Luca, we'll need to meet again. I know this is premature because you are so young, but you need to give some thought to naming a beneficiary down the line. You can change it at any time, but a name should be in place."

"I understand, Mr. Germond. I'll think about it. Thank you for your help."

"Do you know what you want to do after you graduate?"

"I think I'll take a year off and travel before I continue my education."

"What field are you thinking of pursuing?" Clement asked.

"I'm thinking of being a writer, or maybe looking at the publishing business."

"So a business degree...?"

"Yes, and a creative writing degree, perhaps at a university in the United States. Just a thought."

"Fascinating. Keep me posted, Luca. I'm glad to hear you have direction. You may not end up there, but having direction at least leads you down a road with detours and other highways you might find even more interesting. Direction is key."

"That's what Ms. Walker says too."

"Good advice," Clement said. Luca stood up to leave. Clement asked him to sit down. There was something else he wanted to discuss.

"Luca, since we're being candid with each other, there is something else I want to say. Gabriel told me what happened to young Harold Brockmeyer nine years ago. There's nothing that can be done at this point, but I wanted you to know that I affix no blame to you."

Luca nodded and hung his head.

"Good. So we're straight?" asked Clement.

"Perfectly. Thank you for your help, sir."

Clement walked him to the door where Luca took his coat and scarf from the tall oaken coat rack and stepped into his new world.

The air smelled fresher, more full of promise, than it had in a lifetime. First stop, the Bank of Lucerne.

CHAPTER TWENTY-FIVE

"Just when I think I have learned the way to live, life changes."
—Hugh Prather

It didn't snow often in Charlottesville, Virginia. Especially not in late March. But when it did, it was a Norman Rockwell painting. Cristin loved the UVA campus, with the famous statue of Thomas Jefferson in front of the Rotunda, modeled after Rome's Pantheon. Between the Rotunda and the Pavilions lay the Lawn, a stretch of green or brown or white, depending on the season. It was an impressive expanse. The brick halls with white colonial-style pillars painted a classic look to a venerated institution. Cristin particularly loved the University Chapel, with its Gothic Revival architecture. She dreamed she would be married there someday.

This morning she was headed to her Dream and Vision Interpretation class. Most people's dreams were tied to their everyday experiences, what she called "level one" dreams. But since Cristin was a child, she had dreamed of people she hadn't known, places she'd never been, and eventually, she identified them to be real, as if she had had a prescience about whom she would meet and where she would go. And then there were dream messages from souls who had passed on, the most recent being from her Grandma Dori, her Great Aunt Tess, and the vision of the Madison Thomas woman.

The class had just finished a month's study of Jung's *Memories, Dreams, and Reflections,* and had moved on to short pieces by Graham Greene, Virginia Wolfe, John Updike, and Gabriel Garcia Marquez, all dealing with dream interpretation. Their discussions of a dream's ephemerality, suspension of physical reality, tangled language, and color and sequencing, stimulated her personal dreaming to higher levels. She was her own interpreter, as every dreamer needed to be. She could construe her own thoughts, feelings, and visions, within the context of her singular understanding. After all, she was the dreamer. But that didn't mean that she couldn't learn from others. Every once in a while, she discovered a philosopher or an author like P.D. Ouspensky, who said "dreams disclose the mysteries of being, sow the governing laws of life , and bring us into contact with higher forces." It infused her world with inspiration and new considerations.

She hadn't had a flying dream for more than two years. And she missed flying, her favorite unconscious experience, by far. When flying, she experienced a liberating lightness, a thrilling otherworldliness. She associated flying with breakthroughs, bursts of creativity, or new thinking. She was due.

This particular class was not taken on-line. She preferred to sit in a classroom with a lecturer and have a chance to interact with other students who had parallel fascinations. Seconds before the prof launched his lecture, she found a place next to her friend Melody.

"Dreams are like thieves in the night," Professor Wiessner bellowed. "Let's examine similes and metaphors for dreaming. Anyone?"

The girl in front of Cristin raised her hand and said, "A dream is an abstract painting we get to view from the inside."

A man behind her called out, "Dreams are like pools of water, fluid and elusive. Pools of subconscious, personal, collective, cosmic unconsciousness that when disturbed by either a subtle point of entry or force, will ripple or storm."

Cristin turned to see the student and saw a blond, blue-eyed man she'd never seen before, with a European accent. She smiled, nodded in approval, and turned to face the professor.

Cristin raised her hand. "A dream is a conversation between your past and future."

The foreigner continued, contributing to the professor's topic. "A dream is a wish your heart makes."

"Good one. But is that *your* metaphor or Jiminy Cricket's?" the professor responded, amused, while the class tittered.

Cristin spoke again. "A dream is a bubble, fragile and surreal."

Melody snickered and whispered, "Do you need me to pass your sparring partner a note?" Cristin felt a wave of heat pass from her chest to her cheeks. She was blushing, a feeling she hadn't felt for a while. She swallowed a pool of saliva collecting in her mouth which only happened when she was excited or aroused.

The stranger continued, "Not my own, but a good question... Seal's song, *Why Must We Dream in Metaphors*?"

The professor pointed his finger at the young man and asked, "Your name?"

"Dane Scardina, sir."

Cristin liked the sound of it. Strong, unusual, mysterious, fitting.

The professor continued. "Mr. Scardina brings up an excellent point. Gregory Bateson writes a dialogue between a father and daughter, where the father says, 'A metaphor compares things without spelling out the comparison. It takes what is true of one group of things and applies it to another. When we say a nation "decays," we are using a metaphor, suggesting that some changes in a nation are like changes which bacteria produce in fruit. But we don't stop to mention the fruit or the bacteria."

"I'll paraphrase the next part because it's close enough. You'll get the gist of it." Professor Wiessner took a sip of water and continued. "With a dream, it's the other way around. The dream would mention the fruit and probably the bacteria but would not mention the nation. The dream elaborates on the relationship but does not identify the things that are related."

Cristin felt a hand on her shoulder and turned to see the handsome stranger mouth the words, "I'll see you after class?"

She nodded and felt the warmth return to her cheeks. She whispered to Melody, "Will you take notes for me today?" Melody smiled affirmatively. Cristin plunged into a different form of dreaming that effectively cancelled class that day.

After class, she folded her laptop and saw Dane Scardina already in the aisle, walking toward the exit. Cristin remembered her mother saying that nothing happens if you're not out there. If she'd stayed in her dorm, she wouldn't be about to meet this gorgeous stranger. *Sliding doors*, she thought to herself.

The weathervane had changed as a blast of cool, winter air greeted Cristin on the steps of the Old Cabell Hall. She peered around a colonnade of white pillars. And there he was, standing under a gingko tree. She walked toward him, and through a smile, introduced herself.

"Hi, I'm Cristin."

"Dane. It's a pleasure to meet you." He extended his hand to shake hers. She would later wonder if he had taken her hand just to touch her.

"I haven't seen you in class before," she said.

"I'm just auditing. The field of the paranormal interests me. It's fascinating, isn't it?"

"I think so. I like your accent. Where are you from?"

"I was born in Italy but raised in a boarding school in Switzerland."

"How exotic," she said.

"Not really. You're beautiful."

His bluntness surprised her. "Not really. You're direct," she said, feeling herself blush.

"Why waste time?" he said. "I'd love to talk with you sometime, when I have more time. Could we meet at the Corner, at Trinity later this afternoon? At about four-thirty? I'll buy you a craft beer of your choice. I like to try American beers. Sort of a hobby of mine."

"That sounds terrific. I'll see you at four-thirty then." Cristin smiled and turned away with the satisfaction of accepting a date. It had been a while since she'd flirted and it was fun. When she was a safe distance, she turned to see if he was gone. But he wasn't. He hadn't moved an inch and was still watching her.

Trinity Irish Pub was located across the grounds of the university and was a common hangout among local university students. It was too cool to sit outside, so Cristin presumed that Dane was inside waiting for her. She was right. He was punctual, not keeping her waiting like American boys so often did. She liked that. As she approached the table, he stood and pulled out her chair. She liked that too.

"I've ordered a sampler of beers and food. I hope that's all right," he said.

"Of course. Thank you." She was unaccustomed to a guy's thoughtfulness. "I must say, you look so familiar to me, but I can't place from where."

"Well, that would be a long shot. Have you ever been to Europe?" he asked.

"I wish," she said, with longing in her voice and eyes.

"So tell me, Cristin. Where are you from? Do you have a family?"

"I'm from Nebraska. My mother still lives there. My father passed a few years ago, and I have one sister Lizzie who just moved to South Carolina. She's a wannabe naturalist and lives there with her boyfriend."

"That's interesting. I have a buddy from school who is a Pat Conroy enthusiast and will probably end up a writer himself, or at least in the publishing business. He's never been to the States but hopes to visit South Carolina as soon as he graduates. Have you been to the Carolinas?"

"No, but after the semester, I'll probably drive down to visit my sister. She's very taken with the area. Causeways, canals, changing tides, fishing boats, lighthouses...you know, all the romantic fixings a place could possibly claim. But tell me more about you, please."

"There's not that much to tell. I've always wanted to travel and The United States has held particular appeal. Tell me about your interest in the paranormal. Are you gifted?" he asked.

"I don't know if I'd go that far. I do seem to have revelatory dreams. I seem to know things that other people don't know, but it's random. I don't make predictions, but I recognize having dreamed about people, events, and places ahead of time. But it's hit and miss. I never really know until it happens."

She suddenly placed where she had seen his face … in a dream with her mother's Aunt Tess. In a lighthouse? But she couldn't place the context and wasn't about to tell him. He'd think her a freak. She changed the focus to him.

"I loved what you said in class today. You're very insightful," she said.

Just then the platters and sampler tray of beer arrived.

"And you're very kind," he replied. They talked against an increasingly loud background of Irish pub music. As afternoon bled into evening, the music morphed from ballads and folksongs to hits by Flogging Molly and The Dropkick Murphys.

Around nine p.m., Damien insisted he walk her to her apartment which was only two blocks away. He was the perfect gentleman and asked to see her the following day. Not on the weekend or next week, not something as vague as "I hope to see you soon," but the next day. She had plans with her best friend Flora that she didn't want to break, but agreed to see him the following day. Besides, she didn't want to appear too available. She did have a life.

That night in bed with the lights out and the room quiet, Cristin revisited the day, a day that seemed longer than any other in recent memory. She'd spent almost six hours with a man she hadn't even met the day before and had later recognized as having seen in a dream. And she would see him again in two days. But why had he appeared in a dream? She rolled over to turn on her nightstand light and retrieved her dream journal from the drawer. She leafed through the pages of entries. There it was. An allusion to a handsome man, in a lighthouse. She'd written in the margin *Fear. Two mothers*. What did that mean?

And what did she know about him? He attended school in Switzerland, had a friend who would be visiting soon, enjoyed craft beers, was fascinated by the paranormal, and was handsome, charming, educated, intelligent, kind, and courteous. Wasn't that enough to know on a first encounter? The only missing piece of her perfect day was that he hadn't kissed her good-night. He should have kissed her good-night.

* * * * * * * * * * *

That night with the lights out and the room quiet, Damien surveyed *his* productive day. He'd transferred his fortune to a bank in Charlottetown to keep it near. He'd Americanized his name, which he'd suggest Luca do as well. He'd met and befriended Cristin Shanihan McClaren without her suspecting his duplicity. *Madam, in Eden. I'm Adam.* He'd laid the groundwork for Luca and him to travel to South Carolina to meet the other McClaren sister. And he hadn't kissed her.

CHAPTER TWENTY-SIX

"Everything is funny if you can laugh at it."—Lewis Carroll

She only took a duffle bag with enough breathing room to bring back a memento of her trip. South Carolina. It sounded exotic. Cristin had read *Gone with the Wind, To Kill a Mockingbird, As I Lay Dying, The Prince of Tides.* She loved the idea of southern hospitality, southern cooking, Dixie belles, and dashing Confederate rebels. Of course, there was the other side...the poverty, racism, trashy trailers, red-necks, Ku Klux Klan, vigilantism. But all in all, being in the vicinity of Charleston and Savannah, was downright electrifying.

Lizzie and Shane picked her up at the Charleston Airport. Lizzie was queen of the delta. This was now her turf and she felt at home. She hugged Cristin like she hadn't seen her in years while Shane flung the duffle in the back of the pick-up truck. They were ready to show her their little slice of paradise. Lizzie talked so much on the way home, she barely finished one sentence without jumping to the next. The whole time, Cristin gawked at the southern scenery and the parade of Greek Revival plantation architecture. They crossed a causeway with shrimp boats lining sandy banks, wrinkled with reeds and bearded grasses. Spanish moss swept the root-knuckled streets, and the ferns grew, untamed and wild.

Narrow, winding roads would lead to the guesthouse Lizzie and Shane had leased on a canal on Fripp Island. Many of the homes were built of stone with charming wooden fences, which

145

according to Lizzie, did not deter the deer who roamed freely on Fripp. Homeowners planted periwinkle and daffodils as deterrents, but springtime was replete with a menu fit for insatiable deer. And charming? Cedars, angel oaks, southern live oaks, and palm trees occupied the yards as permanent residents and sinecures of the area. The windows of the homes were screened and the homes themselves, wrapped with porches and adorned by hanging baskets, dripping with runaway pothos.

They drove off the road, through an open gate, and onto a dirt driveway that wound past a large white wooden house on a raised lattice foundation. Lizzie explained that raised foundations were common in the area because of fluctuating water levels from the canals. Cristin drank in the humid smell of marshlands and the wildlife they contained. Behind the home were two small buildings, a guest house and a boathouse next to a dock.

Lizzie pointed to the guest house. "This is where we live." She affected her best southern accent. "Ain't it darlin', darlin'?"

"It's charming, Lizzie." Cristin was amazed how small the living space was that she was about to share.

"Don't worry, big sister," Lizzie said, "you get to stay in the big house while the owner is away."

"Are you sure?"

"Yeah, Ruby knows you'll be there. Besides, we can't very well ask you to sleep on the floor, can we?"

"That's kind of you and Ruby," Cristin said, relieved that she would have separate, larger accommodations.

"But first, come in and see our place," Shane said. "Then I'll take you up to the big house."

Flowering bushes and perennials lined the perimeter of the guesthouse.

"Look at the azaleas and the lilies! I can't wait until spring to see the peonies bloom. And in the back, hydrangeas and a rhubarb patch. Cris, this area is crawling with plants and animals. You stick anything green in the ground, it grows. Oh, and my God, the birds. Painted buntings, woodpeckers, all sorts of warblers. They even have one called the prothonotary warbler, and his nickname is the swamp canary. Isn't that the cutest? I'm not just in heaven. As Ruby says, 'I'm in pig's heaven', whatever that means." She laughed her glorious, full, unapologetic laugh that Cristin had always envied.

The guesthouse was indeed small. The kitchenette was in the same footprint as the eating area and living room, in the shape of a square, a small square. A bedroom with a confederate flag on the wall and a bathroom completed the floorplan.

"We rent it furnished. Obviously," said Shane. "But for the time being, it's home. Let me get your bags, Cris, and you can get settled in the big house. We picked up dinner at the Shrimp Shack so we don't have to leave the property tonight."

The big house was huge with a back entrance at the lower level with steps leading up to a wrap-around porch lined with bird feeders. Large screened windows provided protection from the mosquitoes and a lofty view of the canal. Inside the house, high wood-beamed ceilings crowned an enormous great room. A copper-studded kitchen had a wrought-iron pot holder above an island that rose out of a sea of used-brick flooring. This was going to be fun.

Cristin changed clothes and met Lizzie and Shane down on the dock.

"So tell us an interesting ghost story, Cristin," said Shane.

"You guys are hilarious. Ghosts are not my curiosity. ESP and dream interpretation are. However, since you asked, I do have a new story that's pretty provocative. A guy in my class named Alex had a number, ten digits long, recur in his dreams. He had no idea what it meant, except it was persistent, so he brought it up in class. Someone suggested it might be a telephone number, which made sense. He was reluctant to call the number until the following night, when he dreamed the number again."

"But there was a message with it: *What you're looking for is under the front steps of the cabin.* This made no sense but he called the number anyway. He said what he needed to say before the person on the other end of the phone could hang up, because he realized it sounded like a crank call. But the person asked him to repeat the message to his wife and said that they would like to call him back in a couple days. The following day, they called him to say that they had driven to their family cabin in New Hampshire that night, with a shovel and a flashlight. Under the steps of the cabin was buried a manuscript that their grandfather had written that had been MIA for over two decades. They were past grateful and wanted to pay Alex."

"Did he say yes?" Shane asked.

Lizzie rolled up the magazine in her hand and bopped him on the head. "That's not the point of the story, Shane." Turning to Cristin, she continued. "My God, that's so cool. Tell another."

"Well, I recently met someone I'd seen in a dream which is a bit unnerving. But his name is wrong. He said his name is Dane, but in my dream, it's close, but different, and I don't remember it. And we're in a lighthouse together. In the dream, that is. And Aunt Tess is telling me not to go in, but I do, and I wake up. Oh, and he has two mothers. Who knows what that means? Maybe he's adopted? Weird. "

Lizzie and Shane exchanged glances, and Lizzie added, "There's a lighthouse in Beaufort-the haunted one I mentioned, but we've never visited it. But tell me more about this Dane guy."

"Dane and I...we get along really well, but so far, it's strictly platonic. He's interested in spending time with me, but he's not interested in me. He says it's because he's getting over a girl who he loved but it didn't work out. So I'm giving him some space. And although we have a great time together, something isn't quite jelling. But in the dream, he's significant to me. I guess time will tell."

"What does he do?" asked Shane, adjusting his chair to see the sunset from a better vantage point and passing a bucket of Carolina fried shrimp that smelled delicious.

"I'm not certain. He's from Europe; I think he has money. I know he's interested in paranormal phenomena, because I met him auditing one of my classes. He has mentioned forensics and criminal law, but we always get sidetracked. He's quite charismatic. Oh, and when I told him about your pursuing a naturalist's accreditation at Clemson, he sounded interested in that too. He loves birds."

"You should bring him down here sometime," Lizzie said.

"I don't know. Maybe. He wants me to meet a friend of his who's flying in next month. He says we'll have a lot in common. Remember my undergraduate minor was American lit? His friend is an American literature nut and loves Pat Conroy's books."

Shane chimed in. "Conroy's a home boy, one of Beaufort's royalty."

"Ask them down, Crissi. I bet they could both stay in one of Ruby's rooms. She loves company. Are they cute?" Lizzie shot a minxish look at Shane.

"Dane is. I don't know about his friend. They're both Italian, if that means anything."

Shane stood up. "I can tell right now this conversation may disintegrate into the uncomfortable zone. I have some work to do at the house, so I'm leaving you girls to talk about boys and makeup and ovaries, and whatever else."

"Shane!" Lizzie yelled.

He smiled, bent over his girl to kiss the top of her head and vanished into the weeping willows.

"He's a keeper," Cristin said.

"I think so too." Lizzie smiled. "So can we talk for a minute about Grandma Dori?"

Cristin nodded.

"What do you know about the woman she killed?" asked Lizzie.

"Not much. We'll need to ask Mom. But frankly, I've broached the subject a couple times, and she hasn't been forthcoming. I think it was a really painful time for the family."

"Yeah, and that was before they knew about Grandma Dori's involvement. Do you think she told anyone else besides us?"

"No. There was no point to spreading it around. I don't think she would have told us if I hadn't been there when it surfaced. This is one of those things that's better kept buried. You haven't told anyone, have you?"

"Only Shane but he'd have no reason to blab. He doesn't know the Monson side of the family. But someday I want to hear the whole story."

Cristin turned and lifted her head to see the remnants of purple and orange disappearing below the horizon. Then she saw it. "Oh my God, what's that?" she screamed.

A thorny alligator had emerged on the bank of the canal and lay in the coarse, brown sand, not thirty feet from them.

Lizzie laughed. "It's a gator, Sunshine. He won't come out on the dock. Relax."

"I guess we don't swim in the canal, do we?"

"No, Ma'am. The canal is to view only. There are all kinds of critters in *them thare watas*. Snakes, snapping turtles. And just as a warning, stay either on the dock or near the house. Don't take a midnight walk on the bank in the moonlight."

"No problem with that." Cristin beamed. "I love talking with you this way. It's been so long since we've felt close. And don't say a word. I know I've been aloof, exclusive with my high school and college friends. I know we didn't get along when we were teenagers. But ever since this business about Grandma Dori, it feels different."

"I know," said Lizzie." I've thought a lot about that dream you had where Grandma said she did it for us. If she did, we shouldn't be distant. It would somehow tarnish her memory, and that's not right. I loved Grandma Dori."

"I did too," said Cristin.

"But you were always so perfect." Lizzie had a hint of malice in her voice. "I could never compare to you. Especially in Mom's eyes. I mean, let's face it, you were named after her dead sister, who she adored. And every time she said your name, she had to think of honoring her love for that auntie we never knew."

"I wasn't perfect," Cristin said. "You always had more friends."

"You always had better grades. And you're prettier."

"No, you are." Cristin raised her voice." And you have a boyfriend. I don't."

They looked at each other in disbelief and burst out laughing. Lizzie opened the cooler and offered Cristin another beer. "One of South Carolina's finest crafts," she said.

"And that's another thing Dane loves. Trying new craft beers."

"My darling sister, you have Dane brain." Lizzie giggled. "You're insane."

"Dane fuckin' brain." Lizzie started laughing uncontrollably.

"You're profane." Cristin snorted, trying to control the spontaneous, runaway interchange.

"Don't complain. Dane reigns." Lizzie was now laughing so hard that she barely articulated.

"Refrain. Refrain," Cristin spouted, doubled over and falling off her beach chair. "Please, stop. Stop talking! Stop laughing! I hurt. I'm still hungry."

"For Chow Mein?"

The girls laughed themselves out, eventually found their land legs, and after a long, heartfelt hug, they stumbled to their respective houses and beds. The last thoughts Cristin had before falling asleep were whether or not the alligator had slinked back into the canal or had moved up on the grass where they'd retreated from the dock; and how good she felt to have her sister in her life, for the first time she could remember.

That night, she dreamed of flying, for the first time in years.

Trisha St. Andrews

CHAPTER TWENTY-SEVEN

"What we see or seem is but a dream within a dream."
—Edgar Allan Poe

In earlier years, Gabriel and Damien had been close, stirring up mischief, trying to live on the edge of school rules and regulations. But after the death of young Brock, they went their separate ways, actually avoiding each other. But the time came when Damien needed to get closer to Luca, and there was no question that Luca's best friend was Gabriel Germond. On two occasions that year, Luca had gone to the Germonds' home for the holidays while Damien went to his mother's home in Italy. Those were excruciating holidays for him. His mind imagined that Gabriel might also be attracted to Luca and be in a position to act on it.

But in school, Gabriel was accessible to Damien. They had a number of classes and a lab together. So Damien befriended Gabriel again, and within months, he had assimilated into a group of friends that included Luca. By the following year, the three of them had become a virtual trio, bound by common interests, humor, and notable to all three of the young men: they had fathers who had known and trusted each other for decades.

The message from Luca that Damien had anticipated for weeks came on a Tuesday afternoon. Luca was hoping to fly into Dulles, hop a plane to Charlottesville, and stay with Damien. Damien returned his call immediately.

"Hey, buddy. That's great news. Book it, let me know the details, and I'll pick you up in Charlottesville. Let the adventure begin."

"Sounds good. Once I graduate on Saturday, I'm a free man. By the way, there's a chance Gabe can join us. That's cool, right?"

In a matter of seconds, Damien felt his plans derail, pain in his gut. There was nothing he could say but yes. He emerged through the wreckage of the sudden request, like a conductor walking away from a crash site, stunned and disoriented.

"Damien? Damien, if it's not okay, just tell me," Luca said.

"No, of course it is. We'll have a blast. How long can you stay?"

"Gabe can't stay long. His class schedule is pretty brutal. Maybe a few days. But I'm buying an open-ended ticket."

Damien's hopes were rekindled, not dead, but on ice that could thaw.

"Excellent. He's such a history buff, he'll love it here. And I was thinking, after he leaves, you and I can drive down to South Carolina? I've met a girl whose sister lives in Beaufort. I think you'll like this gal. She has a fondness for southern writers, so you'll probably have a lot in common with her."

"Sounds good. I'll take an apartment of my own so I won't infringe on your lifestyle, but I appreciate being able to acclimate for a few days at your place. I'll call you when we land."

"Perfect. See you then." Damien's heart pounded with anticipation of what he'd dreamed about for close to four years. He paced his apartment. Gabriel was a fly in the ointment, but just a minor detail in the overall scheme of things. Regarding Luca, most lovers started out as friends, and friends they would remain for a while longer. Luca certainly wouldn't need to take his own apartment, but they'd talk about it after Gabriel left town. They would finally have time to travel, maybe camp, hike, shoot rifles. He laughed out loud at the absurdity and thrill of the thoughts. Elated with the scope of possibilities, one thing he knew for sure—he wouldn't give up. He would make Luca love him.

He'd read stories about men who didn't have gay inclinations, who with the right man, changed their minds. It was possible. It was more than possible; Damien was the key to Luca's mother's retribution. Luca had no idea what Damien had already done for him. He would not only be grateful, but feel indebted to him, the man who loved him above all others.

Damien felt himself stiffen with the thrill of the coming days. He undid his zipper.

****

In one of his political classes, Gabriel studied the American Founding Fathers and had become a disciple of Thomas Jefferson's wisdom and insight into the strengths and weaknesses of democracy. Gabriel wrote a paper based on a journalist's interview with an American professor named Forrest McDonald. McDonald had dissected and analyzed the functions of the American presidency, and concluded that there are two primary but diverse functions of the office, rarely being found in the same person. Ruling and governing. Jefferson was one of the few who'd successfully exemplified both. He personified the hopes and dreams of a nascent country with exquisite poise. In his paper, using Jefferson as his paragon, Gabriel compared presidents who had only one or neither of these talents, to their discredit and their country's distress.

In his final American literature class, Luca examined three early nineteenth-century writers, dissimilar in style. Nathaniel Hawthorne, Walt Whitman, and Edgar Allan Poe. He was particularly interested in Poe, not because he was the finest writer, but because his content was provocative, often dark and vulgar. Luca admired him because of his courage to write what he did, despite the disapproval of the Transcendentalists and lauded writers of his time. He was a maverick and true to his mind.

At the tender ages of twenty and eighteen, respectively, Gabriel Germond and Luca Gherardini had landed in America and were headed to where Thomas Jefferson and Edgar Allan Poe had each walked the hallowed grounds.

****

Damien was at the airport to greet them. He first saw Luca's striking demeanor, his dark Mediterranean eyes, dark skin and dark, thick hair. His gorgeous body descended the escalator at baggage claim, while Damien's heart pounded and his body stiffened in anticipation. Luca was in America, finally.

Then he saw Gabriel who waved to him, ignorant of the sacrifice Damien was making to be civil and hospitable. But his jealous heart needed to be curbed while he kept his eye on the prize. Luca was about to meet Cristin. Gabriel was a collateral nuisance, not worthy of his envy or time.

After dropping off their duffle bags at Damien's apartment, they headed to the Virginian, a local watering hole for university students.

"So what's the deal with this Cristin chick? You talk about her a lot but you're not interested?" asked Gabriel. "Why waste time with someone you can't make time with, you know?"

"She's just cool. You'll see. I, for one, think men and women can be friends." Damien flashed his broad, mischievous smile.

Gabriel persisted. "Is she gay? I mean, why would she hang out with you so much if she wasn't attracted to you?"

"No, she's not gay. I told her I'm getting over a relationship gone south with another girl, and I need time. I can only be friends now."

"Any truth to that?" Luca asked.

"No. It's just a little white lie."

"Is there such a thing? It sounds to me like you're stringing her along, buddy," Gabriel said.

"Not for too much longer. Don't worry about it. We're cool. Oh, and by the way, I suggest you Americanize your names. She knows me as Dane, and you as Luke and Gabe."

"What the…? You're telling us now? Why?" Gabriel asked.

Before there was time for a response, Damien opened the door and entered the bar. Gabriel and Luca quizzically looked at each other and followed him.

"Never a dull moment," said Luca, shrugging his shoulders.

"There she is," said Damien, pointing to a pretty woman, already seated across the room.

Cristin had secured a table for five near the bar and was waiting there with her exotic, dark-haired friend. The women stood to greet them. Cristin gave Damien a hug and extended her hand to both of the others, then introduced her girlfriend before sitting. "This is my friend Flora. Flora, Dane, Luke and Gabe."

"We've seen your photos," Flora said with an exotic accent. She smiled at Gabriel.

"Welcome to Virginia. Welcome to America, for that matter. Are you feeling jetlagged yet?" Cristin asked.

"No, we're pretty pumped to be here. I imagine we'll feel it tonight," Gabriel replied.

"Dane told me that you're going to school in Spain, Gabe. You didn't fly together then?"

"Actually, we did. I lived in Switzerland so I visited my family for a day. Then Luke and I flew out of Lucerne."

The waitress, a brown-eyed beauty named Holly, introduced herself and asked for their order.

"Where are you from?" asked Luca, struck by her southern accent.

"I'm from Athens," she said. Then seeing their perplexed looks, she added, "Athens, Georgia? Alls anybody has to do is hear me talk and they knows I ain't from Greece." She paused a moment, then added, "I'm just messing with y'all." She quickly glanced around the room to check her tables filling up. "So what will be y'all's pleasure today?"

Holly took their order and left them to their conversation.

"So Flora, Dane tells us that Cristin is from Nebraska, where are you from?" asked Gabriel.

"I'm Persian," she said.

"Iran?" he asked.

"Yes. I have a student visa and hope to live here. My aunt will sponsor me for citizenship. She lives in Alexandria." She paused, "Virginia, not Egypt."

"Good one," said Gabriel, He laughed but sensed the table was tense with the subject, so he dropped it. He knew that with this many people, the conversations would overlap and become elliptical, and at some point, he would find his orbit and circle back to her.

When the drinks were served, Flora's martini was lacking.

"They forgot my olive," she said.

Luca asked, "Does a martini need an olive?"

"Does a martini need an olive? Does a haunted house need a ghost?" asked Flora.

"That's a question for Cristin," said Damien.

The boys from Switzerland stared at Cristin.

"How much have you told them about my field of study, Dane?" she asked. She lined up the saltine crackers on the table in front of her.

"Nada. Care to explain?"

"Ahh. My undergraduate degree is in American Literature, but my graduate studies are in parapsychology. Hence, the ghost joke."

Luca watched Cristin's perfectly shaped lips as she spoke. "How long have you studied the paranormal?" he asked.

"I've had unusual experiences since I was a little girl. The so-called paranormal and I are on regular speaking terms. I didn't have much choice. It's as much a part of my life as my birthday. It's dreaming that particularly intrigues me."

"How so?" asked Luca. The sound and the pace of her voice was mesmerizing, low like a cello, playing a love ballad.

Cristin talked about dreams, and Luca concentrated on her lips, her voice, her eyes, and the way she gracefully floated her hands. He wanted to take her home with him.

Damien stared at Luca. There didn't appear to be attraction between Luca and Gabriel. Maybe Damien had been paranoid.

But more importantly, Luca was talking to Cristin. It wouldn't be long before Luca knew his fate. The one act of love he could show his dearly departed mother. The debt he would owe Damien for setting the whole business in orbit. Unrepayable.

Cristin continued. "Dane tells me that you love American lit too. He'll have to take you by Edgar's room on campus. Edgar Allan Poe was a student here at UVA, you know."

"I know. *What we see or seem is but a dream within a dream*," Luca said.

"Yes! One of my favorite quotes!" Cristin squealed with delight. "Dane, he knows one of my favorite quotes," she said, looking at Damien adoringly.

"I think Edgar may have been a bit mad. History hasn't been kind to him, you know," Dane said, in his detached Platonic voice.

Cristin leaned into Luca, enough to press against his arm, and for him to feel the breath of her whisper. "I agree, but don't say that aloud around here. He is revered at UVA."

"I always thought he was British," said Flora. "With the funny hat and magnifying glass?"

"You're thinking of Sherlock Holmes," Cristin said. She turned to the men. "Flora is a brilliant biochemist, not a literature buff."

Gabriel nodded politely and smiled at Flora.

She smiled, and drank him in with her deep almond eyes.

"Flora, I have a question. I hope it's not impolite. But I'm a political science major, so I'm naturally curious about global relations. You mentioned you want to be a U.S. citizen. How does your family feel about it, considering the anti-American sentiment in your country?"

She stared at him with her enormous eyes, rimmed with thick, long black lashes, and he imagined how beautiful she must be, naked.

"They're not happy because we won't see each other often, especially if travel restrictions are imposed by your government."

"Soon to be your government. Go on, please," he urged.

"My parents understand. It is a better life here. But they're older. They can't start again. They can't leave their friends, relatives, and familiar way of life."

"But you can?"

She paused, looked at him intently, as if deciding whether she wanted to continue the conversation.

"Please, I don't mean to put you on the spot. I'm just curious," he said.

"It's okay. I've been asked these questions before. The answer is, I'm young, and I'm selfish enough to want a better life. I am free here, and I am not free in Iran. One cannot speak out against the government there."

"I presume you're Muslim?"

"Secular Muslim."

The table of women next to them suddenly burst into a banter, so loud, that conversation throughout the bar ceased, and scores of heads turned their way. They squawked like seagulls on a jetty, until the manager appeared and asked them to lower their voices. The disruptive outburst had been a conversation killer.

"So Cristin, when are you going back to South Carolina?" asked Damien. "I told Luke that your sister lives there, and he's a huge Pat Conroy fan."

"You guys can go anytime. They love company. Just let me know."

"Count me out," said Gabriel. "I won't be here that long, and if I took a side trip, it would be to Washington D.C."

"I love D.C.," said Flora. She and Gabriel exchanged glances.

"Maybe you could join us," Luca said to Cristin.

Cristin smiled, then turned to Dane. "I'd like to show you the area. I told my sister all about you, Dane."

Luca stared at her without self-consciousness.

"Well, we'll see," said Damien. "Luke, Gabe, let's head back to my place. Ladies, thanks for saving the table and meeting us here. We'll see you soon."

"I hope so," said Luca, standing and addressing only Cristin.

"I'll make sure of it," she said.

CHAPTER TWENTY-EIGHT

"A man lives by believing something: not by debating and arguing about many things."—Thomas Carlyle

Damien's place was spacious. They walked in, and he dimmed the lights. He and Gabriel sprawled on the sofa, and Luca landed in a supine position on the carpet in front of them. Luca lit the joint, took a hit, and passed it to Damien. Damien tasted the imagined sweetness of Luca's lips on the joint and passed it back to him.

"Hey, what about me?" Gabriel asked.

Luca passed the joint. "Sorry, man."

Damien grudgingly lost the illusion that Luca would taste his lips, as well. They were all quiet for a few minutes, adjusting their eyes to the darkness and passing the pleasure.

"So Luca, what are you going to do when you grow up?" Damien asked, feeling his hit immediately on top of the beer he'd consumed. "I mean, are we ever going to really grow up? Is there a year when we look at ourselves in the mirror and say, 'Man in the mirror, I've arrived. I'm now a grown-up.' Or at age fifty, do we realize we're closer to death than birth, so we must be a grown-up? Do we fall into it or achieve it?"

Luca stared at the ceiling, as if the answer was hidden within the perimeter of the water stains. His mind whirred and he relished the safety net of his surroundings.

"I dunno," he said. "But I like to think about shit like that. My favorite class at school was philosophy. When I write my first book, I think I'll have an antagonist who's a religious guy who becomes a prosecuting attorney. I mean, that situation is wrought with moral dilemmas. I mean, the Golden Rule? I think we live by it but it isn't an absolute. For instance, it disregards room for the imposition of justice, like jailing criminals. There are so many philosophical unknowns, and they'll never be resolved. Mind-boggling. I mean, is there a God? What are numbers? Is there life after death? Should a few be spared to save many? Why is there something rather than nothing? It goes on and on. Did you ever see *Inherit the Wind* with Spencer Tracy and Frederick March?"

"Whoa. We have a philosopher in our midst," said Gabriel.

"And a movie critic," Damien added.

"Okay here's one for you," said Gabriel. "What if you came across a car accident and found your wife and her lover, who you didn't know about until that night. They're both gravely injured. You have a better chance of saving the lover by applying pressure to a neck wound. Who would you help and why?"

"Your wife," said Luca, "because you love her and even though she dissed you, you still love her."

"Do I have to save either one of them?" asked Damien.

"Yes!" the others responded.

"I'd save the lover because he stands a better chance of surviving. Your wife doesn't love you anymore or she wouldn't have cheated. You can deal with the lover later, if you want."

Damien lit another joint, and silence filled the space as they passed the joint and indulged themselves in the privacy of their own thoughts.

"I have one," Damien continued. "You and your father are in a concentration camp and have been captured after trying to escape. You are ordered to kill your father. If you do, you will be spared. If you don't, you, he, and another innocent man will be shot. Would you pull the trigger?"

"I couldn't kill my father," Luca said.

"You never had a father," said Damien.

Momentarily, the room grew cold.

"I did in my heart. I couldn't do it."

"Even to save an innocent man's life? Forget your own. You'd probably want to kill yourself anyway after killing your father," Damien said.

"We come back to a question I threw out earlier. Should a few be sacrificed to save many? Should one innocent be sacrificed to save another? I don't know the answer. Choice is a freedom and a burden. One of my favorite writers from Virginia is William Styron. And we all know the question he posed in *Sophie's Choice*. It haunts me," said Luca.

Gabriel spoke. "I would kill my father because he would want me to, to save my life and the life of the innocent man."

Damien responded. "And may I point out, you have a great father. If your father was an asshole, you'd still kill him, but for a different reason."

"My turn," said Luca. "You are an eyewitness to a robbery. But the robber gives the money to a local orphanage. Would you turn him in?"

"I would," said Gabriel. "He's a criminal with a big heart, but a criminal nonetheless. A civilized country must have laws that are abided."

Damien laughed and passed the joint. "I wouldn't turn him in. I'd ask to be his partner and go down in history as a modern-day Robin Hood."

"I've got one," said Gabriel. "Suppose you discover your passport is missing, which actually happened to Luca. Let's say there is a stamp, and you need to find out who was the thief. What would you do?"

"That's not a dilemma where you have to make a choice," said Damien. "It's just a mystery." Damien's felt his pulse racing in his temple, his wrists, and his gut.

Gabriel broke the tension "Okay, my last question. You pride yourself in being an honest man. A frightening-looking character comes to your door with a chainsaw in his hand and asks if your mother is home, and she is. What do you do, tell the truth or lie?"

"Lie! No brainer! Next," yelled Luca." And don't say it's because I never knew my mother so I shouldn't feel so vehemently."

Everyone laughed.

Damien said, "Is it crazy how saying sentences backward creates backward sentences saying how crazy it is?"

"What the hell?" said Luca.

"Damien, your mind boggles me. It's just one of his weird word games. You know, saying something forward that you can also say backward. What's it called?" Gabriel asked.

"It's a form of palindrome," Damien replied. "Okay, seriously, just one more situation. What if someone you loved asked you to kill someone?"

The moment following the question was stillborn, ending the amusement of the discourse.

Gabriel broke the abyss of silence. "I guess I'd have to say that no one I love would ask me to kill someone else. What kind of a question is that?"

"I'm serious. Indulge me for a moment. If someone murdered your mother, let's say, and your father was old and infirm, and asked you to avenge her death, would you?"

He backed away from the question, giving it room. It was like a thought that he wanted to stoke, but if he blew too hard, the flame would die.

Gabriel looked incredulous, with a faraway stare as if he couldn't remember if he'd locked his apartment. He finally said, "That's such a random speculation. I can't even wrap my mind around it."

"Luca, what about you?" Damien prodded as his heart pounded.

"I agree with Gabe. It's like Pangaea. We'll never know because we'll never experience that context."

"But if you did experience the context, what would you do?" Damien persisted.

"I know," said Gabriel, interrupting. "I pretty much know my answers before the question is asked. I wouldn't do it."

"Why?" asked Damien.

"Because as much as I love my father, I am my own man and have my own moral compass. There would have to be circumstances, incomprehensible to me at this moment, as stoned as I am, that would make me use someone else's compass, which I wouldn't do, not even my father's."

"What about you, Luca?" Damien asked again.

"I guess you never know what you'd do until faced with the question. It's too abstract for me. Tonight. But I have one more question," said Luca.

"Damien, are you seriously not interested in Cristin?"

"Not at all," he said as he stood from the sofa and stepped over Luca. He turned on a dim light on the coffee table and looked back at Luca who was still lying on the floor.

"Do you mind if I give her a shot?"

Damien's chest seized up in pain as he felt blood rushing from his head to sustain his anguished heart.

"Why should I?" he responded.

CHAPTER TWENTY-NINE

"Some people see things as they are and say why? I dream things that never were and say why not?"—George Bernard Shaw

Damien would never forget the first time he was approached by a boy. One would think that an all-male boarding school would be a breeding ground for sexual experimentation with raging male hormones and access to girls limited to weekends. But even then, the school hours and curfews were so strict, opportunities were infrequent. He had heard rumors of boys investigating sexual preferences, but experimenting didn't mean that a guy was homosexual. Besides, these were just rumors. And weren't rumors the devil's playground? That's what his mother had taught him.

The boy's name was Jean-Claude, nicknamed JC by his classmates. Damien thought that was blasphemous, despite his distaste for his mother's fanaticism. Jesus Christ was the Son of God and shouldn't be likened to any mortal. But then, his class was demographically secular; very few students from religious families. This fact made the labeling JC more pardonable. They knew not what they did.

Jean-Claude was a homely boy, not popular with his classmates, but bright and an excellent study partner. He was an upper-classman which implied deference. There was most certainly a pecking order, a class system within the conservatory that superseded mere matriculation. Damien and Jean-Claude were paired to complete a project for their sociology class, debating welfare of the group as opposed to profit to the individual. Damien argued that capitalism undermined the group ethic. JC argued that capitalist individualism was endemic to the advancement of culture.

During their final late study session in Jean-Claude's room, Damien announced that he needed to take a break and stretched out on the bed to rest his eyes. He briefly fell asleep and woke to Jean-Claude unbuttoning his shirt. Surprised and not wishing to shame his upper classman, he removed the boy's hands and rebuttoned his shirt.

"I'm sorry," Jean-Claude said. "It won't happen again."

"We won't speak of it," said Damien. "Let's wrap up our arguments."

Jean-Claude nodded, humiliated, and began to speak. "As Ayn Rand said in her novel *Atlas Shrugged*...."

Damien heard a muffled voice of indistinct words in the back of his brain but computed none of them. He was disgusted with himself for feeling aroused. He slammed his book shut.

"You know what, I'm going to take off."

Jean-Claude hung his head and didn't say a word.

Damien returned to his room and vowed to himself that he'd never mention the incident to anyone. But he *did* think about it. He tried to get to sleep that night but tossed and turned, trying to ignore his arousal. Until he couldn't any longer. He serviced himself while envisioning someone else unbuttoning his shirt, then unzipping him, turning him over and climbing on top of him. It was another man. Dark, handsome, strong, and forceful. But Damien wasn't gay. He was just experimenting with fantasy.

The following day, he looked at Jean-Claude and felt repulsed. He intellectually took him apart in the debate and came out on top. Jean-Claude was negligible. A non-entity.

"Why were you so hostile?" Jean-Claude asked him after the exercise.

"I wasn't hostile. I was in control," Damien said.

"Fuck you," Jean-Claude yelled and walked away.

"We already know how *that* turned out for you," Damien yelled back with satisfaction.

During the next two years, he experimented five times. He first dated women. A girl named Giselle from the affiliate boarding school who was extremely attractive. He'd seen her at a dance and thought he wanted her, until he talked to her. She talked in an abrasively high-pitched voice. But she was intoxicatingly lovely and he thought he could navigate his way past her sandpaper voice and vacuity. So he bedded her. Once.

His second conquest was an older woman named Rietta from his village. She caught his eye at a local farmers' market one Saturday when she squeezed a white zucchini to test its ripeness. When their eyes met, she smiled and continued to fondle the squash without taking her gaze from Damien. He, in turn, focused without blinking. An hour later, they were at her art studio, filled with oil nudes and erotica, where they made love for hours. It was at that studio that he found himself staring at the paintings of men in the act of lovemaking while he repeatedly nailed the female *artista*.

His third and most complicated encounter was a local girl named Violette whose father owned the butcher shop, the *metzgerei*, in town. She was plain but willing, and threw herself at him at a local tavern one night. He felt weak, sufficiently inebriated, and obliged to be taken. So she took him to her father's shop, where amid the slabs of beef, she climbed on top of him and pumped him inside her until he burst.

The act was quick, but the aftermath was not. She stalked him for weeks and told him that unless he continued to be her lover, she would report him to the authorities. She was underage. Worse, she intimated that her father was known as "the butcher" for reasons other than his occupation. After weeks of sleepless nights, Damien turned to his school counselor, if for no other reason than to name his murderer if he were to go missing. The counselor laughed out loud and told him that he was one of many victims of the renowned Fraulein Violette Hempler. It seemed that her modus operandi was to lure many an SCB student to her father's butcher shop in the middle of the night and scare them into becoming her full-time lover. The counselor assured him that she was not underage and quite harmless, despite her convincing threats. Her father was an upstanding member of the village counsel and aware of his slutty daughter's escapades.

Despite his experiences with women, Damien continued to dream about men. It was time to decipher whether or not his dreams were shedding truth on his nature or cruelly lying to him.

Rumor had it that Josef Heidigger was inclined to experiment with boys. Josef was a year ahead of Damien in school, which meant they rarely crossed paths. But one thing that Damien now recognized about his own nature was his methodical relentlessness in pursuing what he wanted. He didn't want Josef for a future partner, but he wanted the experience. He was ready.

His mother had taught him that God worked in mysterious ways. This time, he would take it literally. One Sunday morning, he attended chapel and seated himself directly behind Josef. He watched his every move. When Josef stood, he pictured him naked, muscular shoulders and trim waistline. When they were asked to stand for the anthem, Damien leaned forward and could smell the muskiness of Josef's neck. He imagined stroking his fingers through his hair.

As they stepped out of the chapel, he edged next to Josef and said, "Hello. I'm Damien Scardina. I think we have an anatomy lab together."

"I'm not taking an anatomy lab this semester," Josef replied.

"Pardon me. I must be mistaken," said Damien, looking him directly in the eye.

Feeling the flush of arousal, Damien turned away when Josef caught him by the arm and said in a low-pitched whisper, "However, I'd like to take an anatomy lab with you. Are you interested?"

Damien felt hairs on his neck bristle and the blood in his head drain to below his waist. He turned, submissively smiled, looked down at the beautiful hand still touching his arm, and met Josef's scrutiny. It was a tacit question that needed to be acknowledged.

It was as if a remote control of the terrestrial sphere had been slowed to pause. This erotic feeling was singular, and male, never felt in the presence of a woman. His whole life had been leading up to that moment, eclipsing the sun into a warm darkness that was transcending and delicious.

What Damien had viewed as a pioneering involvement with an upperclassman to experience technique and pleasure, escalated into a rapacious affair that left him wanting variety and novelty, and someday, love.

Then there was Luca Gherardini. Luca was a year younger than Damien; Luca, a boy with no family, unaccountable to anyone. Beautiful Luca, with the gorgeous Mediterranean coloring of his father and stunning beauty of his mother. Yes, he'd heard his parents speak of Luca, even alluding to the fact that the Gherardini son was a beautiful child. But he was a child no longer, and Damien realized that his boy crush had transformed into something much deeper.

It was a magical night that he'd relived a thousand times. Damien was included in a holiday at the Germonds' home during his final year at SCB. Gabriel had invited both Luca and him for Christmas. They all slept in the beds and sofas in Gabriel's bedroom. The first night in the house, Damien lay on top of his covers and stared at the brooding moon outside the bedroom window. And at Luca. Damien became so bothered, so heated, so stirred, that he couldn't bear it. How could something so good feel so inaccessible? It was that night that Luca became the object, not only of his desire, but his affection. Damien realized that he wanted it all, sex and love, a future with someone he couldn't bear to live without. He sleeplessly stared at Luca's body and incorporated every dream and reality he'd experienced with another into one irrepressible fantasy. That night, he fell in love with Luca Gherardini and knew that Luca would someday love him too. Luca was his future. Luca was his world.

CHAPTER THIRTY

"A story untold could be the one that kills you."—Pat Conroy

The first time Luca met Cristin alone was two days after Gabriel returned to Spain. He'd signed a short-term lease on a townhome and became the beneficiary of the greatest luxury he'd ever known—privacy to conduct his own life, his own business, his own way. Damien had been hospitable, but Luca preferred his own space. He had waited a lifetime to be without roommates. He sensed that Damien was disappointed, but Damien was a big boy; he'd get over it.

Luca's first night in his own home was a rite of passage, not akin to scarification or a vision quest, but euphoric nonetheless. He lay awake half the night, thinking about his good fortune and the lovely Cristin McClaren. He wanted to smell the shampoo she used, kiss the back of her neck, and kiss the inside of her legs. He wanted to swim in the green pools of her eyes and mesh his fingers in her thick, auburn hair. He wanted to feel her tongue in his mouth, taste her, and feel her climax while he was inside her. He was mad for her, bothered thinking about her. His lust became torment. He jumped up from his bed and broke his manic obsession in a long, cold shower.

He'd been with other girls. His first sexual experience was disappointing, because neither she nor he knew what they were doing, other than something they shouldn't be doing. The forbidden mystique was a rush, but it ended in emptiness and a feeling that there must be something more. Cristin was uncharted territory. She was special. She was someone he wanted in his life, for a long time. Maybe forever. He needed to tread lightly and make no mistakes.

Tomorrow he would lease an Audi R8 and offer to take her for a drive in the country. Perhaps to the Middleburg equestrian country, where the hills would be seamed with roller-coaster white fences, upholstered with enormous sycamore trees, and peppered with black stallions that snorted and galloped next to the fence lines. And he and Cristin could laugh and talk and touch and kiss and….

He slipped into sleep like an owl silently flying into a primordial forest.

It only took a couple hours to prepare his blueprint for the perfect day and have it stamped and approved by his board of directors, namely Cristin.

She wore a hat to contain her long, curly hair. When they finally slowed their pace on the windy roads of Hunt Country, she shook her hair free. It blew like fragile red kelp in breezy waves of light.

"I love this countryside, Luke. It's truly beautiful. You know what Pat Conroy said about beauty?" she asked.

"Remind me," he said, smiling.

"*You must appreciate beauty for it to endure.*"

"*South of Broad,*" he said.

"Good one. His books come alive in the South. You'll have to go to Charleston, Luke. It is a jewel in the crown of the South. The history, the homes, and the gardens. You have to see Boone Hall Plantation. Scenes from *Gone with the Wind* were shot there. And the food? Well, the food is yummy. Do you like southern cuisine?"

"I've never tried it. Do you like wiener schnitzel?" he asked.

"I've never tried it. We may have some adventures in sight. You can stay at my sister's place when you go to Carolina. Maybe I'll tag along." She smiled.

It was a smile that spoke to him, as if she'd whispered, *I think I have a crush on you. I know I have a crush on you.* But it was just a smile. Luca smiled before speaking. He wanted the moment to last.

"That would be nice," he said.

Cristin blushed and continued. "You know, Conroy said South Carolina is not a state. It's a cult."

"What do *you* think he meant?"

"I guess we'll have to go there to find out," she said.

Luca stepped on the accelerator, and Cristin squealed with delight. He took curves fast and straightaways faster, slowing down only when approaching civilization. Throughout the day, the villages, spotted with charming antique shops and tack stores, came in and out of view. They talked and talked and talked; stopping at a café, a farmer's market, and at one point, taking a walk.

"By the way, in case I haven't told you, I love your accent," Cristin teased. "Tell me about *your* life."

"There's not much to tell. Boarding school. No family."

"You never knew your parents?"

"No. But in my father's defense, he died when I was very young."

"And your mother?"

"That remains a mystery. But why inhabit the past when you can look forward to the future, right? I forgot who said that."

"*You* did," Cristin said, adoringly.

"And Conroy said, 'Hurt is a great teacher.'"

Cristin stared at him with a look Luca had never seen before. An amalgam of sadness and respect. She took his hand and held it for a minute while she gathered her thoughts.

"You'll have to meet my mother someday. My dad died but my mom, Trina, she'll like you, Luke."

"That's another thing. My name isn't Luke Gerard. Dane thought we should Americanize our names. But his real name is Damien and mine is Luca. Luca Gherardini."

"Oh, I like it. Very Italian."

"That's me. Dane wants to be known as Dane, so let's keep the name change to ourselves. But that brings up something else I'd like to discuss."

"Shoot."

"I'll just throw it out there. Were you and Dane romantically involved before I showed up?"

"Oh God, no," she snapped. "Not that it couldn't have happened, but he wasn't interested in me. He was in anti-rebound mode, you know. Or so he said. Anyway, he never even kissed me good night. And now that I've met you, that possibility isn't possible anymore."

She smiled, her eyes crinkling at the corners, her one dimple buttoning her right cheek.

Luca stared at her mouth as she spoke and thought of Conroy's words in *The Prince of Tides*: "She pronounced each word carefully, as though she was tasting fruit." He chose not to share that thought with her.

"I want you to know that I did tell him I'd like to see you. To tell you the truth, I can't imagine any man not wanting to be with you."

Cristin's eyes widened, and her cheeks filled with color.

"Nevertheless, I don't want to flaunt the fact that we're going to be seeing each other. I think he's a bit sensitive to it."

"I wonder why. Maybe you're the one being sensitive. You don't mind if I still call you Luke? I just met you that way. It feels more natural to me."

"No problem. But Dane is my friend so I'd rather err on the side of caution and not display you, if you know what I mean."

"I think that's thoughtful of you. I'll be sensitive...for a while."

That night, before retiring, Luca checked his phone. There were three texts from Damien asking where he was all day, and one text from Gabriel: *Call me. I want to hear about your date, Romeo.* He elected to return Damien's call in the morning. But Gabriel was probably already awake in Spain so he placed the call.

He answered on the third ring. "So how did it go?"

"Brilliant. She's wonderful, Gabe. I really like her."

"Does she feel the same?"

"I think so. I'm seeing her again tomorrow. We're going to take an afternoon tour through Monticello."

"Outstanding. Thomas is my man."

"I know. I'll be thinking of you," said Luca.

"I appreciate the sentiment, but no, you won't."

Luca laughed. "You're right. I stand corrected."

"So what does Damien think about you dating his friend?"

"I haven't really told him. You were there when I asked him if he minded and he said no, so I've taken him at his word. But I don't think he'd be real pleased. Something's not quite right with Damien and me, but I can't put my finger on it."

"He seemed edgy to me too. He isn't in school, doesn't have a job. I think he's lost his compass. Taking a break from women? Since when? I mean, I'm in school full time, very focused, and I think about women all the time. By the way, I've talked to Cristin's friend Flora a few times."

"No way."

"Yeah, I really enjoy her, but we've decided just to be friends. Geographically undesirable, you know?"

"Ha! Got it. Did I tell you I've leased a townhome not far from the campus? I don't think Damien was happy about that either. But I mean, guys live together when they can't afford any other option, right? I like my space."

"You like having your place to bring Miss McClaren back to share it, buddy. You can't fool me."

Luca laughed.

"I talked to my father the other night about the Damien vibe I had when I was over there. He gave me some insight into the dude. I mean, I know he's our friend, but Damien has some serious baggage."

"So do I," Luca reminded him.

"Yes, but you've got your act straight. I'm not so sure about Damien."

"What do you mean?"

"My father said that his mother's side of the family was pretty screwed up. You know how religious his mother is. Well, according to my father she was to the far right of that mother in the movie *Carrie*. Apparently Mr. Scardina loved his wife but had his hands full. She was in and out of institutions. And Mariana's brother, also named Damien, committed suicide. So the family has a history of mental illness, and you know that our Damien is on some kind of medication. I've never talked with him about it but maybe it's for depression? And while I'm thinking about it, a bit off subject, did you ever notice that key he wears now around his neck? What's that about?"

"I don't know," Luca replied. "The next time I think of it, I'll ask him."

"I didn't mean to be a downer, buddy, but I thought I'd pass on that inside scoop from dear old Dad. I'm sure Damien's okay. Just keep your ear to the ground. I've got to get to class. Big test in physics today. E equals MC squared. Have fun with Miss Cris and let's talk sometime later this week."

"Hmm. Will do. That's a lot to digest. Good luck on the test, man. *Ciao.*"

"*Ciao.*"

Luca terminated his cell connection to the other side of the world and sat at his desk, staring out the window at the large tree that blocked his view. At night it was lit by a flood light at its base, and the leaves fluttered in the night breeze, mesmerizing him like a changing kaleidoscope with unpredictable patterns. He'd always thought that life would have predictable patterns. From chaos comes order. But it was turning out that each day, with each new bit of information and experience, life wasn't predictable at all. From order comes chaos, from which to find new order, and the cycle would renew itself.

He mulled over what Gabriel had shared about their mutual friend, but none of it was revelatory. Damien had entrusted Luca with his life's complications and angst long ago, at least some of it. And Luca had honored his promise, not to repeat what he knew. But when all was said and done, all that really mattered that night was that he had kissed Cristin, and she had kissed him.

CHAPTER THIRTY-ONE

"She had awakened something in him that had slumbered far too long. Not only did he feel passion, he felt the return of hope."
—Pat Conroy

When Cristin wasn't at Luca's place, he was at her apartment. They became inseparable, two people who didn't know how they'd survived the first part of their lives without the other. Luca didn't talk to Damien about his love affair, and the only people whom Cristin had told were her sister and Flora. They were discreet. The world would know soon enough. But in the meantime, it felt more special to be intimately inconspicuous and alone together in the world.

Cristin took a break from her studies, and they spent the entire afternoon and evening in Luca's bedroom. He loved the touch, the smell, the taste of her, and he loved their tenderness in talking afterward. She was a treasure he had found and would keep. Luca cracked his window open to feel the breeze. He turned on some Ed Sheeran in the background, and made love to Cristin, over and over again.

"I took a class in English poetry once, and the melancholy romantics like Keats, Shelley, Byron, they really got to me," he said.

"You are such a romantic. I love you for that. Which was your favorite poem?"

"That's a tough one. That's like asking who your favorite composer is. It depends on my mood. But Lord Byron's *She Walks* in *Beauty* ranks right up there. Keats? *Ode to a Nightingale.* Shelley? His *Love's Philosophy.* But if I thought longer, I'd probably change my mind," he admitted.

"*Love's Philosophy?* That doesn't sound very romantic."

She had challenged him.

"Really? Listen to this." He recited.

The fountains mingle with the river
And the rivers with the ocean,
The winds of heaven mix for ever
With a sweet emotion;
Nothing in the world is single;
All things by a law divine
In one spirit meet and mingle.
Why not I with thine?

See the mountains kiss high heaven
And the waves clasp one another;
No sister-flower would be forgiven
If it disdained its brother;
And the sunlight clasps the earth
 And the moonbeams kiss the sea:
What is all this sweet work worth
If thou kiss not me?

He rolled her over in bed and kissed her deeply.

"I will love Shelley forever." She smiled. Her auburn curls adorned his satin pillow case like gilded primroses. Her jade eyes with golden specks were wide with admiration. He would never forget her just that way.

He heard an owl outside his window.

"Do you hear that? You know I love owls. Did I ever tell you that?"

"No, but I have an owl joke. What is more amazing than a talking owl?"

"I don't know."

"A spelling bee." She giggled and covered her mouth as if she was embarrassed.

"That reminds me of an owl palindrome that Dane likes. You know how he has outbursts of Bible quotes, nursery rhymes, lyrics?"

She crinkled her brow, looking confused.

"Well, he does. He interjects seeming nonsense into conversations. Sometimes it's hilarious; other times, I seriously question what goes on in his mind. But anyway, this is it ... *Mr. Owl ate my metal worm.*"

"That *is* weird," she said. She grabbed the pen and paper from the nightstand and wrote it down, then read it backward. "It works," she said. "But it's not Shelley." She winked at him and smiled. "When I was in grade school, we had a hopscotch rhyme that went, *The wise old owl sat on the oak/ The more he heard, the less he spoke.* But this started with you telling me that you like owls. It's your story. Tell me a story, Luke."

"You're messing with me. You know Pat Conroy said and I quote, "The most powerful words in English are 'Tell me a story.'"

"So tell me an owl story. Please? Why do you love owls?"

"Because I identify with them. They are solitary and strong. And I admire them because they are wise and omniscient. They know what people don't know, because they're awake at night, with acute vision and hearing. I find them fascinating. And I guess I do have a story, a short one. When I was a young boy at the conservatory, there was a large eagle owl in a fir tree on the cliff outside my window. Eagle owls are strong and impressive in flight. I called him Fluffy."

"Fluffy? That's so cute, Luke."

"I saw him roosting during the day once. He had a thick neck and a large head. He turned to stare at me with fierce, yellow eyes, scary for a seven year old. So I never looked again, but I loved it when he hooted to me at night. When the other kids would go home to their families during the holidays, Fluffy was my only friend."

"That's so sad. You really were alone?"

"Technically, there were adults at the school to watch out for me, but the kids were gone. When I look back on it, I was a lonely kid. I still have deep, sad feelings that become too hard to access anymore. But I remember that when I fended for myself, I had to make a choice between being beaten or being strong. I chose to be strong like Fluffy. I've never told anyone that."

Cristin leaned in and kissed him gently on the mouth. Then she smiled as if he were the only person in the world and she adored him.

"Now tell me something you've never told anyone," he asked.

"All right. But this is a big one. Brace yourself. I discovered a few months ago that my Grandma Dori killed someone to protect my sister and me."

"Whoa! That is a big one. Are you serious?"

"Perfectly. It was so upsetting to my mom that she didn't share a lot of details about the woman, but she promised she would someday."

"Your grandma must have really loved you. I don't know anyone who would kill for me," he said.

Cristin's entire body visibly shuddered. "That was strange. I wonder where that came from. Luke, I really don't want to talk about it right now. I'm sorry I brought it up. This is our time together, and I want it to be about just the two of us."

He rolled her over to spoon her. "Okay, then tell me more about your dreams."

"Well, I don't remember not dreaming. I look forward to going to sleep every night, and apparently a lot of people don't even remember their dreams."

"Do you ever wonder how many dreams we actually have every night? Maybe you think you remember them all but are only remembering a fraction of them," he said.

"I know. The mind is an amazing computer. My favorite dream by far is flying. And I always say the same thing every time I fly."

"What's that?

"Why don't I fly all the time? I know how. Why don't I always fly? Have you ever flown in your dreams?"

"No, I can't say that I have."

"Well, you'd remember it. It is the most liberating, thrilling feeling I've ever had, in a conscious or subconscious state."

"Except for loving me, right?"

"Of course. Except for loving you."

"Maybe you and Fluffy will go for a flight together some night. Do animals ever talk to you in your dreams?" asked Luca.

"Yes, of course."

"What would Fluffy say to you?" he asked.

"He'd say that he watched over you as a child and brought you to me, all the way from Switzerland, so I could watch over you for the rest of your life." Cristin rolled over and snuggled into his chest to hold him tightly.

They fell asleep when dusk melded into darkness. Luca woke long enough to pull the blanket from the bottom of the bed to cover them together, as if they were one body. He had never been as happy. Everything he'd ever felt, said, and done, had made him the person he was at that moment. He wouldn't change places with another living soul.

Before morning dawned, the owl hooted again. Luca whispered over Cristin's bare shoulder, "Did you hear that?"

She snuggled and whispered, "Befriend the darkness within you." Then she slipped back into slumber.

In the morning, she sat up in bed, dizzy and out of breath.

He was startled. "What's going on?"

"It's nothing. It happens to me from time to time. I have low blood pressure. Sitting up too fast makes me dizzy. The out of breath thing passes. No worries."

"That's not normal, Cris. I want you to have a physical exam."

"After finals, I promise, just for you. Don't worry. I'm fine. See, I've already recovered."

"Well, you stay in bed for a while, and I'll bring you some juice and toast. Marmalade, right? We'll pump you with sugar."

"That sounds healthy. But you're probably right. They always give you orange juice after you've given blood, which I haven't done in years and should do. Just add it to my constantly growing to-do list."

He made a continental breakfast for them and entered the bedroom with a tray and a coral rose he'd picked from the pot on his balcony. She squealed with delight, as he placed the tray on her lap and then pulled the sheet over his legs to join her. It was then that he remembered the shadowy statement she'd made in her sleep.

"Cris, this morning, I heard the owl outside our window and asked you if you'd heard it. You said *befriend the darkness within you*. Do you remember saying that?"

"No," she admitted. "But it's something I would say so it doesn't surprise me."

"What did you mean?" he asked. He swallowed his first bite of toast.

"Well, the owl is a nocturnal creature. In the spirit world, the owl is the animal of clairvoyance. He sees and knows what's there. He can intuit what others can't, the essence of true wisdom. So in order for us to have a glimpse of what he knows, we need to befriend the darkness, his world, the night. Remember Athena in mythology? She always had an owl on her shoulder to light her blind side, allowing her to speak the whole truth, as opposed to a half-truth. The owl is your friend, my darling. And I'll go a bit further to say that because you have an affinity with the owl, at least in some cultures, the owl would be your spirit guide. Or as the Native Americans say, your personal medicine."

"Hmm. That's interesting but how does it work?"

"Open yourself up more to the image and belief in the owl's wisdom. Tune into his call, which I think you've been doing your entire life."

"It's the first sound I remember as a small child in Italy."

"You are fortunate. Not many people have such a definitive affinity with an animal as beautiful as the owl. Wisdom can come to you through dreams or meditation. Be open to its suggestion."

"This is a bit beyond my comfort level, but you are the one with the developed ESP, so I'm listening." He smiled adoringly at her.

"There is a downside, if you want to know, but being aware can be helpful. When you befriend the darkness, ask it what you may be in the dark about. Are you deceiving anyone? How? And by whom are you being deceived? The owl asks *Who*."

"I've been deceived all my life. Or maybe I should say betrayed. But now, I can't imagine who in my inner circle would deceive me."

"Just remember, the owl is your friend. Always be aware and he will serve you well. By the way, you don't have to share any of this with anyone. Most people would think I'm weird,"

"I don't. I think you're brilliant and extraordinary, and I love you, Cristin McClaren." He removed the tray from her lap.

"I love you too, Luca Gherardini," she whispered as he rolled back on top of her.

****

Damien killed Cristin in his dream that night. *It's about time*, he said under his breath. *She has to go.* He'd had enough sleepless, fuckless nights. His anger, his loneliness, his frustration were arming him to go into battle and win the war. Luca was seeing him less, and Cristin, more. His plans of having Luca to himself every day had shattered when Luca moved out to be on his own. Now Luca's hours away from Damien were a constant threat. They weren't hours spent with him, in a bed, against a wall, on a staircase, under the stars. All because of her.

Damien hadn't foreseen Cristin as a possible romantic interest to Luca. He needed to tell Luca of Sofia's mandate soon. If Luca didn't have the mettle to go through with it, Damien did. He would kill for Luca.

****

Cristin violently shook and screamed, but she couldn't exit the nightmare on her own. Luca grabbed her and held her closely, saying loudly, "It's all right. It's all right. It's just a dream. You're safe with me. Cristin. Cristin, wake up."

Cristin revived and held him close.

She sobbed. "Someone was trying to kill me."

"No, my darling, you're safe. I won't let anyone hurt you, ever."

"Someone was trying to kill me," she whispered.

CHAPTER THIRTY-TWO

"The devil can cite Scripture for his purpose."
—William Shakespeare

Damien believed in fate, in the sense that a single decision could alter his life, or at least his day. A decision to go or not to go, to do or not to do. Like cosmic providence, a human decision could change plans, paths, and opportunities. But the truth was that he didn't accept fate. He manipulated the players and opportunities to his advantage and deemed it fate.

He counted his blessings: I'm off my meds, I have money to burn, *my mother lies over the ocean,* and *Gabe, Gabe, gone away. Don't return another day.*

Damien now needed Luca to himself. South Carolina was demanding an audience. His father said, "Great things have no fear of time." And as his mother said. "Patience is a virtue, sayeth the Lord." But Damien was now out of time, and definitely, out of patience.

In South Carolina, they'd be alone. South Carolina would be the venue. When Luca heard the reason for having met Cristin McClaren, whatever feelings Luca had for the bitch would detonate. Yes. It was an awesome vision. Damien had almost lost track of the superficial reason he'd fabricated that he and Luca take the trip. Oh yes, because Luca wanted the see the places that Conroy described in his novels. Yes. And to meet the other sister and know who she was and how she would suffer when she lost Cristin. Yes. All of the above.

Damien clung to the belief that Luca fantasized about him. There had been positive signs. He fantasized that Luca would come to him, submissive and ready. After all, Luca didn't mind when Damien gripped his arm or touched him on his knee. When Luca stayed at his apartment, they both slept in the nude. They'd grown up in a boys' dormitory, slept without clothes, and taken communal showers their entire lives. That was at school. Watching Luca sleep in his own apartment had been a nightmare. Damien so longed to touch him but couldn't. But soon he would share his feelings. The horizon of his vision was narrowing.

Damien timed the trip to occur during Cristin's exam week, anticipating that she would not be able to join them. He promoted it to her as a guys' trip. Cristin graciously acquiesced, not only because she should study, but because she was tired. She arranged with Lizzie that Damien and Luca could stay at Ruby's big house.

Time evaporated on the drive. Damien played his favorite American bands—Nine Inch Nails, Red Hot Chili Peppers, Foo Fighters. He slapped out drum rhythms on the steering wheel while Luca played the air guitar. Twice, Luca punched him in the arm and grabbed his knee with his nails during the exhilarating peaks of the blaring music, and Damien imagined Luca's nails on his back, as they climaxed, together.

They drove down the freeway through North Carolina without seeing Appalachia, the Blue Smoky Mountains, or the islands. In other words, they didn't see North Carolina, except for one long detour to the outer banks. Damien insisted that they see the Cape Lookout Lighthouse.

They entered the low country of South Carolina, and Luca saw Conroy's homeland as if he'd painted pictures, not written words. The city of Beaufort presented itself like a delectable menu of entrees and a variety of choices for anyone.

The salt marshes were inundated with birds and flooded with ducks feeding before sunset. The backdrop of radiant pinks and oranges reflected in low-lying stratus clouds and higher cirrus powder puffs.

"God, it's beautiful. I knew it would be," Luca said. "The vibe is just what I expected."

They drove across the causeway and saw two bald eagles and an osprey. When they arrived at Fripp Island, sun streamed through a dense tree canopy, and the magnolia trees welcomed them with offerings of lotus-like blossoms.

"I can't believe that after this long drive I'm saying this, but let's drive to the far end, to the sand dunes, before it gets too dark. I can see them on the map. We're so close."

"Yes sir, captain," Damien replied.

They parked the car and took a walkway through trees draped with wild grapevines and tangles of moss. The air smelled of salt, sea, and critters. The dunes were light brown, almost white, stenciled with sandpiper feet, and bordered by the ocean on one side, and fields of sea oats and grasses on the other.

"You can drop me off here for the night," said Luca.

"Ha! I don't think Cristin's sister would appreciate that," Damien responded. "But I do understand. It's beautiful."

His impulse was to kiss Luca, but at that moment, Luca bent over to pick up scattered shells in his path. *Maybe tomorrow*, Damien thought. *Tomorrow.*

A half-hour later, they drove past the open gate and down the driveway of their vacation destination. In the back where the driveway ended, Lizzie and Shane were barbequing on the grill.

"Hey there!" Lizzie greeted them as they exited the car. "I'm Lizzie and this is Shane. Welcome to Dixie."

They all made polite small talk before Lizzie directed them to the big house. She told them that they'd cooked up some ribs and shrimp, with okra gumbo on the burner inside. Dinner was in an hour, and they were to come down for drinks as soon as they were settled.

The men took their duffle bags to the back of the house and up the stairs to the screened porch that extended the length of the house. On the porch were gray chaise-lounges, wicker tables and chairs. They entered the residence through a sliding glass door on the upper level to find themselves in a large master bedroom. They both dumped their duffels, walked through the great room and kitchen, then downstairs to explore the lower level, where they discovered three smaller bedrooms.

"I can stay down here, if you want," Luca said.

"Naw. Leave your stuff upstairs. We'll probably end up on those big cushy sofas in the living room anyway," Damien said. "Let's go down to the guest house. I'm starving."

Damien grabbed his opportunity to touch Luca's back to usher him ahead to the back door, and he felt no resistance. The tide was up so the canal was full, and as the evening unfolded, the cicadas and invisible insects filled the fluid humid air with staffs of staccato.

After dinner, they all walked up to the porch.

Lizzie's cell phone rang and she answered.

"Well, speak of the devil. Hey, Ruby. We're waiting for the storm and sitting on your porch with Cristin's friends ...yeah...great...haven't seen a painted bunting yet. You promised me a painted bunting...ha!...see you tomorrow. Bye."

"Have you ever noticed how charming it is when a southerner says bye? It's more like *baa*. And pie is *paa*. So cute."

"Ruby's coming home early?" asked Shane.

"Yep. And she's bringing her brother."

"They're a pair to draw to," Shane added.

Damien tried not to show his disappointment and felt the anger squat in his chest like he was about to burst. Anger lived in him like a hungry wolf, and if he fed the wolf, the wolf became stronger and not likely to be contained. *And I'll huff and I'll puff, and I'll blow your house in.*

He waited for Lizzie to go inside for some ice, and while Luca and Shane were engrossed in conversation, he silenced her phone and looked for a number. Then he replaced it back on the glass table top before she returned.

"So tell us about the woman who owns the house. Ruby's her name?" asked Luca.

"Yeah, how would you describe Ruby, Shane?" Lizzie smiled as if daring him to define the undefinable.

"Ruby is a southern girl, but not from here. Her parents moved here twenty years ago. Originally from Kentucky. Thick accent, charming as hell, and she has a heart as big as Georgia. Obviously. Lizzie and I came down here on the fly without anything but our duffels and my job. We didn't want to stay in an apartment, so we shopped for a guesthouse, in hope of being on some land with the perk of a big house. We got lucky. Ruby isn't here much. This is hurricane country so she feels good that we're here to watch her house. Big rainstorms aren't uncommon. We're supposed to have one tonight as a matter of fact."

Storm clouds gathered from the east as they talked about what they were going to do the following day in Beaufort. A sudden rain hit the canal.

"You should have taken that there flag down, Shane," Lizzie said in southern drawl. She pointed to the Confederate flag on the pole in the yard near the dock.

"If the truth be told, that's not in my job description, baby girl."

"I ain't laying blame, just puttin' words to truth," she replied.

"You best perish that thought," said Shane, and then they both burst out laughing.

"When you get Ruby and big brother Rhett together, that's how they talk. It's a dog and pony show, hilarious. Just a warning. Shane, let's make a run for it before the storm. You boys have a good night. We'll see you tomorrow."

They grabbed a huge umbrella next to the door and ran like squealing puppies across the lawn. Their observers watched the umbrella invert and the pelting water soak them to the skin in a matter of seconds. A sudden descent of darkness and sheets of rain obscured the canal and added privacy to the homes on the opposite bank.

"They're nice," Luca said. "Lizzie's really different from her sister, don't you think? She's kind of in your face, in a good way. Cristin is more relaxed." Luca paused, thoughtfully. "I love the way Cristin hesitates before she speaks, a slight inhale, like a grace note, before the melody begins. Have you ever noticed that?"

"Jeez. Not really. It begs the question, what do you notice about me?" Damien asked.

"I noticed that you weren't pleased to hear that Ruby is coming home early tomorrow."

"You're right," Damien said. "I was hoping to have a little down time without having to talk to strangers who we'll never see again. I need time to talk with you, without being interrupted."

"We had all day in the car."

"I was concentrating on driving."

"So you have something specific on your mind?"

"I do, but let's go inside where it's warmer and quieter."

The thunder rumbled in the distance. Nature was about to perform a wild and violent act in the sky over South Carolina.

He watched Luca lie on the end of the deep, ample sofa, one bare, muscular leg bent and the other leg straight, his arms crossed behind his neck. Damien lay down on the other end, so they could talk face to face. This would be their only night together, and Damien knew he would need to tread lightly on the seeds he was about to plant.

"So what's on your mind?" Luca asked.

"All right. Here goes. Years ago, Clement Germond asked my mother to look through my father's papers for a letter from your mother addressed to you in a missing file."

"What?" Luca raised his head from the sofa.

"Well, I found the letter. You can't tell Clement, because he wanted it, but I know what he would have done with it."

"What are you talking about? Where's the letter?"

"It's back in my apartment. I don't carry it with me."

"What did it say?"

"Don't get angry. I'm just the messenger. Your mother named someone who she thought was responsible for her death, if she died prematurely, which she did." He paused and sighed with angst. "She wanted you to find the person responsible...to punish her."

Luca sat up straight, swinging his feet to the floor, and stared at the coffee table as if he were waiting for its four legs to walk it out the door. His eyes blinked rapidly.

"What are you talking about? Why didn't you tell me this before? Who is this person? What gave you the right...?"

"Luca, Luca, Luca. We had to speak privately. We haven't had time alone. No one else could hear this, only you. If I'd handed over the letter to Clement, he wouldn't have shared it with you. You know that. It's too volatile. Considering your history at SCB, he may have thought you would act on it. Your mother didn't want Clement to read her plea for your help. She wanted you to read it, only you. And because Clement asked my mother to find it, I acted on your behalf. I found it. I didn't know what was in it. But when I read it, I recognized that the contents were explosive. I did you a favor."

"You had no right to read it. You should have handed me the letter and let me read it, only me."

"You're probably right but I was protecting you. And maybe it was something I could help you with. The secret is safe. I'm on your side."

Luca jumped to his feet and paced the room, repeatedly throwing one fist into the palm of his other hand as if it were a baseball glove.

"What the fuck! What the fuck!" he yelled.

Damien said nothing.

"I mean, what am I supposed to do with this shit? I thought the drama of my life had ended. I could look forward to some smooth sailing. And now this?"

"I'm sorry. I'm just here to help you."

"You're right. I'm sorry for jumping on you, but you must admit, this is a shock. That's an understatement. Someone killed my mother?"

"Yes. And now you can decide what to do."

"I need to find the person. What was the name?"

"I don't have the letter with me, so that will have to wait. But I will help you find the person."

"You don't remember the name?"

"There were a couple of names. I read it quickly. All I remember is thinking is that you had a right to know what your mother wanted."

"You're right about that. Thank you for looking out for me. Clement would not have shown me the letter if it was inflammatory. You're a good friend." He stared at the rain pounding the windows, hearing it pummel the roof. "I'm tired. I think I'll crash here on the sofa. You go ahead, take the master. I'm probably not going to sleep much anyway."

"No, I'll stay out here with you."

"No, please, I want to be alone."

Luca stood and hugged Damien, hard and long.

"I love you, man."

"I love you too," Damien said, holding on longer than he should have, but not as long as he wanted to.

CHAPTER THIRTY-THREE

"Loose lips sink ships."—Anonymous

Sleep was not kind or abundant that night. Lying in bed, Luca felt more awake than he felt during his waking hours, adrenaline rushing and heart pounding, until finally in the early hours of the morning, he finally slept. When he woke, he left a note for Damien and walked to the dunes. Morning fog had skulked its way from some cryptic home at sea and captured the beach at daybreak. Luca stood by himself, in dense fog, knowing that in hours, daggers of hot sun would puncture the atmosphere's thin skin, and the coolness of the morning cloud would vanish as mysteriously as it had arrived.

The air smelled of brine and sea lavender. When he breathed deeply, he felt the first relief he'd experienced in hours. *Nature is a healer*, he thought, *even if only temporarily*. All night his mind had been spinning with questions—*What kind of retribution has my mother implied? Did she name her killer or has she left clues? Am I to launch a manhunt? And then what? Turn the culprit into the authorities? Or handle it myself? I need to read the letter. And why does this even bother me? My mother didn't love me. Why should I care about her? And how long had Damien had the letter? Gabriel had said that he'd caught Damien in a lie. He hadn't been back to see his mother in months. Why had he lied? Was he lying about this?* The questions chased each other like weasels until he felt dizzy and disoriented. He inhaled the sea. *Nature is a healer. Nature is a healer.*

He turned his back to the ocean and noticed blue herons impaling breakfast on the shore of the interior lagoon, a couple hundred feet inland. Seagulls squawked and pelicans maintained their V formation overhead, all minding their own business and unaware of his. He looked down to see the fresh wash of gifts deposited on the shore from the night's storm. Piles of shells, a sand dollar, fans, a sponge and one starfish—all treasures from the sea, but now devoid of water and about to feel their first sting of direct sunlight. He reflected on the previous night and Conroy's image from *The Prince of Tides:* "Lightning flashed around the island; thunder played its favorite game of scaring the crap out of all the shivering mortals below." That's exactly how he'd felt the night before. Scared. But not necessarily by the thunder.

He turned to walk home, oblivious to the humming golf carts, peopled park benches, reflections of yards in neighbors' picture windows, and the deep bloodshot stain of the soaked birch bark.

He wanted to talk to Cristin, but it was too early to call her. He no longer wanted to shield Damien from his most precious relationship. Maybe Luca had imagined the jealousy. Seriously, why would Damien be jealous of Cristin? Luca didn't care anymore. He loved Cristin and wanted to spend the rest of his life with her. He couldn't refrain from talking to her any longer so he called her. She didn't answer.

When he walked in the door on the lower level, Damien was walking down the stairs.

"Where did you go?" he asked.

"Just went for a walk. I had trouble sleeping."

"Sorry. I understand. I talked to Lizzie last night in the kitchen, and she suggested that we take a look at the lighthouse after we take that town tour. It's a brick and cast iron tower with a bell. It's not operational, but there's a rotating light that turns on from dusk throughout the night to mimic what it must have been like at the turn of the last century."

"Seriously? " Luca questioned him.

Damien took him by the shoulders. "I promise, it isn't far. Listen, Luca, don't stress about what I told you last night. We'll handle this later, together. You're finally here in this wonderful part of the world. Let's enjoy ourselves. The rest will wait."

"I have a lot of questions."

"I know. They'll wait too. Let's go have some fun."

"Damien, stop! I want to go back to Virginia and read that letter. How are we going to find the woman? I mean, where do we start?"

"I have some ideas. There were a couple addresses that could help us."

"I want to leave today," said Luca.

"No. This is my vacation too. I should have waited for a few more days to tell you."

"Which brings me to another question. How long have you known?"

"Not long. We'll leave soon, in a day or two, if it makes you happy, I promise." Damien paused. "A couple days won't make any difference. The main thing is that now you know, and we can talk freely. You'll make the right decision. You always do. This is our time to enjoy and decompress before you handle the heavy stuff."

Luca felt the pit in his stomach grow bigger. He thought back to Gabriel's concern about Damien, and he felt compromised. He didn't feel safe. He called Cristin again. No answer.

After they returned from the lighthouse, they heard a horn blaring, as a car in the driveway approached. Ruby Lynne and Rhett George had arrived. Luca and Damien surveyed the advent of the owners from the screened porch as the southerners were about to reclaim their homestead.

Rhett George led the way with both bags in tow. He was a hulk of a man, wearing a beard and overalls, farmer style. His gray ponytail lay on his back like a sleeping snake. All he was missing was a bear on a leash. Luca and Damien stepped out from the porch to greet him.

"Well, ain't you a handsome looking couple," he remarked.

Blood rushed to Damien's face and drained from Luca's.

"I'm Rhett with two Ts. Welcome to Fripp with two Ps. Ha!"

The boys offered to take the bags and he declined, pushing past the screen door and marching into the house.

"Evenin'. I'm Ruby Lynne. Ruby for short. You two are a tonic to look at. Happy you're staying with us and the kids. Are you moved downstairs?" she asked. She swatted at a fly that was attracted to her scent.

"Yes, ma'am," they said in unison.

"We'll convocate on the porch with the kids for cocktails in a half-hour. Has everybody ate?" she asked.

The guys nodded their heads and turning away, Luca mouthed *convocate?*

Damien mouthed *has everybody ate?*

One half-hour later, they met their hosts and "the kids" on the porch. Ruby made Bloody Marys with celery and crab claws and God-knew-what, sticking out of the tops of Mason jars. Rhett George drank bourbon, straight.

"Here, Luke, you set next to me. You boys can have your conjugal later," said Rhett, throwing his head back and laughing hard. Luca looked uneasy, slightly shaking his head. Damien smiled, but barely.

"Rhett George, mind your manners," yelled Ruby. "Don't you mind him. He's just an old hillbilly. We're mighty happy to have you here. Any friends of Lizzie and Shane's are friends of ours too, right Rhett?"

"Give me the benefit, Ruby. You don't have to make apologies for me. They know I'm just jestin'. "

"So Rhett, what do you do in Kentucky?" Damien asked.

"In my younger years, I dug coal. Work's too tough for me now." Rhett leaned back into his chair, took a long sip of whiskey and sighed. "I love visitin' Ruby down here. So tell me, how do you know the kids?"

"We're friends of Lizzie's sister, Cristin," Damien said.

"We knew that, Rhett. Pay attention, boy," said Ruby.

"Truth be told, I forgot. Any one up for a game of Truth or Dare?"

"That's an evil game. We don't want to bring our guests down, Rhett George," Ruby said.

"I'm in," Damien said without hesitation.

"All right, Dane. You're on. Truth or dare?" Rhett asked.

"Truth," he responded.

"Have you ever slept with a man?"

"No," he quickly replied. So much for truth. But considering their host's previous innuendoes about his relationship with Luca, Rhett George wasn't safe. He was also ready to play hard ball which would make for an interesting evening.

"Luke, truth or dare?" Damien asked.

"Truth," Luca replied. "Go easy on me."

Everyone laughed.

"Describe the weirdest dream you've ever had."

"The weirdest dream? I guess it would have to be when I met my mother. I don't have any memory of my mother. I was dumped at a boarding school when I was three. So that was pretty weird."

"Well, cry me a river, boy. I wasn't expecting that answer. What was she like? In the dream?"

"Well, I've seen pictures. She was beautiful on the outside, but she was as mean as a snake in the dream. I probably shouldn't have brought it up. You want a truth or dare?"

"I'll start out with a truth," said Rhett.

"Tell us about a skeleton in your family closet."

"That's an easy one. But I should ask—you boys spook easy?"

They shook their heads in rapt attention.

'Well, my aunt killed my brother's wife. We don't talk about it much but when we look in the rearview, the bitch had it comin'."

Ruby shot him an evil eye.

"Far's I know, it's true. Just putting words to truth, that's all."

"Shane, truth or dare?" Ruby asked.

"Dare."

"Good. About time," Rhett exclaimed. "Act like a gorilla for the next minute. Ruby, set the timer."

"Ready, set, go," Ruby yelled and started laughing.

Shane turned his back and dropped his arms so his knuckles dragged on the ground, then turned around, pumped his torso, and bellowed like a gorilla. He pounded his chest while he jumped and ran the length of the porch and back.

Lizzie finally took a breath from laughing. "Well, a dare certainly proved to be more entertaining! I'll always remember you that way, honey," she said.

"I did it though, didn't I?" he said, laughing himself.

"Let me put that on the list of things I never want to see again," roared Rhett. "Lizzie your turn, honey. Truth or dare?"

"After that display, I think I'm safer with truth."

"Okay, let me ask," said Ruby. "Have you ever been jealous of someone, like really jealous?"

"That's easy," said Lizzie. "My sister Cristin. You've all met her. Except you, Rhett George. I was jealous of her and angry at her for years. And she hadn't done anything wrong. She was named after my mother's sister who died. I used to call her Saint Cristin, because in my mother's eyes in particular, she could do no wrong. She pulled straight As, had cute boyfriends and everybody liked her. I was always Cristin's little sister, not my own person. But we're older now. I realize she didn't do anything to deserve how I felt about her."

"So your aunt must have died young?" asked Damien, digging for details.

"Yeah. Since we're telling the truth. She was murdered."

Damien started putting pieces together. *Had Sofia murdered Cristin's aunt? Is that where it started?* He had more information than anyone else in the porch and felt the power.

"By who?" Ruby asked.

"Somebody."

"They never caught the murderer?" asked Damien.

"Let it go," said Luca.

"Technically, no. But I agree, let's go on. I don't like talking about it," said Lizzie.

Damien was sitting on a keg of dynamite, and not far from lighting the match.

The game continued for a while until Rhett and Ruby retired. Lizzie stood shortly thereafter and announced in her finest southern drawl, "It's now time for me to get my beauty sleep, y'all. Don't stay up too late, King Kong. She turned her back and with arms dramatically extended like Norma Desmond in *Sunset Boulevard*, she said, "Nighty night "and exited the screen door.

"She's really fun. You've got your hands full," Luca said to Shane.

"That's a wild story about her murdered aunt," Damien said, adding fuel to fire, not willing to let it go.

Shane digressed. "Yeah. She grew up in the shadow of her sister, that's for sure."

"And they never caught the guilty party?" Damien persisted.

"Well, they may have."

"That sounds intriguing. What happened?" Damien asked.

"For years, her family hunted for the woman they suspected of a number of crimes and finally found her. In Vancouver, of all places."

"What did they do?" asked Luca. This was the kind of story one only heard about on the news.

"They didn't have to do anything. The woman died years ago."

"How?"

"The girls have reason to believe their grandmother poisoned her, to protect them. Pretty solid evidence to support the theory. But don't say anything. They just recently figured it out and grandma is dead, so they're committed to bury the secret with her. No good would come from telling the police at this point, and grandma's memory would be tarnished as a criminal. She was an unsuspected vigilante defending her kin, as Rhett would probably say."

"That's a mind blower," said Damien and turned to his friend.

"Luca, has Cristin told you that story?"

Luca shook his head, guarding her secret.

"Did you just call him Luca?" asked Shane.

"A nickname," said Damien.

"Okaaay," Shane replied, drawing out the last syllable. "Well, like I said, don't mention it. It's a private matter. I probably shouldn't have said anything. But it's just one of those nights, talking the truth and all."

Damien nodded and assimilated his newly-acquired information with contrived composure. Luca's mother had been murdered by Lizzie's family, because she'd murdered someone in Lizzie's family.

Luca shook his head and turned to Damien.

"That Italian P.I. I told you about? He told me my mother died in Vancouver. Remind me never to go there."

CHAPTER THIRTY-FOUR

"Absence is a house so vast that inside you will pass through its walls and hang pictures on the air."—Pablo Neruda

On Friday, two figures walked into Damien's apartment in Charlottesville, not laughing, not talking, and not acknowledging each other's presence. Damien turned on the living room light and dumped his bag on the rug in front of the coffee table. Luca followed him and did the same.

"Where's the letter. I want to read the letter, now," Luca demanded.

"I'll get it. But I have to warn you, there's something in the letter I haven't told you."

"What the hell?"

"You have to trust me on this one, Luca. I've thought this through, and you'll see how much I've helped you when you read it." Damien's voice faded as he disappeared into the bedroom to procure the purloined letter.

Luca paced. He knew his life was about to change, not necessarily for the better. He had played every possible scenario in his head: *Would he be able to find the person responsible for his mother's death? Would there be proof or would it be conjecture that someone had killed her? Would he avenge her death? Or would he walk away from her perverse entreaty? He didn't even know her. She had abandoned him. Why would he do something heinous in her name? Because she was his mother?*

Damien walked back into the room with the letter in hand and asked Luca to sit. They both took a seat, and Damien handed the letter to his friend. Luca stared at it, noticing that his name was on the outside of the envelope.

"Why did you open this when it was addressed to me?"

"It was unsealed, and I wanted to make sure it was the letter in question and not some bank statement that Clement probably already had."

Luca paused, then stared at his friend with eyes as cold as a shark.

"When did you find it?"

"Why does that matter? Read the letter, Luca. I'll explain and you'll understand, I promise."

Luca opened the envelope and unfolded the letter. It was the first time he'd seen his mother's handwriting, the first personal aspect of her that he'd yet witnessed. He read the words to himself while Damien watched his face fill with horror as he read the last lines.

Family is critically important to these people so the death of one of their own will be the most passionate revenge.

"She was a monster," Luca said under his breath. But then his eyes fell on the following revelation:

My oldest friend Trina has two daughters, one named Cristin McClaren. She would be the greatest loss to all of them because she represents a loved one who died years ago. Concentrate on her, my son. Stay invisible to these people but find a way for that family, particularly Trina Shanihan McClaren, to know that Cristin's death is payback. They ruined my life.

Peace be with you my son. I'm truly sorry we didn't know one another. I have never asked anything of you but I trust you will do this one thing for me, Luca. Make them pay. Please.

Love,
Your mother, Sofia

Luca looked up in utter disbelief and said, "Cristin? She wants me to kill Cristin?"

Damien nodded.

"So you read this letter and found Cristin for me?"

"I would do anything for you, Luca. Anything."

"What are you saying? What have you done?"

"I've found her for you. Your mother has asked you to do one thing for her. I have found the person who must pay for your mother's death."

Luca jumped to his feet and hit the wall with his fist. His face was pumped with anger and dark curls of hair fell forward onto his forehead as he shook his head with both hands in frustration.

"I can't kill Cristin. I'm not a murderer."

"No one would know. I would do it *for* you, if you want. I would do anything for you, Luca." Damien's eyes filled with tears. "You don't get it, do you? I love you. I love you, Luca."

"I don't want you to love me. What the fucking fuck! Fuck! I don't want you to do this for me. Promise me you won't hurt Cristin!"

"*Honor thy Mother* is one of the commandments in the Bible, Luca. You can't let this go without retribution." Damien was now standing and his voice ferocious, his face tense with mania. "What do you think I've been doing for these past months in the United States of America? I found this letter last year and protected your right to hear it, knowing that Clement would never have shared it with you. Why do you think I went to Nebraska? To talk to Cristin's mother, to find out where Cristin was. Why did I audit a class in dream psychology, for god's sake? Why do you think? To meet her! Why do you think we went to South Carolina to meet Cristin's sister? So we could better plan how this reprisal can be played out."

"So you knew Cristin's name when we were in Carolina. You lied when you said you didn't remember."

"I was protecting you. I knew this would be shocking, and there were too many people around."

"I don't want your protection, Damien."

"Yes, you do. You're just upset. This could never have happened had *I* not found the letter. *I* put you closer than you could possibly have been on your own to carry out your mother's wishes. You are her only child, her only son, and she asked only one thing of you."

"But what she asked of me is to murder someone!"

"She was your mother!"

"That is fuckin' twisted, and you know it!"

He clenched his fists and punched the air. "I need to talk to Cristin and find out what her family did to my mother to initiate this degree of vengeance. Do you think she knows? Does she know who I am?"

"Of course not. She doesn't know who I am either. We have to remain Dane and Luke, two random guys she knows from school. If the name Luca Gherardini surfaces, we have to call the whole thing off."

Cristin already knew Luca's legitimate name, and it hadn't made any difference to her. She hadn't recognized him as a threat. She was an innocent party.

"Stop talking that way. There's nothing to call off. And you need to stay away from her. Promise me, Damien, promise me that you will not harm her. I love her, Damien. Not you, her."

Damien looked like he was expecting a grenade to explode in his face. The blood pooled from his head to his gut and he felt faint. His voice deepened. Slowed. "Luca. Luca, you're in shock, you don't know what you're saying."

"I'm perfectly lucid. I love Cristin. Nothing can happen to her. Please listen to me. You're my friend and I wish you well, but I'm not in love with you, Damien; and I certainly don't want you to prove your love to me by acting on a maniacal order from my dead, murderous mother."

Damien continued. "Luca, forget me for a moment. Think back to the other night in Carolina on the porch. When we were playing Truth or Dare? There was something said that I hadn't known before, but we need to address it. Shane said that the girls recently discovered that their grandmother killed a woman in

Vancouver who they thought had killed their Aunt Cristin. Read this part again." Damien pointed to the sentence in the letter that read, *she would be the greatest loss to all of them because she represents another person who died years ago.*

"So my mother killed their aunt, and they finally caught up with her? Is that what you're saying?"

"Yes. It's the only scenario that makes sense. I've had more time to think about this, but after hearing what Shane said the other night, I think that woman in Vancouver was Sofia. If so, their grandmother killed your mother. They as much as admitted it."

"Because my mother killed someone they loved. No matter how you slice it, my mother was a murderer."

"She was still your mother," Damien said, still in love, still believing there was hope.

Luca looked at his friend, whose eyes implored him for understanding.

"I need to be alone. I'm going for a walk."

"I'll go with you," Damien said. He grabbed his jacket, and visibly shaken, made a move for the door.

"No. I want to be alone. And don't follow me. Stay away from me."

Luca slammed the door behind him and walked into a world he'd never seen before. A world, now colored by fear, confusion, and shame. *Who was he anyway? Was he like his mother, not yet knowing what he was a capable of doing?* He wasn't a killer. But it sounded as if Damien would take a fall for him, which couldn't happen. It sounded as if Damien was anticipating a premeditated murder on Sofia's behalf. Luca needed to talk to Cristin.

She lived five blocks away. She hadn't answered his messages or texts for a few days. Up to this point, he'd presumed she'd either lost her recharger or misplaced her phone. It wasn't like her not to return his calls.

What if Damien had already hurt her?

Every few steps he took felt like a mile. When he arrived, his heart pounded as hard as the knock on her door. No one answered. He knocked again. No one answered. There were neither lights nor any signs of life inside. So he waited. He sat across the street on a park bench so he could see her front door when she returned.

For the few minutes he was able to sit still, he took a walk through his life. He'd always felt different from the world around him, because everyone had a family, even if it was just a cousin or grandfather. He'd had no one. It took him years to learn that he wasn't unworthy, just unloved. But not because he was unlovable. It was because he didn't have a family.

It was a circle of pain that had no end; it just spun round and round, year after year, and inside that circle, he relived a maelstrom of sadness that set up a gyrating gravitational force from which he couldn't escape. Who would abandon her child? It was ultimately heartless and damaging, and he hated his mother. To first find out that she had lived for years after he'd been deserted and had not once tried to reach him, see him, hold him, tell him that she loved him? And now, to find out that she had asked him to carry out the unthinkable. And in honor of her? There was no honor, either for her or about her. Was he not thinking clearly? Was his fury at her decision to leave him as a child obscuring his judgment of her? Could there have been extenuating circumstances? Had she stayed away from him to protect him from someone evil? Was she maternally bereft through no fault of her own? Or was she a monster?

He'd endured years of stealing tears, disguised from his roommates, ashamed of his neediness, furious at his aloneness. His sadness and anger riddled holes in his spirit until he thought his sieve of a heart could never hold love for anyone until he met Cristin. He needed to talk to Cristin.

A cyclist sped through a puddle in front of him, splattering muddy water on his jeans. Luca jumped to his feet. "Fuck you!"

But the cyclist was far-gone and unaware of his malfeasance.

The sun had gone down and the air had turned brittle and unforgiving. He hadn't thought to bring a jacket. The wind had come up, and he felt the water seep through his jeans and turn his skin cold and wet. Where could she be this late? The library, the bookstore, at Flora's apartment? She hadn't expected him back yet. But what if something had happened to her and she couldn't reach him? *I need to keep her safe, but I can't if I'm not with her.*

But what had Damien said? He would be willing to *handle* it? Why would Damien put his life on the line for him? Did Damien really believe that Honor Thy Mother bit? He knew that Damien's mother was fanatically religious. But Damien himself wasn't, was he? He certainly wouldn't harm Cristin, would he? Why? In the name of what? Love? That's what he'd said.

Luca had been so shocked to discover the target of Sofia's requested reprisal, he hadn't circled around to the love declaration. Was it an I love you, buddy, like a brother? Or an I love you because we share history and we need to count on one another? Or a different kind of love?

The shocking, front-page, boldly-typed headline in Luca's mind had been that his mother was a killer, and Cristin the target of her posthumous revenge. The parenthetical statement- *I love you*- was buried on the back page. If Luca had bothered to read further at the time, he would possibly have discovered what Damien had meant. If he was the object of his friend's affection, the world was an insane asylum. He'd address it later. Cristin must be his *only* focus.

He couldn't just sit there. He ripped a piece of paper from the garbage bin next to the bench and scribbled a note to Cristin. He stuck it beneath her welcome mat, so that she'd see it if she returned. He then ran to the library and checked the floor where she always studied with Flora. Cristin wasn't there but Flora was. He ran to her. The chair screeched against the wood floor as he sat down.

"Flora, where is Cristin? I can't find her."

Flora jumped. "Ah. Luke, you startled me. I haven't seen her for a couple of days, maybe three."

"But you've talked to her, right?"

"No, actually, I've been so busy studying for finals, I haven't. You look worried. I'm sure she's fine."

"I don't think so," he said.

"You're scaring me. What's going on?"

"She hasn't answered her phone in three days and she's not at home. Where else could she be, Flora? Think."

"I have no idea. I'm sorry. Did you try her sister's house? Maybe she went to Carolina to surprise you?"

"During finals week? And I don't have Lizzie's number. Do you?"

"No. How about Dane?"

Luke felt a helpless horror tremble through his body.

"He says he doesn't know. Flora, if she calls you, call me. I'm desperate to know that she's safe."

"I promise I will. Please call me when you find her. Please?"

Luca nodded. He ran down the library steps, past the book store that was closed, and back to Cristin's apartment. His note was undisturbed, and there was no sign of life.

By the time he reached Damien's apartment, the lights were out. He banged on the door, but no one opened it. The panic he felt at that moment was like none other he'd ever experienced. Where was Cristin? Where was Damien?

CHAPTER THIRTY-FIVE

"When life events mimic shattered glass, carefully locate the pieces then gently pick them up."—Gina Greenlee

When he heard the words "I love you," he was spooked, Damien thought to himself.

It all just spilled out like a dam breaking. All those years, holding back the swelling logjam of love, anxiety, fear, sexual tension, patience, and anger. It just spilled. He should have informed Luca of Sofia's bidding only. He shouldn't have told him that he loved him. It was too much to process at once. Now it was his turn to process. Luca and Cristin were lovers. He screamed, long and loud, until his face was red and the vein on his forehead knotted as if it would burst.

Hours before, Damien had shadowed Luca to Cristin's place, to the library, making the rounds even to his own dark apartment. *All around the mulberry bush, the monkey chased the weasel.* Luca deserved the agony. It was pay-back. By the time Luca gave up, he'd returned to his own place at four a.m. The night was finally over.

But in hours, Luca would be up again, and Luca's search for Cristin would resume. Damien needed to find her first, to discredit Luca and prevent their interaction prior to Damien's mission. *Where was she?* She wasn't answering her phone so something was wrong. But because Luca hadn't found her either, the race was on.

213

If Luca did find her first, he'd tell her everything. Maybe even tell her that Damien loved him. But maybe he'd just tell her that he'd found a letter from his mother that referred to her family members, involved in his mother's life. Maybe he'd just press her for information. Maybe he wouldn't tell her about the revenge appeal. Maybe he would be satisfied to connect some dots and walk away.

No, he wouldn't walk away. He loved her. He wouldn't hurt her. He wouldn't fulfill his mother's appeal to him. And he wouldn't come back. Damien could see it in his face and hear in his voice. Luca was not coming back. To him, anyway.

"No, no. no, no, no! I refuse to be ignored!" he screamed into the deafness of his apartment. He pounded the air with clenched fists and moaned guttural animal sounds.

All that planning for nothing. It wasn't right. It upended the story. His story, Sofia's story, Luca's story. Sofia would have been enraged that her only son had fallen in love with the person she had marked as the target of her revenge. It was wrong. Luca was ripping out the thread of a brilliant, masterful tapestry. Against God's commandment. It was now up to Damien to redirect the plan that was spinning out of control.

Old Mother Hubbard went to her cupboard to get her poor son his meds. But his mind was clearer, sharper, more passionate when he didn't take them. No meds. He needed a strategy, a course of action, a detour to the target. *A man, a plan, began. A man, a plan, a canal, Panama.* Stop! A plan.

Luca could not be with Cristin. That was his first objective. He'd need to turn her against him. She must reject him. If he couldn't have Luca, neither could she. *Jack fell down and broke his crown and Jill came tumbling after.* He was making progress.

He paced the room with heavy, deliberate steps. He could tell her that Luca was planning to harm her all along, that he'd only become close to her to carry out his mother's wishes, to destroy her. He'd show her the letter. His index fingers punctuated each thought as if directing an orchestra.

The letter would prove that Luca knew who she was and tracked her down to harm her. He would tell her that Luca sent him, an innocent party, to meet her. Damien had never read the letter and was unaware of Luca's intentions. Damien thought he was helping Luca meet a girl.

If he's told her that I declared my love for him, I'll deny it. He's the one with the screwed up childhood. He's the one suspected of Brock's death. He's the one in therapy for years. He's the one with the monster mother. He's the one with the name! Luca Gherardini, son of the devil. Her family won't let her near him ever again. Yes!

He swiped the air with both arms and distended fingers as if ending the fourth movement of the New World Symphony. He grabbed his cell phone and noted the number he'd lifted from Lizzie's phone in South Carolina. He took a disposable phone from his desk drawer, the one he'd bought that no one could trace or identify. He entered the pilfered number into the new phone, then texted *I'm not dead* to Trina McClaren and set his backup plan of slow torture into motion. He would make them all pay. *Someone* had to be an advocate for Luca's mother.

On his real phone, he called Cristin again, then Luca, then Cristin, then Luca, then Cristin, then Luca. No one was answering. They were ignoring him. He threw his phone across the room. It bounced off the wall and landed on the floor with a thump. He picked up his disposable cell and sent another message that read *Tell no one.*

Then he realized that he needed backup, someone to support his version of the story, someone on *his* side. Gabriel. He retrieved his hurled cell off the hardwood floor. It still worked. He placed the call. No one answered. He needed Gabriel to answer his fucking phone. He looked at his watch. It was only five-thirty a.m. in Spain. He left an urgent message to return his call. What else could he do? He took a deep breath and faced his front window. The last time he'd looked outside, the sky was the color of tangerines, watermelons, and grapes. But now a darkness had washed the paint from the sky and plunged to the earth like a lead curtain. The light of the street lamp was obscured by a blanket of fog, leaving only a gray glow. Outside looked cold and empty and numbing.

By the time his phone finally rang, he was breathing like a stallion after a race. Damien laid out the contents of the damning letter and his sincere concern for Cristin's safety to Gabriel, just as he'd planned to tell Cristin to cover himself and bury Luca.

"This is crazy. Do you really think he'll hurt her?" asked Gabe.

"I think he's going to do it."

"You have to go the police, Damien. If Cristin's life is truly in danger, you have to go to the police."

"I've thought of that but there is no evidence. All he's done that can be proved is spent time with her. What should I do, Gabe?"

"Go to Cristin. Tell her everything you've told me. She could get a restraining order against him, and at least the police would be alerted to the potential danger."

"Okay, that's good. I've been trying to reach her. But that's the key, you're right. Thank you."

"I'm in shock. When I've talked to Luca recently, he sounds so happy. I'd never imagine he'd be plotting to kill this girl that he says he loves."

"But that's just it. It's all a sham. He doesn't love her, Gabe."

"And the irony of it is, he and I have been concerned about you," Gabriel said.

"Me? Why me?"

"You just didn't seem yourself when I was there. Writing off women? Making up that story that you'd told Cristin that you couldn't be involved with her because you were getting over another girl?"

"Well, you can see why I said that now. Cristin was Luca's mark, not mine. That whole charade of asking if it was all right if he had a go at her, was for your benefit only, buddy."

"That explains why he's asked questions about you," Gabriel said.

"What did he ask?"

"Oh, bringing up your Biblical references as if you were brainwashed by your mother. I even asked my father about you. Sorry pal, but I was trying to find some sanity in a rift that had opened between you two. Maybe I shouldn't have asked him because none of this is my business, but I didn't know how to respond to Luca. Anyway, my father told me that your mother had some emotional troubles that your father concealed as well as he could. And your uncle had committed suicide. That's all I know."

"I guess the skeletons in my closet are on a rampage."

"Everyone has them. Call me when you hear from Luca and when you reach Cristin. Keep me apprised. I care about all of you, you know."

"I know. That's why I knew I could call you. And there's one more thing, Gabe. Luca is definitely not in love with Cristin. He made a pass at me last week. He isn't interested in women."

"What? That's a curve ball. Are you sure you haven't misinterpreted whatever happened."

"No. I didn't misread him. Trust me. And one other thought, Gabe. Let me reach Cristin before you try to contact Luca. He doesn't know yet that I've intercepted the letter. I want to give him a chance to recuse himself. But if I don't reach him soon, I will tell Cristin."'

"Got it. Makes sense. *Ciao*."

Damien disconnected. He picked up his disposable phone and texted, *Beware, the son.*

217

CHAPTER THIRTY-SIX

"Der Teufel steckt im Detail."—Friedrich Nietzsche

The devil is in the detail, as Clement had been taught. Detail in application or in solving a problem. Time and again, he discovered a detail in a legal case that might have changed a consequence, perhaps determined conservatorship or other aspects of estate law. He was not a trial lawyer, but he appreciated the concept of "the detail" in any branch of law, in any branch of living, for that matter. Interpretation, based on the detail of investigation could alter a decision, a judgment, an outcome.

* * * * * * * * * * *

"Son, what's going on? Talk to me." Clement sat up from his easy chair and planted his feet on the floor. There was usually a buoyancy in Gabriel's voice when he called his father. This time there was not.

"Dad, I'm concerned about Luca. And since you are his executor and you know his history, well, I need to talk with you."

"What has he done?" asked Clement. He felt like he'd been punctured, like his body was slowly leaking his life force.

"Nothing. Yet. But apparently, he possesses a letter written by his mother, Sofia. And the letter requests he take revenge on a woman in the United States, a girl named Cristin."

Clement felt the hair on the back of his neck bristle at the mention of Sofia. He watched Fiona walk into the room in slow motion. He motioned with his hand for her to sit down. He put his index finger to his lips, indicating that she was not to interrupt. She attentively took her place across from him.

"Does he know where she is?"

"He has found her, Dad. I'm afraid the girl's in danger."

"Damn!" Clement jumped to his feet. "I knew such a letter existed but didn't know where it was. How did Luca come to find it?"

Fiona's mouth opened, inhaling audibly. Her eyes widened, revealing her horror, as she recognized the topic of concern.

"That's not clear."

"Then where did you hear this?" Clement stared at his wife as he waited for the answer.

"From Damien. He discovered it in Luca's backpack. He wanted to go to the police but there is nothing but implication that Luca may harm her. So he's trying to reach Cristin to warn her."

"Good. This girl is innocent, Gabriel. She shouldn't pay for Luca's mother's mistakes."

"What did his mother do?"

"She apparently was an evil person, son. Her requesting him to seek revenge is not a surprise, but Luca coming into possession of the letter is. If he's gone to the trouble to find the girl, she is in danger."

"Do you really think he'd hurt her?"

"His counselors assured me he would not harm anyone. But why else would he track her down? Mere curiosity? I doubt it. This is distressing. Do you know if he's contacted her, or met her?"

"Dad, I've met her. When we visited Damien a few months ago. And Luca claims he's in love with her, but that may be a cover."

"Have you talked to Luca since your talk with Damien?"

"No, I called you right away. Damien asked that I hold off calling Luca. He wants to get to Cristin first to warn her to stay away from Luca. Her safety is the most important thing, don't you agree?"

"Yes, I do. But when you hear that Cristin is safe, call me. Right now I need to warn Cristin's mother. I have her number somewhere in the file."

"Why? How?"

"I'll explain later. You were right in contacting me, son. There may be something I can do to avert a tragedy. Is there anything else I should know?"

"No. That's it. That's all."

"All right. Goodbye then."

"Goodbye."

Clement disconnected.

"Fiona, I need to retrieve my notes in the Gherardini file. I'll be right back."

Moments later, he walked to the dining room table, his limp more pronounced with his advancing age. He slapped down the notebook on his desk. Fiona turned on the overhead light and held both her breath and her remarks until she couldn't any longer.

"Clement, what is going on?" she whispered, her voice trembling.

Fiona's words floated out the door.

"Clement, what is going on?" she said in stronger voice.

"Ah, as you've surmised, that missing letter to Luca from his mother has surfaced, and he's gone after one of the American women. After I met with him regarding his inheritance, he seemed normal, balanced. How could I have been so wrong? Where are my notes?"

"What notes, Clement?"

"Remember, I told you, that Luca had mentioned going to Italy and talking with the man who was the private investigator in Sofia's disappearance? Vinnie someone?" He rifled through his papers. "And do you recall how a few years back, after young

221

Brockmeyer's death, I found a letter in the Gherardini estate file addressed to Luca from his mother, to be opened when he turned eighteen? I was concerned that the contents might prove to be volatile, so I opened it, remember? To possibly protect him from himself?"

Fiona nodded, cupping her hands over her mouth like a oxygen mask.

"Considering Luca's compromised mental state at the time, I made the decision not to share the message with him. Where are those blasted notes? The message, as you recall, alluded to revenge but also referred to another letter that would name the details, the people, the victims, if you will. He couldn't carry out a revenge if he didn't know who they were, but better yet, if I didn't share the first letter with him, he'd never be aware of her request, or should I say, demand, and he wouldn't look for the second letter. But we never found that missing letter, or the cited passports or a safe deposit key in those files, Fiona. It was as if the other file had vanished. I even asked Mariana to search Santino's home office. Twice."

Clement found his notes.

"Here!" he said as he repeatedly struck the name on the page with his index finger. "Vinnie Vingiano was the P.I.'s name. He owns the local tavern in Castiglione. He agreed to talk with me, because I was a friend of Luca's father and had Luca's best interests in mind. He told me about the American women who'd hired him. He assured me that when he met Luca, he did not share the fact that these women were hunting for his mother, or the fact that they believed she had killed people, people they loved. What good would it do? And Vingiano was right. Sofia was dead."

Clement found Trina's number.

"Trina's daughter must be the Cristin that Luca has located."

"Clement, this is dreadful."

"And here in the margin, I've written that the Americans, the Monson women, suspected that she'd killed eight people, to their knowledge. Trina's younger sister, Cristin Shanihan, and her own parents in a fire, in Iowa, in 1994; Tia Monson's friend Yvette Vandal, in Grenoble, France, in 1996; Sofia took both Cristin's and Yvette's identities after their deaths; Katie Shepard's son Shep and a pilot in a plane crash over the Pyrenees in 2000; and possibly both Rudolpho and Nico Gherardini, in Italy, in 2005 and 2006. Eight total. And there have been others."

"Rudolpho must to be rolling over in his grave."

"I need to warn this Trina woman. It looks like her daughter is the focus of Luca's vengeance."

Clement dialed the number and waited for Trina to pick up.

"It's the middle of the night in the U.S., Clement." Fiona wrung her hands as she paced back and forth in front of him.

"Her phone went directly to voice mail."

"Hello, this message is for Trina McClaren. My name is Clement Germond. I'm calling from Switzerland, Mrs. McClaren, regarding your daughter Cristin. This is urgent. This is not a prank call. I am the attorney for the Gherardini estate. Please return my call as soon as you receive it. Thank you." He hung up.

"You didn't leave your number, Clement," said Fiona.

"It registered on her cell phone. If I don't hear from her soon, I'll call again."

Clement continued. "Do you recall how I agonized about opening that letter addressed to Luca, nine years ago? It wasn't my place to open it, but at the time, we thought Luca may have killed the Brockmeyer boy which now begs the question--did he? Was Gabriel mistaken? As it turned out, the letter *was* explosive. I did my due diligence in trying to find the other letter, Fiona, I really did, but not for the intended reason. I wanted to intercept it so the women referred to were never found, and this whole cycle of mania would end. And now that I've learned more about Sofia from Vingiano, I believe these women were victims, Sofia's victims. And her reprisal, even from the grave, stems from the fact that they hunted her so relentlessly, they made it impossible for her to resurface. And this is her retaliation for not being able to be visible to enjoy her billions.

"From what Vingiano told me, the American women are good people, and it's highly unlikely that they are responsible for her death. Sofia was an angry, ruthless, tormented soul who had no qualms about involving her son whom she abandoned, and pleading for his retaliation on her behalf. I thought I had controlled the damage by not sharing the letter in my file. But the devil is in the detail—there was another letter. The whole scenario is sickening. And it doesn't appear to be over, Fiona."

CHAPTER THIRTY-SEVEN

"They're back."—Poltergeist II, 1986

On the day Luca and Damien came home from Carolina, Cristin's neighbor had found her collapsed on the sidewalk in front of her home and called nine-one-one. She regained consciousness in the ambulance, with sirens blaring, needles in her arms, and electrode patches on her chest.

"What happened?" she'd later remember asking as paramedics took her blood pressure and bandaged her throbbing head which hit the pavement when she fell. The inside of the ambulance whirred in a dizzying dervish, turning fuzzy and dark. Before she heard their answer, the world went away.

After she was admitted and stabilized, a nurse found and recharged her cell phone to search for a contact number. She found the name Mom in the address book and called Trina. Trina immediately placed an urgent call to her daughter in South Carolina.

"Mom, what did they say happened? Is she okay?" Lizzie asked.

"They couldn't tell me. Someone found her unconscious in front of her house. That's all I know. They found my number and called me. They promised to call back when they have an update on her condition."

Trina clutched her chest with her free hand.

"I'm in Boston with Katie, but I'll be leaving to drive down in a few minutes. Lizzie, do you know any of her friends in Virginia who could go to the hospital? I hate to think of her all alone."

"Yes, a couple of them, but I don't have their numbers. I'll be there as soon as I can. Can we talk to her?"

"No, she's in ICU. The nurse has her cell phone. Thank you, sweetheart. I'll see you soon."

Was it possible for a drive to go any slower? Time was curious that way. It went quickly when you were happy and slowly when you were distressed. Now time would unfold the pages of a story that Trina hadn't anticipated reading. If only she could fast forward to read the ending.

Nothing could happen to Cristin. That was all that mattered. Her little child had grown up and now lived in a world far away, where Trina could no longer protect her. Little children had little problems. Big children had bigger problems. There was no way around it. The world was a scary place.

She turned on the radio, then turned it off. She turned on her CD of Martina McBride, then turned it off. She was preoccupied with thinking about Cristin only, lying in a hospital bed, unconscious and alone. Crazy-making thoughts that didn't help but she couldn't shut them out. *Was Cristin conscious? Was she in pain? Would she live? Would she die before Trina got there?* Trina felt panic but couldn't drive any faster. She banged on the steering wheel with the stiff open palms of her hands. She opened her window to feel a cold blast of air. Anything to derail her negative, fearful thoughts.

When she checked her phone again, there was a text from a number she didn't recognize. It read, *I'm not dead.* What could that possibly mean? It must be a mistake, but a poorly timed one. *I'm not dead?* It wasn't from Cristin's number. Cristin wasn't even in possession of her phone.

When she'd passed the outskirts of Bridgeport, Connecticut, she discovered another text: *Tell no one.* It was a mystery, but not a mystery she had the energy to solve at the moment. She called the hospital. Cristin was conscious but wasn't allowed to accept calls yet. At least she was conscious. That had to be positive news.

When Trina arrived at the hospital in Charlottesville, she stormed into the building like a madwoman. Where was ICU? She first tried to decipher a large, complicated directory but had trouble even locating the *You Are Here* arrow. She resorted to asking directions of strangers. The first man didn't speak English. The next man was holding a baby and yelled, "Can't you see I have a sick child? Ask someone else." Finally a woman pointed to the elevators.

Trina entered the elevator, out of breath. Balloons that read "It's a girl" filled the small space, and the excited baby welcomers were ready to party. It infuriated her. What about her daughter?

The next elevator was empty and cold. She felt alone and afraid she wouldn't make it in time to talk to Cristin. She followed multi-colored arrows on shiny, antiseptic-looking tile floors, around corners, down hallways, and through swinging doors. She arrived at the bright ICU nurses' station and tapped on the counter to draw attention to her sudden appearance. A robust nurse in a pink uniform and a wide apple-doll face turned to acknowledge her with a quizzical smile.

"I'm Cristin McClaren's mother. I just arrived from Boston, and I'd like to see my daughter, please."

"Mrs. McClaren, I'll alert the doctor that you're here. You'll need her permission to see your daughter. Please take a seat, and we'll try to reach her."

In the waiting room, with their backs to the nurses' station, Lizzie and Shane hadn't seen her arrive. But when they heard her burst into tears, they jumped to their feet.

Lizzie consoled her mother.

"What have they told you?" Trina asked.

"Not much," Lizzie replied. "Mom, this is Shane. Shane, my mother, Trina."

"I'm sorry we're meeting under these circumstances, Mrs. McClaren. May I get you a water or a cup of coffee?"

"Please, call me Trina. It's nice to meet you, Shane. You have good manners. I appreciate your driving up with my daughter. And yes, I'd love a water, thank you."

Trina looked back to her daughter. "Nothing can happen to her, Lizzie."

"Sit down. She'll be all right." Lizzie put her hand on Trina's knee. "You look so tired."

"I am tired. The stress is exhausting. I'll be much better when we talk to the doctor. Not knowing what happened is excruciating." Trina mumbled through her tears. Her cell phone text-messaging pinged again.

Shane handed her a glass of water. She nodded in appreciation and gulped down the drink.

"And on top of this scare, I'm getting strange messages on my phone that have unnerved me."

"Let me see." Lizzie took her mother's cell phone.

"I'm not dead? Tell no one? Beware, the son? What kind of sicko would send you messages like these? Is someone angry with you?" Lizzie asked.

"Not to my knowledge. But I have to tell you, this throws me back to those terrible years when that woman stalked our family." Trina shot a glance at Shane with questioning eyes that Lizzie quickly translated.

"Mom, I told Shane everything. He knows about Grandma Dori too, but it won't go any further. Right, Shane?"

"Of course. Don't worry about me, Mrs. McClaren," Shane said.

"But since you brought it up, are you sure she's really dead? Could she still be out there, and the Grandma Dori theory is erroneous?"

"The body was positively identified as Madison Thomas. And Maddie Thomas was the name that Sofia Gherardini used when she escaped from Italy to Canada. There were photos taken. She's dead."

Trina cupped her hands against her mouth and shook her head. "What caused Cristin to lose consciousness? I'm so worried.

I just need to know that she is all right. That's what I need to focus on."

Her phone buzzed again. "Unknown number. I don't have the energy for an unknown number. If whoever is calling needs me badly enough, he or she can leave a message. I'll listen later."

The door from ICU opened and a slight, young Indian woman approached them.

"Hello, Mrs. McClaren?" she asked as she extended her hand. Trina jumped to her feet, nodded, and shook the diminutive hand.

"I am Dr. Abha Manjunath. I am your daughter's attending physician. Please sit down and we'll talk."

Trina pulled her chair forward to be close to the doctor's every word.

"Please tell me she'll be all right."

"Your daughter will be fine. She's resting comfortably."

Trina sighed aloud, aware that her voice was shaking.

"However, your daughter has indications of early kidney disease, specified by her symptoms and her bloodwork. Do you have any history of kidney disease in your family, Mrs. McClaren?"

"Not to my knowledge," said Trina, "but I am adopted, so I don't know my comprehensive medical history. I could probably find out, if it's important."

"Merely a point of interest. Knowing one's medical history alerts us to potential medical problems. I believe that if you delve further, you'd find that there is a history of kidney disease, as your daughter is young to have these indicators. But until we run further tests, we won't know how damaged she is. However, I am optimistic that she can be treated. Kidney disease isn't necessarily fatal."

Trina gasped.

"Many people live long, happy lives with some stage of kidney disease. If early enough, she'll possibly not even need dialysis. If not, she may become a candidate for a transplant down the line."

"A transplant?"

"The worst case scenario, Mrs. McClaren."

"What were her symptoms, doctor? Why was there no warning?"

"There were plenty of warning signs that your daughter apparently did not share with you. She chose to ignore them herself, which is not unusual. It is very common for people with symptoms that aren't debilitating, to be in denial. No one wants to know he or she is ill. Cristin's symptoms could have been attributed to a combination of not getting enough sleep, malnutrition, drinking too much alcohol, stress--all potential behaviors of a college student. But she has been fatigued for some time now; she's had back and leg pain, nausea, swelling of her ankles, dizziness, to name a few symptoms."

"Oh, Mom, when I was with her last fall, she did get dizzy. She had to put her head between her legs. And she told me how tired she was. I just presumed she was burning the candle, you know?"

"When can I see her?" asked Trina. "When can she come home?"

"You can see her shortly. I'll check in on her to make sure she's awake. Now that we've identified the problem, we'll be moving her from ICU until the tests are completed. Then I suggest that she take a hiatus from school, and rest. I am also recommending that she be an outpatient at MUSC for the foreseeable future, so her health is monitored."

"MUSC?"

"Oh, excuse me, the Medical University in Charleston, South Carolina. They have a world-renowned nephrology department. She would be in excellent hands. Now, if you'll excuse me, I'll check in on our patient."

Trina stood to shake Dr. Manjunath's hand and thank her.

"Good Lord. How is this possible?" Trina said. "I want to find another hospital in Nebraska though."

"But Mom, Charleston isn't far from where we are. I could take her home with me."

"My head hurts. I can't think that far ahead," Trina said. Her cell phone had pinged while they'd talked to the doctor. She had another voice mail message from the unknown number. But there were signs on the walls admonishing people not to use their cell phones in the immediate area, so she continued to ignore both calls.

The ICU door opened, and a nurse announced that Trina could see her daughter, then Lizzie, but only one of them at a time.

Trina shot through the door into the sterile white room, filled with machines, monitoring her precious daughter. A disturbing sight.

"Oh darling girl, you've given us such a scare," she said.

"I'm so sorry, Mom. I was so scared." Cristin tried to be brave but couldn't disguise the fact that she had been crying.

"The doctor says you're going to be fine, sweetheart. Please don't be frightened. Please don't cry."

"I can't believe I'm in the hospital. And you and Lizzie are both here." Cristin swallowed hard. "Mom, they aren't giving me my cell phone yet. I need to call someone. May I use your phone?"

"Of course, but maybe you'd better wait until we're out of ICU, honey. We're not supposed to make calls in here. Who do you need to call?"

"The guy I've been dating. He was out of town, and I ran out of charge, then this happened, so I haven't spoken to him in a few days. He has no idea where I am. I know he's worried." She started to cry.

"Cristin, honey, you're going to be fine. I didn't know you had a boyfriend. What's his name?"

"Luke. Luke Gerard. I really need to talk to him."

"As soon as you're in a private room."

"Mom, I'll need to drop out of school for a while. And the doctor talked to me about MUSC. I like the idea. I could stay with Lizzie."

A handsome dark male nurse with a deep voice like a young Morgan Freeman came into the room. "Your time is up, Mrs. McClaren. We're getting ready to move your daughter to her room soon."

"May my other daughter have a few words with her first?" she asked.

"Yes, but only a few words," he replied.

"I'll be brief," Lizzie said to Morgan as she whisked by to sit at her sister's bedside.

"Oh, Lizzie." Cristin shook as she grabbed her sister's hands and waited for the door to close.

"We were so scared. But you're going to be fine. Please don't worry," said Lizzie.

"I know I'll be all right. Thank you for being here. I'm so happy to see you,"

Cristin burst into tears.

"What's going on?"

"I need to tell you something else but you can't tell Mom. She'd freak."

"Okay, you have my word. What's wrong?"

Midst her sobs, Cristin whispered, "I was pregnant. I lost the baby."

Lizzie paused before answering.

"Luke's baby?"

"Yes, of course. I need to talk to him. He must be so worried."

"I'm so sorry. Did you know you were pregnant?"

"No. And only you and I will ever know...and Luke."

"I really need my phone. Try to get it for me, okay? And Lizzie, if I'm going to have to be an outpatient, I want to go to South Carolina, to be near you. It will be closer for Luke as well, although I know he'd follow me back to Nebraska. But I don't want Mom hovering over us. You understand?"

Lizzie nodded furiously.

"So you'll support me on that decision?" Cristin continued.

"Of course, I will. Let me try to get your phone so when they move you, you can call him privately."

"Thank you, Lizard. I love you," Cristin said, midst her tears.

"I love you, too, Pris."

When Lizzie walked back into the waiting room, Shane was leafing through a health magazine.

"Your mom is down the hallway, in a cell phone area. I just gave the nurse your cell number to tell us what room Cristin will be assigned to. She told me to tell you and your Mom to go have some dinner."

"Shane, we can talk later, but I need to warn you that Cristin wants to come to Carolina to be with us for a while, and do the outpatient deal at MUSC. Is that all right with you?"

"Of course." He smiled and wrapped Lizzie with a heartfelt hug.

Lizzie hugged him back. "Thank you. You're the best."

Then she saw her mother, disoriented and unsteady on her feet, holding onto the door jamb.

"Mom, what's going on? You look as pale as a ghost."

"I returned a call from that unknown number. I feel woozy, like I'm seasick. I need to sit down."

Shane helped her to a chair.

"Mom, who called you? Who was it?"

"A man named Clement. From Switzerland." Trina's voice trembled. "He is the executor of the estate for the surviving son of that horrible woman. This is an unending nightmare."

"Why would he be calling you?"

"Because her son is now eighteen, has inherited a fortune, and has come into the possession of a letter of revenge, targeting Cristin." Trina started sobbing.

"Targeting her? What are you saying, Mom?"

"This son is out to harm her. This Germond man called to warn me. I could hear fear in his voice, Lizzie. He found my name in a file that had been shared by the P.I. I hired to find Sofia Gherardini, one of the many aliases this monster used. She had a son. I knew that, but it was so long ago. He was young and had no way of knowing the history between his fugitive mother and our family. But this Luca is in the United States and knows who Cristin is."

Shane flinched. "Did you say Luca?"

Trina nodded.

"Wait a minute, Lizzie, when Dane and Luke came to visit us in Carolina, after you went to bed one night … when we guys were talking, Dane called Luke *Luca*. I swear he did. I even questioned him. He said it was a nickname. Think about it – the accent? Is Luke Luca?"

"Oh my God, Mom. He's Cristin's boyfriend. She's in love with him."

"I don't believe it. This fucking nightmare isn't over," Trina barked. Heads around the waiting room turned in her direction.

"Let's go into the hallway," Lizzie said as she cupped her mother's elbow in her hand and steered her out of the waiting room.

On their way out the door, Trina looked down again at her phone. Another text message had been delivered, which read, *I am my mother's son*.

When Trina looked up, her pupils were as dark and intense as black holes.

CHAPTER THIRTY-EIGHT

"There is a time for departure, even when there's no certain place to go." —Tennessee Williams

Hospitals used to smell of ether. This one smelled like bleach. A nauseating tradeoff that even permeated the cafeteria.

Trina took a seat in the corner, as far away from the other hospital visitors as possible. "I'm not hungry," she said. If there had been a rabbit hole through which she could escape, she would have burrowed into it and spiraled down until she fell into an alternate universe.

"Mom, you have to eat something," urged Lizzie. "Please, I'll bring you some soup. Then we'll talk. Come on, Shane."

Trina watched her daughter disappear around the corner. She felt her emotions eroding and erupting at the same time, like a living geological oxymoron. Her anxiety grinded down her faith in her fellowman while a cataclysmic eruption of fear from her core threatened ruin for all who lived in her village of loved ones. *How did Luca Gherardini know her cell phone number? What else did he know? Where was he? How was she going to protect Cristin? And Lizzie for that matter? And herself? Was this Luca really his mother's son in every sense of the word? Why was he sending her cell phone messages, if not to terrify her?*

Even if she could have inferred the answers, her mind was working too fast to process them. While thinking of one concern, she was obsessing about the next. Clement Germond implied that Luca had a history of troubled behavior, but Clement hadn't wanted to elaborate. He only called to deliver the message that he was concerned. Very concerned.

Trina buried her face in her cold hands and felt her pulse beating in her wrists and in her gut.

"Here, Mom. Chicken noodle, your favorite."

Trina looked up through reddened eyes. "We need to keep Cristin away from her phone. She said she was frantic to call this boy. As soon as she has a private room, she's going to want to tell him where she is."

"I know, Mom. But the nurse told Shane that she'll let us know as soon as they transfer her. You have time to have your soup. Please."

"This is a hospital, Lizzie. We have to be her advocates. We have to protect her."

Trina jumped to her feet, bumped the table, spilled the soup, and charged out of the cafeteria. She careened into an elderly woman with a walker and almost knocked her over. Lizzie followed, apologized to the infirm woman, then raced ahead to catch up with her mother.

"Mom, Mom! Wait! Wait for me." She dodged wheelchairs, carts, and groups of visitors in the crowded path. "Mom, Cristin will want to know why you don't want her to have her phone."

Trina kept her frantic pace. "I'll have to tell her the truth, and she'll have to listen to reason."

Trina's phone rang, another number she didn't recognize. This time, she answered.

"Hello, Mrs. McClaren?"

"Yes, who is this?"

"My name is Dane Scardina. I'm a friend of Cristin's. I haven't been able to reach your daughter for a few days. Have you heard from her?"

The voice with a foreign accent sounded vaguely familiar. Trina tried to place where she'd heard it before.

"Dane? Why are you calling me? How did you get this number?" she asked.

"I know your daughters. I'm a friend. Luca hasn't been in touch with you, has he?"

"Did you say Dane? Let me talk to him." Lizzie grabbed the phone from her mother.

"Dane, this is Lizzie. What the hell is going on? Luke is someone called Luca? He's sending my mother threatening texts, and he's after Cristin? What the fuck?"

"Thank God I reached you, Lizzie. Does he know where Cristin is?"

"No, I don't think so. We're on our way to Cristin's room to warn her not to contact him. What's happening?"

"Room? Where are you?"

"We're at University Hospital. Cristin collapsed and they're doing some tests."

"Is she all right?"

"It's complicated. She'll be okay but what's going on with your friend Luke...or should I say, Luca?"

"How did you find out?"

"Some attorney from Switzerland discovered that your friend knew where Cristin was. I'm so confused. All we really know is that she's in danger, and Luca is dangerous. If he's dangerous, why is he your friend? Did you know this all along?"

"Absolutely not. And he's not my friend anymore. As soon as I found out that he intended to hurt her, I tried to find her, then you and your mother. Lizzie, I've been going crazy for a couple days now. It's a long story but I promise you, I'll share every detail. At all costs, don't let him know where she is. Cristin needs to call the police to file a restraining order so Luca can't come near her. Then I guess, you'll need to hire an attorney, to figure what else you can do. I don't know. Call me after you've told her. I just need to know she's safe. "

"Thank you, Dane. I'll call you later."

Trina stepped into Lizzie's face like it was an interrogation. "What was that about?"

"Dane is, was, Luca's friend. He's been out of his mind with worry ever since he put it together that Luca was after Cristin. We can trust him, Mom."

Lizzie's phone pinged.

"Cristin is in room 471. Let's go. I'll text Shane."

When they found the room, Cristin was sitting up in bed with her cell phone in hand, shaking.

Lizzie marched over to the bed and snatched it from her.

"Why did you do that? I need to call Luke. He has to be worried sick about me."

"His name isn't Luke," said Lizzie, "it's Luca. Luca Gherardini."

"I know that. He told me that a long time ago. Now, give me back my phone."

Trina and Lizzie exchanged panicky glances.

Trina began, as calmly as she could. "Cristin, listen to me. What you don't know is that Luca is the son of that woman who stalked and killed members of our family. He didn't tell you that, did he?"

Cristin flinched.

"According to the executor of his estate, Luca has methodically tracked you down to hurt you, because his dead mother claimed our family was set on destroying her."

"And didn't we? Destroy her?"

"Cristin, stop it. You're not listening."

"*You're* not listening, Mother. *Neither* of you. Now either you give me my phone or I will call the nurse."

Lizzie looked at her mom and said, "I'm leaving for a while. You can handle this, Mom." She walked out of the room with the coveted phone in her hand.

"Lizzie! Come back here. Give me my phone!"

"Cristin, please listen to me. If you've ever loved me, you must at least listen. He has become close to you, entrenched himself into your life, so he can hurt you. His family attorney called me from Switzerland this morning to warn us."

"This can't be true. I love Luca and he loves me."

"You can't love him," Trina yelled.

"I can and I do. I do love him, Mother. I was pregnant with his child, and I just miscarried. I love him, and I will continue to love him and someday have his baby."

Trina lashed out. "Pregnant? Thank God, you're not anymore."

"Get out of my room! I don't want to talk to you anymore...ever!"

"Cristin, I'm sorry. I shouldn't have said that. But you need to hear me out, honey. Your Luca has been sending me threatening texts. He is dangerous, Crissie. Do you really think I'm lying to you?"

"This is what I think. I *think* I will survive my kidney challenge. I *know* you're lying to me."

Trina started to shake. A coldness spread through her like she'd fallen through a crack on an icy pond. Her words didn't surface, just dangled near her legs in the subzero, swirling, and debilitating water. She stared at the blank, icy white wall of the hospital room. She wanted to freeze the world, freeze her daughter's insanity, freeze her fear, freeze her life, and take a breath. But she couldn't.

"Mom, are you all right?" Cristin asked.

Trina inhaled. "Just let me catch my breath."

"Okay. Okay."

"I want you to do me a favor. Please."

"I'll try," Cristin said.

"Your friend Dane called earlier to warn us that Luca was dangerous."

"Dane called? He called *you*?"

"Yes. He corroborated the attorney's claims, and then some. Cristin, he's a very good friend to you. He was senseless with worry about your safety. Will you talk to him? Now?"

Cristin nodded. Trina called the number Dane had used to contact her and handed Cristin the phone.

"Dane, this is Cristin."

"Oh Cristin, thank God you're all right. I've been so worried."

"So what they're saying about Luke/ Luca isn't true, right?"

"I'm afraid it is."

"How long have you known? How did you find out? Or were you aware of this from the beginning? You introduced me to him, Dane."

"No, no, you have it all wrong. I thought I was matchmaking. He'd already found you online, knew who you were, and convinced me that he was infatuated with you. I had no idea there were ulterior motives. I would never have put you in that position, Cristin. Please believe me. Recently, I discovered a letter that his mother wrote to him before she died. It implicated that your family hunted her down and destroyed her life. She requested that Luca take revenge against you specifically because you were the namesake of someone who set off a maniacal set of events. Does that make sense?"

"My Aunt Cristin. But this has nothing to do with me. It's not logical. It's not fair."

Tears streamed down Cristin's face.

"I should have known earlier," Damien muttered.

"What? What should you have known earlier?"

"Late one night, when we were visiting Lizzie, Shane shared with us that you'd discovered that your grandmother had poisoned the woman who had hurt your family. The look on his face was disturbing, as if he were taking it personally. But I couldn't put my finger on it. I asked him about it later, and he blew me off. But I could tell that he didn't know that piece of the puzzle, until then."

Cristin swallowed hard. "He never let on. Not once. I really thought he was in love with me."

"He was getting close to you, to set you up. Promise me you won't try to reach him, you won't talk to him. He doesn't know you're in the hospital. And by the way, I hope everything is okay."

"I'll be fine. I won't call him. I'll just disappear. It looks like I'll be having some outpatient time somewhere else. I won't be back to school. And I won't go back to my place. My mom and sister can pack me up."

Cristin heard her voice crack and knew that she was ready to cry again, and didn't want to.

"Dane, I had a dream about you before I met you. We were in a lighthouse. I guess it was telling me that you were to be a dear friend, a guiding light. Thank you."

"I'll be in touch, angel. Goodbye."

Cristin handed her mother the phone and broke down sobbing.

Trina climbed into her daughter's hospital bed and held her like she'd held her as a little child. Cristin was safe, at least until they decided what the next step would be. Trina wouldn't be leaving her side that night.

CHAPTER THIRTY-NINE

"Three blind mice. See how they run."—Author unknown

Three people. Three calls. Whether it was something good or something bad, it always came down to the number three. His mother had taught him that. The Trinity. There were twenty-seven books in the New Testament. Three times three times three equals twenty-seven. The cock crowed three times. And on and on. Damien came from a family of three. He and Luca and Gabriel had been a triumvirate of best friends. Trina, Cristin and Lizzie. And now, there was a triangle comprised of Luca and Cristin and him. This one would be broken, however. All three's did not survive.

He had spoken to Cristin. Luca couldn't get to her, because he didn't know where she was. Damien was certain that neither Cristin nor anyone in her family would reveal her location. They were too traumatized. But what if Luca might call local hospitals? One problem solved and another surfaced.

So this is the way it was going to be. Cristin would move out of area for her treatments, and Damien would make it his business to find out where she was going, but he couldn't surface at the hospital. The mother would recognize him as the nice young man named Mario who had a dog named Wolfgang and had recently settled in Lincoln, working for Mutual of Omaha. It would not be seen as a coincidence, but a threat, and he needed to preserve the trust of the family. And the family *did* trust him. After all, it was *he* who informed them of the danger Luca represented. Well, he was the second person. Clement Germond, a thorn in his side, had beaten him to it. Germond's communiqué was most likely based on the call he'd received from Gabriel informing him of the conversation he'd had with Damien. Clement now had every reason to believe that Luca had found the letter and was inspired to act on his mother's prompting. After all, hadn't Luca been sending threatening messages? Who else had a motive to kill Cristin McClaren? Yes, the call to Gabriel had proven to be valuable. It reinforced the family's fear of Luca and strengthened their faith in himself. All was going according to plan, but time was of the essence. It wouldn't be long before Luca told them a different story.

Trina McClaren seemed like a nice person. But the fact remained, her mother killed Luca's mother. *An eye for an eye.* It stood to reason that her daughter's death would be a violation of natural order, and therefore, an appalling loss. In turn, Sofia Gherardini's death had been a violation of natural order, and the scale of justice must be balanced. *Defend the oppressed. I can do all things through Him who strengthens me.* What had at one time seemed the way to win Luca's love had now mutated into a path to be God's servant and a means to punish the oppressors. His actions were no longer born of passion, but anger. Justifiable anger. *The righteous will rejoice when he sees the vengeance.*

Gabriel, Luca, and Cristin. He lined them up in his mind like targets on a fence. He picked up the phone and placed a call to Spain. *Take me out to the ballgame.*

"Damien, what's happening?" asked Gabriel.

"Have you heard from Luca yet?"

"He's called but I wanted to hear from you first, so I haven't talked with him. He sounds desperate to find Cristin. Have you found her?"

"Yes, but he won't. She's moving out of the area. She's safe."

"Thank God. Where is she?"

"I'll tell you but you have to promise that if you talk to him, you can't let him know. At all cost, don't let him know. "

"I hate lying to a friend, but I promise I won't say anything. "

"She was in a hospital. She's being moved to an out-of-state facility. I don't know where. All I know is that she collapsed and was rushed to the emergency room. She's okay though."

"That's good. Did she contact the police?"

"I told her to. She probably has by now. She's going to get back to me and let me know what her plans are. And thanks for talking to your father, Gabe. The whole thing is so implausible, I don't know if her family would have believed only me. But coming from your father? Well, he gave the story credibility. Please thank him. He probably saved her life."

"I will. He's a prime mover, that's for sure. So how did Cristin take the news? She must have been shocked."

"It was tough. She didn't believe her mom until I spoke with her. She needed validation because the news came from Clement, who she doesn't know. She thought her family was crazy and colluding against them. She really thought Luca loved her. So sad."

"He talks like he does," said Gabriel. "It's all quite confusing, but if what you tell me is true, and there's no reason to believe it isn't, he's really fucked up. Is it possible that he hunted her down with ill intentions, and then fell in love with her? Maybe changed his mind?"

"No way. Remember, he told me he loved me, not her. We have to keep him away from Cristin. She needs to disappear."

"What a mess. It's surreal," Gabriel said.

"*See how they run. See how they run*," Damien said, under his breath.

"What did you say?"

"Oh nothing, just me being warped. Nothing."

"All right. Keep me posted. If there's anything either my father or I can do for you, let us know."

"I will. Thanks for listening and be sure to thank Clement. Bye."

The story was believed. "Yes!" he said aloud. *Bam. Strike one.*

245

He opened his window. The vendor below grilled sausages and onions. The aroma wafted up to his floor. Damien was hungry, but Damien was busy at the moment.

A minute passed. Luca called. Damien didn't answer. Luca called again. This time, Damien answered.

"Why haven't you answered my calls? Where's Cristin?" Luca yelled. His voice was unhinged and demanding.

"One answer at a time. I haven't called you, because the last time we spoke, you made it clear that you wanted to be alone, that you wanted me to, how did you put it? Stay away from you? I'm merely honoring your request. Why should I answer your calls?"

"Because I've called over a dozen times, that's why. Where's Cristin?"

"How the hell should I know? You're the one in love with her. Maybe she doesn't feel like returning your calls. Maybe, it's over."

"But she hasn't been home in days. I think something's happened to her. Have you hurt her, Damien?"

Damien hung up.

The phone rang again, and again, and again.

When Damien answered after the third call, Luca's voice was softer. Chastened.

"I'm sorry. I shouldn't have accused you. I'm just panicked. And the way we left things between us, I didn't know what you were thinking, that's all. It's not like her to ignore my calls. Something's wrong. I can feel it. I'm really worried. Damien. Has she talked to you?"

"I'm staying out of it," he said, as his foot reached across the floor to step on a spider.

Silence.

"Damien, before you say anything, I want to talk to you about what you said that night...about loving me. I was so disoriented when you shared that letter, all I could think of was Cristin. I had to find out what she knew about her family's involvement with my mother. I am in the dark. I know nothing except for the few things the Italians told me. I know my mother wasn't an angel, but

I don't even know what the accusations against her are, and if they're legitimate. If Cristin could share what she knows, or her mother could enlighten me, maybe we could work through it. But if my mother told the truth, if the letter was true, Cristin and I don't have a chance. I am devastated. But one thing is certain, Damien—I would never, ever hurt her."

Luca paused, and Damien could hear the resignation in his voice. "I know there's a chance that after we learn the facts of this god-awful story, she and I won't be able to be together, but I still need to talk to her. To explain. To assure her that I won't hurt her. More importantly, I need to know where she is. Is she in a ditch somewhere next to a road, in a hospital, sick, dead? I've called the police, the hospitals, and no one knows anything. If you know where she is, I beg you to tell me."

Luca paused again and took a deep breath.

Damien didn't respond. He just paced.

"I've had time to think about what you said. And I didn't acknowledge it, but I want to now. I had no idea that you loved me. And although I could never love you in the way you'd want me to, I will love you as a friend. It will have to be enough, Damien. You have to be true to yourself, and so do I. If you love me, you want me to be happy, and be myself. Please. I'm very sorry I couldn't respond that night with anything other than I needed to be alone. It had to hurt you. That being said, promise me you won't harm her for my sake or in the name of my mother."

Damien withheld his words of comfort. He sat down and sighed. "I can't think about her right now. My heart is broken. But I'm glad we've talked. Can I see you?"

"I don't think that would be a good idea. Promise me."

"I hear you. I hear you. Can we talk again tomorrow?" Damien asked.

"Yes. Call me when you want to talk or you've heard from Cristin. Thank you for answering my call. Goodbye."

Bam. Strike two.

Damien stared at the brick fireplace. *And everywhere that Luca went, the lamb was sure to go.* No, Luca was lost to him now. But Damien felt satisfaction in the control he now brandished over him. Damien knew where Cristin was, and Gabriel and his father believed *his* story. *He* could be the son Sofia wanted. *He* could still kill Cristin. *He* still had the money. He'd lose himself in the world and find a man who could love him the way he wanted to be loved. He was still the king of the mountain, strong and invincible. He flexed his arms, and yelped.

His phone rang again. It was Cristin. He felt like a rattlesnake, ready to strike. Damien donned his best concerned voice.

"Hi there. How did the tests come out today?"

"Not great. But they're releasing me tomorrow so that's good. I started the process of filing a restraining order as you suggested. It will be difficult for him to find me. I'm moving away. I'll do whatever I need to do."

"So where are you going? And don't worry, if there's anyone in the world who won't tell Luca where you are, it's me."

"I know. I trust you, Dane. For a while, I'll go directly to Lizzie and Shane's and stay in the big house. It's close to where I need my treatments in Charleston. After I'm healthy, I'll move on, probably change my name. Eventually my family needs to move past this nightmare."

He prodded. "I get it. Will your mom come down south as well or is she going back west?"

"She'll go back to Nebraska. As long as Luke doesn't know where I am, I'll be safe."

"Have you thought he might check the local hospitals?

"Yes, the front desk and nurses' station has been alerted not to release my name."

"Have you thought he might go to Lizzie's, looking for you?"

"We're going to file a restraining order down there and hire a security guard, until I leave. Could I ask a favor of you, Dane?"

"Of course, anything."

"Before I'm released tomorrow morning, my family is moving my personal belongings out of my place. Thank God I rented it furnished. I don't have much. Could you keep Luca away from my home tomorrow morning? I don't want my family to have to interact with him."

"That's going to be tough. He doesn't want to see me. It ended badly when I confronted him about harming you. I'll see what I can do though."

"Thank you." She didn't disguise her anxiety well.

"How are you feeling, Cristin? About Luca."

"Frankly, I feel like a different person. Cynical, untrusting, frightened, fretful, disappointed, confused. Pick an emotion, any emotion, and I'm probably feeling it. It's all very perplexing, but most of all, I'm devastated that what I was certain was real is not. It will be long time before I trust again."

"I'm so sorry," Damien commiserated in words and smirked at his disguised duplicity. She was miserable. Poor little fucker. She had no idea what she was in store for. Moving away? Changing her name? Not able to trust again. Boo hoo. She'd never get that far.

"I'll be getting a new cell phone number, but I'll text Lizzie's cell number to you after I hang up, so you can be in touch with me through my sister for the time being. Thank you again for being such a good friend, Dane. I'll never forget you."

"Always. Would it be all right if I visited you in Carolina?" he asked.

"Of course. And don't worry about me. Eventually, I'll get over this. It hurts like hell but they say time is a healer. Bye."

"Bye." *Bam. Strike three. You're out.*

Damien walked to his window. The vendor below was closing shop. The frogs in the stream behind the apartment complex croaked. The world was going to sleep.

Damien smiled.

Three blind mice. Three blind mice. See how they run. See how they run.

CHAPTER FORTY

"Three things in human life are important: The first is to be kind. The second is to be kind. And the third is to be kind."
—Henry James

The day opened its curtain on the morning from hell. Already Damien had asked to see him. Luca knew he should never have opened the door to talking to him, but he was desperate to find Cristin. And maybe, just maybe, Damien had discovered some clue as to where she was.

He dressed and got into his car. It was raining. The gutters on his street, clogged with leaves and debris, backed up water into the middle of the boulevard. The grayness of the sky matched the limited visibility of both the road and his life. He recalled the quote by E.L. Doctorow that said something about writing being like driving at night in the fog. You only needed to see a few feet in front of you … Something like that. Whether it was true or not, it gave him hope. His immediate focus was to drive to Cristin's house to see if she was there. One step at a time.

He turned the corner and saw two parked cars outside her apartment building. One with a Massachusetts license plate. The other, a Virginia squad car. His heart thumped and sped up like an accelerator switch had flipped on inside him.

Luca parked his car, hitting the curb, and ran toward the police car. An officer stepped out and blocked the sidewalk. "May I help you?" he asked.

"Yes, I'm glad you're here. I was going to the police station this morning anyway to report a missing person."

"What are you doing here, sir?"

"This is my girlfriend's apartment building, and she hasn't been home for days. Is she in there? Is she all right?"

"What is your name sir? May I see some identification?"

Luca raised his voice in alarm. "My name is Luca Gherardini. Has something happened to Cristin McClaren?"

A second officer exited the car.

"Your identification please, sir," the officer demanded.

Luca fumbled for his international driver's license, trying to remain calm. His hand shook as he relinquished his license to the officer.

"Please. I am her boyfriend. I'm very worried about her."

Luca looked up at the bedroom window of the apartment and saw Lizzie and an older woman, looking down at him."

"Lizzie, Lizzie!" he shouted. "It's me. Luke! Is Cristin in there? Is she with you?"

The two faces defrosted from the window.

"Luca Gherardini, you are officially informed of a filed restraining order to stay away from Cristin McClaren."

Luca's mind started to spin. The cops looked distorted, one-dimensional. He shook his head in protest. "No. What? Why? I don't understand."

"You will be served today, and you can read what it means. I need you to leave the premises. Now, sir."

Luca moved his weight from one foot to the other, moving closer to the officers. His breathing accelerated, and the sound of his voice amplified. "But this is terrible mistake. Cristin would never forbid me from seeing her. I love her."

"Sir, step back. If she wishes to speak with you, she will call you. You cannot go inside this house."

"This is why you're here? To prevent me from entering her house?"

The officers stepped toward him.

"Let's not have any trouble. Please leave...now."

Luca looked up at the window. There were no longer two faces. He got in his car and drove home. Something was going on that made no sense.

He walked into his house, desperate to talk to someone sane, someone who was not a threat. Someone he could trust. Cristin wouldn't speak with him. He didn't want to speak to Damien. And Gabriel *wasn't* returning his calls. Who else did he have in the world? Then it hit him. Clement had said, *if you ever need a father to talk to, I will be there for you, I promise.*

He looked at his phone to check the time. It was early evening in Switzerland. Luca went to his study and pulled the inheritance folder from his file cabinet. Clement's name and home number was handwritten on the card appended to the inside cover. Luca walked to the refrigerator and opened a strong German beer. He then took a swig, sat down on his sofa, and called Mr. Germond, attorney-at-law.

Fiona answered.

"Mrs. Germond, this is Luca Gherardini. May I please speak to Mr. Germond, please?"

"Luca. What a surprise. Yes, let me get him for you. Just a minute."

Luca could hear muffled words exchanged in the background but couldn't decipher what was being said. The wait felt interminable. The conversation between husband and wife half way across the world was unintelligible and vexing. Why didn't he just take the receiver and talk? Luca heard Clement's footsteps approaching the phone.

"Hello, Luca. This is a surprise. Where are you, son?"

The choice of the word *son* was instantly comforting to Luca.

"Mr. Germond...," Luca began.

Clement interrupted. "Please, you may call me Clement, Luca. I sense this is a personal call, not a business call?"

"Yes, sir. It is. You once told me, Clement, that you would support me, that I could call on you if I needed advice."

"Yes, I did."

"I need your help."

"Go on."

"Damien Scardina found a letter from my mother in his home in Italy which he recently shared with me. The letter requested that I avenge Sofia's death by taking the life of another, a young girl in The States. This is going to sound twisted. Damien thought he was doing me a favor by finding the girl, and giving me the opportunity to kill her, in the name of my mother. He's very religious, or at least, his mother is. He started spouting off scripture, among which was *Honor Thy Mother*, as if he thought I should kill this innocent girl, to honor my mother."

"What have you done, Luca?"

"Nothing. I've done nothing, and I'm not going to. But the problem is complicated. Damien told me that his objective in laying this absurd ground work, was to win my heart. He claims he's in love with me. And believe me, no one could have seen this coming, but I fell in love with Cristin McClaren. Not only would I never injure or harm her, I'm in love with her, Clement. And this is the problem...Cristin is missing. Well, not actually missing. I discovered this morning, thank God, that she's alive. But she's filed a restraining order against me. Why would she not want to see me?"

"Luca, she's afraid of you. That is the primary, compelling reason to file a complaint of this nature."

"But why? She doesn't even know about the letter, or the fact that my mother was the woman her family hunted down years ago."

"Yes, she does," Clement said soberly.

"How could she possibly ...?" Then it hit him. "Damien?"

"Yes."

"But how? How do you know this and why would he tell her? I was never the danger to her. *He* is."

There was an agonizing silence at the end of the line that held secrets of its own.

"Luca, Damien has already spoken to Gabriel, and told a story, contrary to yours. A convincing one. It was so iron-clad, it was difficult not to believe."

"That explains why Gabriel is not answering my calls. I thought he was my friend."

"He is, Luca. We both are. But as I was saying …."

"Don't use the word but. It negates what you just said."

"All right. Considering your ability as a writer, your ability to concoct stories …."

"Wait a minute. Because I write fiction, I'm a liar? That's like saying because someone can act, they are always acting. That's colossally unfair."

"Let me continue, son."

His request was met with silence. Clement inferred, angry silence.

"Considering your background, your years in therapy, your mother's imbalance …."

"I won't listen to this. My mother's sins are not mine. I told you I worked through my abandonment issues. You think I'm crazy? Try Damien on for size. His access to mania and depression is through a constantly revolving door. Who knows where it will stop Happy/sad. Strong/weak. Funny/morose. Uplifting/terrifying. It's part of his charm. He's the one with the crazy mother, the crazy uncle. I'm as sane as you are, Mr. Germond, although I can't speak on your behalf, after listening to you judge me. I have called the wrong person."

"Luca…."

"Good night. Clement."

Luca hung up. His right leg pummeled the floor like an autonomous appendage with a mind of its own. His head reeled with the thought of the impending danger. He had to control his fury. He would find Cristin and explain. He'd have to. Her life depended on it. But how? He needed help. He could no longer count on Cristin, Damien, Lizzie, Gabriel or Clement. He was an island, alone and abandoned. Once again.

But he was also a survivor. Yes, he could still walk away from it all and start over somewhere he wasn't known, but he loved Cristin. He was still concerned for her safety. Damien was the key.

Darkness covered the streets like a heavy, lead blanket. The rain had come and gone like island weather all day, but cold and brooding, not tropical. He drove to Damien's home. *This* is what Damien wanted. To see him. He slammed on the breaks and bolted to the front door of the apartment building. He could see Damien's window from the street. Dark. He bounded up the stairs and pounded on his door. No answer. He pounded harder. No answer.

Finally a woman from a neighboring apartment came into the hallway.

"What's the problem?" she yelled.

"I need to talk to the man who lives here," he yelled back.

"He's not home. I saw him earlier. He looked like he was going on a trip. A duffle bag, you know, a cooler."

Luca stared at her without responding. The woman vaporized through her door.

Where had he gone? Where was Cristin?

Outside the apartment, alone and with no plan or direction, Luca stood next to his car. He heard a train whistle in the distance. He stared at the moonlight dancing in a puddle of water on the sidewalk, like a cosmic lightshow. How could he see beauty when his world was shattering?

He took his cell phone from his pocket and dialed the last person, the only person, he had left to turn to.

CHAPTER FORTY-ONE

"A man's conscience and his judgment is the same thing; and as the judgment, so also the conscience, may be erroneous."
—Thomas Hobbes

It was a bright morning in Lucerne. Clement looked out across the lake, beaded with silver sequins, reflecting light from millions of miles away. How could he explain its existence and have such difficulty processing Luca's phone call? One was scientific, the other involved a human being. Human interaction was a complicated amalgamation of choice, perception, character, or lack thereof, not an equation or a proof.

Where would he begin? Talking to Luca had been confusing to say the least. Either the boy was telling the truth, or he was a master of deception. Like his mother. Ordinarily, a circumstance such as this would not have been his business, but this *was* his business, ethically if nothing else.

When Clement became an attorney, scores of years ago, he'd never imagined such responsibility with an estate file. It was partially the reason he'd chosen this branch of the jurisprudence. Less stress. It had seemed straightforward, predictable, rather like an accountant's job. As long as he understood the intricacies of the law and carried out his clients' wishes, he was safe. No pressure, no hassle. But now, toward the end of his legal career, he was faced with an ethical issue of discovery. An innocent party's life was in peril. And as far as he could decipher, he was the only one who had the tools to ascertain who was more likely to be telling the truth, Damien or Luca.

I was never the danger to her; he was. He is. Those were Luca's words that now haunted Clement. What if Damien was the potential assailant? Could that possibly be true? And if Luca was right, it was unfair to infer that his mother's sins were his; that because his mother was a murderer, so was he. That was a theory Clement had laid to rest after talking to Luca's counselors. So why had he brought it up again? Apparently because he'd believed Damien's account of what was happening in America, without hearing Luca's side of the story. And why had he implied to Luca that just because Luca was a writer, it was easy for him to create a twisted fantasy and act on it? He'd insinuated that Luca was either a liar or a psychopath. That was a foolish non sequitur and utterly unfair to the boy. He may be an innocent party, as he claimed. *If he was telling the truth*.

Secondly, Luca's reference concerning Damien's mental stability had unnerved him. He had never considered that Damien may have had issues. Santino had shared his concern about Mariana's mental health problems on numerous occasions, but not once had he referred to Damien inheriting any disorder. Though once he *had* mentioned medication. And hadn't Gabriel referred to Damien's meds? Both times, the implications were shared in passing, and Clement disavowed any gravity or concern.

What he knew didn't brand Damien as emotionally disturbed. Clement had never had reason to talk to school counselors about the Scardina boy. And Damien's communication of concern to Gabriel seemed real and convincing. As if he'd been set up as pawn in Luca's design to kill Cristin. He may be an innocent party, as he claimed. *If he was telling the truth.*

Thirdly, no matter how he perceived it, Clement was about to compromise his friendship with one of his oldest friends, either Luca's father Rudolpho or Damien's father Santino. He'd never foreseen that he'd be in the position of judge. If the tables had been turned, he would have expected both of his old friends to watch out for Gabriel's well-being. Now, it appeared that Clement would not only need to discern which son was telling the truth, but take a stand. Exonerate one and condemn the other. But before he could balance the scale of justice, he had to accept the fact that he'd already alienated Luca by doubting him. Who else did the boy have to talk to?

When Clement looked out the window, a wind had stirred. The sequins that had sparkled so brightly had fallen off the fabric of the lake's surface, replaced with sapphire nubs of dark velvet. He needed to make a move, although not certain of his course. But inaction was a form of action, and although the most prudent form at times, this was not one of those times. He could smell it.

He went upstairs to change his clothes and informed Fiona that he was driving to the conservatory for a chat with Dr. Landis.

"The psychology department head?" she asked.

"Yes, dear."

"Have you made an appointment?"

"No, I can't take no for an answer. It will be easier for me to bully my way into her office if I'm there."

Clement appeared at the bottom of the stairs in his tweed suit and navy tie, Fiona's favorite. Just as he was about to leave, the phone rang. He barked, "I'm not home."

But before he could escape, Fiona had answered and said to the caller, "He was just about to leave but I'll catch him…Professor Walker."

"Clement, Emily Walker is on the phone."

Clement's agitated furrowed brow relaxed into a wide-eyed curiosity, as he turned to take the phone from his wife. The only time he'd had an interaction, intimate enough to receive a phone call at his home from Emily Walker, had regarded Luca.

Clement affected his most distinguished and gracious tone. "Hello, Emily. To what do I owe the pleasure of your call?"

"Clement, I think you can guess. I need to speak to you about Luca. I received a call from him a while ago, and he's distraught. He mentioned he'd spoken to you earlier, and that you are aware of the position he finds himself in. Could I meet with you right away?"

"Yes, of course. I was just on my way out the door, on my way to the school. Could I meet you there, in let's say, a half-hour, more or less?"

"That's excellent. Could you come to my office?"

"I'll see you there."

Clement hung up and turned to Fiona. "I don't know where this is going to lead, but I don't mind saying that I'll be relieved when this whole mess is cleaned up, off my plate, finished."

****

Clement sat across a desk from Emily Walker.

"Thank you for coming, Clement." She smoothed her skirt over her knees. "Would you care for a water, coffee, tea?"

"Water, please."

She reached into the cooler next to her desk and handed him a bottled water.

"Please, let me speak first," she said.

Clement nodded.

"I heard from Luca out of the blue today. I know, as instructors, we're not supposed to become close to our students, but you know that through the years, Luca has been an exception for me. He was an excellent pupil, a promising and gifted writer, and he needed someone to talk to. So I did take a special interest in him. I'm gratified, as a mentor, that he thought he could call me. Nevertheless, he is panicked that he's being set up by his former classmate, Damien Scardina, and when he called you, you didn't believe him."

Clement shuffled uncomfortably, readjusted himself in the chair. He heard his neck crack, and most likely, so did she.

"I do believe Luca, Clement, but *our* difference in opinion is not my concern. As was explained to me, he may take the fall for the death a young girl, but in his mind, that is secondary to the jeopardy she's not aware she's facing. He thinks Damien is dangerous, and Luca doesn't know where to turn. The police have issued a restraining order against him, not to come near the girl, which ties his hands to help her. And it suggests that he is already guilty of an offense, of which he has no knowledge. He believes that Damien is responsible for poisoning the girl's family against him, by turning some already extraordinary facts in his own favor. I don't know all of the details, but apparently, there is history between Luca's biological mother and the girl's family. And now there is a vendetta which Luca wishes to neutralize and rectify. But according to him, Damien may carry it out, as a retribution in honor of Luca's mother and as a punishment for Luca scorning Damien's amorous declaration. Clement, never in my wildest dreams, did I see this coming. But Luca needs our help."

Emily stopped talking and resumed smoothing her skirt.

Clement nodded once, took a long drink of water and a deep breath. He then communicated the story that Damien had shared with Gabriel.

"After hearing Damien's story, and considering Luca's background, I may have reached the wrong conclusion," Clement said. "What I haven't considered is Damien's history. I know very little about the lad, despite the fact that he was my friend's son. But at this point, I concur that Luca deserves the benefit of a doubt. When I received your call, I was on my way here, to meet with Greta Landis. Perhaps she can shed some light on Damien's integrity and his medical history. Do you have anything else we need to discuss?"

"Only one thing," she said, her face wrought with worry. "Time is critical. A girl's life may be at risk. And Luca's life, let us not forget Luca. He was already abandoned once, Clement."

Clement stepped back into the now windy day. Leaves swirled around his ankles. He pulverized their crunchiness beneath each step, like he had when he was a boy, but with more strength and less relish. He reached the office of Greta Landis to find three students, one girl and two boys, scheduled to see her. He looked at the first name on the list, explained to the receptionist that his visit was urgent, and took a seat among the waiting few. He watched the students, busy on their cell phones, interacting with God-knows-whom. Most certainly, not with each other. Adults weren't good role models, he'd decided. He'd watched adults do the same—play solitaire, check their Facebook accounts and text their friends instead of living in whatever waiting room they found themselves. People, in general, were losing touch with one another, because of their damned cell phones. It was *1984*, as predicted. A waiting room of soulless automatons.

He turned to the girl, the first on the waiting list, who looked like a lost sheep… with blonde bushy hair, a long nose, and a tiny mouth that promised a bleating sound if she opened it.

"Do you believe the change of weather?" he asked in a quiet voice, keeping his eye on the receptionist.

Bo Peep freed her eyes from her phone and looked at him, at a loss for words, as if he'd just transmuted into a wolf.

"It was beautiful this morning. Now it's cold and windy. I always say, if you don't like the weather in Lucerne, just stick around, it will change. The one certainty in life is change."

She said nothing, turning her back to signal that she didn't want to talk to an old geezer who couldn't mind his own business.

Clement smirked. Kids were great at body language, but he understood what he was doing, and persisted.

"Tell me, how many hours do you play that Candy Crunch game?" he whispered. "I've never understood why someone would waste his or her time playing an asinine game like that."

The young girl stood up, obviously frazzled, and because there was nowhere else to sit, she walked to the receptionist's desk and spoke in a muted voice. She turned, shot an evil eye toward Clement, and left the room. *No wonder she needed therapy*, he thought, not without guilt.

"Mr. Germond, you may go in now. We've had a cancellation," the receptionist announced.

Clement opened the door to what had earlier seemed an impenetrable sanctum and found Greta standing to greet him.

"What a surprise, Clement. I haven't seen you for over a year. To what do I owe this pleasure?"

"One guess."

"Luca Gherardini?" she asked. She looked frightened. Guilty, as if she'd released Luca into the world without caution, but with her blessing.

Clement sensed her crisis in conscience. "Luca Gherardini is part of equation, but no."

He heard her deep breath and took a seat as she motioned that he do so.

"Please tell me that he's doing well," she urged him. She coughed in her hanky as if expelling a bad memory.

"I'm here to discuss another former student. Damien Scardina."

"Clement, you know I cannot discuss students with you."

"No, I know no such thing. First of all, he is no longer a student. And secondly, you discussed Luca with me. So tell me, Dr. Landis, how does this work? How can I gain your confidence without compromising your position?"

"I need to hear the urgency of the matter. Let's start there. Let me get Damien's file."

"He has a file?"

"Yes, although I don't know how helpful it will be."

She walked to her file cabinet and pulled it out. Without opening it, she folded her hands, indicating that she was ready to listen.

Clement conveyed the two stories as he understood them, then paused to assess her reaction.

"So, if I am to construe this correctly, you are trying to determine if Damien Scardina is capable of this degree of manipulation and menace. Correct?"

"Correct. I need to know if he ever came to you because of any aberrations of behavior or sociopathic tendencies."

"Not exactly. But he was on medication that I monitored."

"What medication?"

"Let's say, that he was prone to mood swings. Depression and mania, if you understand me."

"He was on medication for a bipolar disorder."

"I can confirm that," she said reluctantly.

"So if he was off his meds, there could be behavioral complications?"

She nodded.

"I know his mother had a history of depression as well. And a proclivity to act out a religious fanaticism. You might not know that."

"Yes, I can confirm," she said.

"And there was an uncle, his mother's brother, who committed suicide."

"Yes I can confirm this as well."

"Is there anything that you can tell me, Dr. Landis, which might be a clue to understanding Damien's alleged behavior? The safety of an innocent girl is at stake."

"Well, Damien was named after his uncle. Let's see...." She read her file notes. "His uncle died a tragic death. Not that all suicides aren't tragic, but what my notes tell me is that he was probably schizophrenic. Very bright. His schizophrenic tendencies were not as easily diagnosed as they would be today."

She coughed again into her hanky, then paused. "Clement, he ended up taking his life after Damien exposed his sexual abuse."

"Of Damien?"

"Yes."

"How did he die?" Clement asked.

"He hanged himself. In a lighthouse."

CHAPTER FORTY-TWO

"There is a time for every activity under the heavens. A time to be born and a time to die."—Ecclesiastes 3:1-2

South Carolina was always there. Even though most people only saw it while visiting, it was always there. Always spread out with wetlands and salt marshes, bordered with sea oats and cattails; its air, thick with humidity and the smell of shrimp.

When Lizzie, Shane, and Cristin drove up the driveway to Ruby's home, Damien was sitting on the dock. He watched them talk among themselves in the car, probably voicing their surprise about his sudden appearance, perhaps wondering where his car was and how he'd accessed their property with the gate closed and locked. No one was waving.

Cristin exited the truck and started toward him, walking around the large patch of crushed grass that had obviously been an alligator's recent resting place.

"Dane, what are you doing here?" she asked.

"I won't stay long, I promise. I've just been so worried about you, Cristin. That's all. Now that I see you're safe, I just want to share what I know with you, and then I'll be on my way."

"Wait, slow down. I need to get the key from Lizzie. Let me get unpacked, and why don't you come up to the big house in half hour or so. We can sit on the porch and talk, okay?" she said.

"That's good. That's good. Privately."

She nodded and turned to leave, avoiding the alligator grass. She stopped at the guest house to get the key, and presumably, to explain to her sister that she wanted some private time with Dane. Lizzie nodded and waved to him, then disappeared behind the door.

He knew he'd taken a chance by appearing unexpectedly, but he couldn't wait any longer, for fear that Luca would somehow find Cristin there before he did. He stared at the yard of ferns and fungi. Cypress trees, pitted with woodpecker holes and rooted in rich, alluvial soil, bordered the south side of the canal. He wondered how long they would live. How long would the canal be there for that matter? Drought, hurricanes, or erosion could eventually erase even this canal from the coastline of South Carolina. Everything and everyone died. It was natural. Everyone was eventually swallowed by time. *Time is the avenger.*

Cristin called to him from the porch. He walked toward the house, stomping through the alligator bed on his way.

"It's good to see you, Dane," she said. She opened the screen door to invite him inside and gave him a hug. "This has been an appalling week. Luke doesn't know where I am, right?"

He adamantly shook his head. "No. He has no idea."

"I have so many questions."

With his back against the wall, Damien took a seat on the rattan chair overlooking the backyard so he could keep an eye on the guest house. There was a bucket with a couple of sodas and beer on ice at the end of the table, so he helped himself.

"Why don't you begin?" he said. He leaned forward. He didn't blink.

"No, please, I'm so tired. Tell me what you know first, and then what doesn't make sense, I'll ask you."

"First let me say, I feel so responsible for your meeting Luca in the first place. It's a long story, but in essence, it was a setup on his part for me to introduce you. I thought he'd found you on-line, and he was interested in you."

Damien told her the same story he'd told Gabriel, ending with how shocked he'd been to find the letter, how betrayed he'd felt to realize he'd been used, and how afraid he was for her safety when he couldn't find her.

"Okay, but changing his name doesn't make sense to me."

"He didn't know if you'd ever heard your family speak of Sofia's son, Luca Gherardini. He didn't want to tip you off. And by the way, since we're being perfectly honest, my name is Damien, not Dane. But you can still call me Dane. I prefer it."

"Okay," She drew out the last syllable as if holding on to a thought she couldn't let go. "He told me your real name. And he told me his real name, so he didn't conceal it from me, which doesn't add up. He wasn't afraid of me recognizing it, not that I would have anyway, because my mother never shared the whole story with us. And he told me that Americanizing his Italian name was your idea."

Luca wasn't supposed to divulge his name. What had he been thinking? Damien acknowledged a definitive hole in the narrative he was trying to sell. He'd have to table it and deal with it later.

"And another thing...if you thought I'd met him online, why all the cloak and dagger? Didn't you think it was odd that he didn't introduce himself as the person I'd met online?"

"He told me you didn't actually meet online. He'd *found* you online, and he wanted me to check you out first. A guy thing. I bought into it," said Damien.

"This is so convoluted," she said. "Until recently, I didn't even know about his mother terrorizing our family. And you do realize—the online deal? That was a fabrication."

"I realize it now. But Luca is an intricate storyteller. I think back to things he's told me, and I have no idea if they are true. It's upsetting to me too, Cristin," he said.

"So this whole affair has been a deception." She paused, regaining composure, steadying the shakiness in her voice. "But what doesn't make sense is if he wanted to hurt me, why did he pretend to fall in love with me?"

"One of his favorite sayings was *Keep your friends close and your enemies closer*. I never thought much about it. He was the writer. He thought differently. And maybe he figured that if he pretended to love you, he'd be close enough. You'd never see it coming."

"It?"

"Cristin, his mother, from her grave, sent him on a revenge mission. He was going to hurt you."

"Well, he's already done that. I'll never be the same. I can't imagine trusting another man after this experience. Except you, Dane. You've been an incredible friend to me."

She leaned forward and squeezed his hand.

"Cristin, you're not quite getting it. He is out to kill you."

Ashes, ashes. They all fall down.

Her mouth opened. She stared through the glass-topped coffee table, as if beneath the wooden floor planks below was a hidden tonic that would wipe her memory and take away the pain. Then she looked up, searching for comfort in Damien's eyes.

"I have been so miserable, agonizing about losing Luca's love, I didn't face what his motivation was, what he was willing to do. I can't imagine him ever hurting me."

"I am sorry to be telling you this, but you need to see it clearly in order to protect yourself. He never loved you, Cristin. His designs on you were methodically vindictive and vengeful."

She started crying. When he stood to sit next to her, she motioned him away, so he sat down. She looked like an injured bird, crossing her wings across her chest, unable to fly.

Eventually, he reached over to take her hands in his like a priest, comforting a confessor. He had her right where he wanted her and couldn't help but feel a deep self-satisfaction. When she lowered her head, he smirked.

"When you confronted him, what did he say he was going to do?" she asked.

Damien groped for a believable answer.

"This is so difficult to talk about. When he and I came to South Carolina, and you decided not to come? A most fortunate decision on your part, I might add. Do you recall how disappointed he was?"

"Of course. But you were the one who discouraged me from coming. He wanted me to make that trip, but I had final exams and then ended up in the hospital. This has all happened so quickly."

"Yes, he wanted you to make the trip. But instead, he was stuck with me. We took a side trip to an abandoned lighthouse. You know he was obsessed with Edgar Allan Poe. Poe's last unfinished work was called *The Lighthouse.* Luca had a fetish about lighthouses."

"I didn't know that," she said. "Remember? I had a dream about a lighthouse, but you were there, not Luca."

"Well, whatever." Damien glossed over the moment. He hadn't thought about Cristin's ESP interfering with his plans. "Anyway, we went to this lighthouse together. Innocuous enough. But what I didn't know is he'd put some rope and a footstool in the trunk of the car. I don't know if he ever told you, but we used to play a game in boarding school. It was a way to get high, cutting off oxygen to the brain and then quickly reviving the player."

Cristin stared at him in disbelief. "That sounds so sophomoric. And dangerous."

"Yes. So anyway, he had a tool to break the rusted lock so we could explore the interior. He always lived on the edge, so this didn't surprise me. Once inside, he tied a noose from the rafter. He placed the footstool and suggested we play the game again. I declined. If you weren't with someone you trust, you could hang yourself. It happened accidentally to a friend of ours, back in boarding school, who tried it alone. Anyway, days later, when we'd returned to Virginia and after I'd discovered the letter, I confronted him about his plan for you. He alluded to this place and how he could get you to play the game. It was premeditated and seemingly so harmless. A stupid schoolboy game."

"I don't believe you. And just for record, I never would have done it, Dane. How could he think I would have done something so reckless?"

"I agree, but a crazy person has crazy ideas. It wouldn't have mattered if you'd gone along with it or not. You would have been at a grave disadvantage. You trusted him, remember? And the good news is that his plan was foiled. It didn't happen."

"And why would he tell you this? You would have gone to the police and told them everything."

"He trusted me. I was his best friend, and he believed I'd be loyal to him."

"This all seems so implausible, so perverse." She nervously twisted the silver bracelets on her wrist. "How did he think he'd get away with it? My sister would have come looking for me. Then the police...."

"But initially, no one would think to look inside a remote, abandoned lighthouse. He'd already purchased an antique, rusty lock to replace the first."

"But the police would have questioned him if he was last seen with me," she said.

"You have to understand how he thinks, Cristin. Luca Gherardini is three things. He's a billionaire, he's smart, and he's devious. He probably already has an alias and corresponding passport. He has probably drained his mother's accounts and set up his own, naming his alias as a co-signatory. He was planning to disappear, to leave the country as soon as his mission was concluded. They wouldn't have found you for days, maybe weeks, and he'd be long gone. I guarantee you that whatever he has planned next, he has an escape plan as well. And I'm here to tell you, Cristin, you need to escape before he does."

"Why aren't we calling the police?"

"I first had to assure myself that you were safe, but I have every intention to contact the local authorities down here. The biggest problem is this is all conjecture. He hasn't done anything illegal yet."

"So we have to wait for him to find me, harm me, kill me, before the police will do anything? My mother said that this is exactly what his mother did, holding my family hostage for years. There was a statute of limitations, all sorts of nonsense. My mother's family couldn't have her arrested, even when they knew she was a murderer. I don't believe this."

"You don't believe me?" he asked.

"No, no. I believe you, Dane. I just don't believe the situation. Until last week, my life was so simple. What I'd do to have that life back."

When Cristin's stress appeared to reach its apex, Damien saw his opening.

"Let's take a ride to the lighthouse. You need to see it to believe it. Then together, we'll drive to the police station."

CHAPTER FORTY-THREE

"Many of us crucify ourselves between two thieves...regret for the past and fear for the future."—Fulton Oursler

"**M**rs. McClaren, are you alone?"

"Who is this?" Trina sounded startled.

"My apologies. This is Clement Germond, calling from Switzerland. Let me begin again. It's urgent that I speak with you. Do you have a few moments to talk?"

His words bit even himself. He could only imagine how he'd startled her. He heard her take a greedy breath.

"Yes, of course."

"Mrs. McClaren, are you with Cristin?"

"No. Why? She's in South Carolina with her sister."

Clement shook his head from side to side and braced himself to deliver the news.

"I am asking for your permission to tell Luca Gherardini where to find her."

"What?" She shrieked. "Why would you do this? Why would you want the man who wants to harm her know where she is? We're working on a plan to protect her, to change her name, so she can disappear, and be safe from him."

Clement continued with a solemn tone.

"I have spoken to Luca, which prompted a conference with his school counselors, Mrs. McClaren. Although the suggestion that Luca had set out to harm your daughter was circumstantially compelling, evidence is not proof. With the information Luca shared with me, I investigated a friend of his who could have been either an accomplice or the primary threat. Indications point to his being a threat to both Luca and Cristin. In truth, I believe that your daughter's danger doesn't lie in the person of Luca Gherardini, but in another young man. His name is Damien Scardina."

"Who is Damien Scardina?" Her voice was laced with terror.

"A schoolmate of Luca's. I don't want to get into the details, because time is of the essence. I'm emailing a photo of Damien to your phone. Can you continue to speak with me and look at this photo?"

"Yes." A torturous silence ensured.

She prompted her email.

"Nothing yet. I'll refresh the system. Just a minute ... here, it's coming." Her heart stuck in her throat as she clicked the icon to reveal the photo. She took in the face, the light hair, and the deep blue eyes. Eyes she recognized.

"Oh! Oh, no." Trina started to shake.

"What? What's the matter?" Clement asked.

"I know this man. His name isn't Damien."

"How do you know him?"

"I met him months ago, while walking my dog. He was from Europe somewhere, working for an insurance company, I think. His dog's name was Wolfgang. But his name wasn't Damien. It was, it was...Mario."

Clement thought for a moment before speaking, then asked the critical question.

"Did you discuss Cristin?"

There was a silence before Trina spoke. "I told him that I had two daughters, and yes, I told him their names." Then after a long pause, through a quavering voice, she said, "I told him where Cristin went to school."

"You need to call your daughters to make sure Damien is not near Cristin right now." Before Trina could react, he remembered something Gabriel had mentioned. "Oh, and Mrs. McClaren, your girls know Damien by the name Dane."

"Dane? Dane? He's their friend, and he knows where Cristin is. We trusted him. Cristin and Lizzie both trust him."

"You need to hang up right now and call your daughters. Damien mustn't be near Cristin. I believe *he* is the danger, not Luca. Call me when you've confirmed that Damien Scardina is not with your daughter. If I were you, I would contact the local authorities in South Carolina. Up to this point, Damien has schemed and lied, but not committed any crime. He has however voiced to Luca that he believes justice should be served in Sofia Gherardini's name, despite Luca refusing to honor her wishes."

"My daughter is innocent. She didn't even know the name Sophia Gherardini or that Luca was her son."

"And Mrs. McClaren, there's one more thing. You're not going to want to hear this, but I believe that Luca Gherardini truly loves your daughter. I think, if anyone can deter this Damien boy, it's Luca. I'll need your daughter's new cell phone number. The other isn't working. Do I have your blessing to tell him where your daughter is and give him her number?"

Clement could hear her aching reluctance from thousands of miles away as Trina McClaren acquiesced to entrusting her daughter's safety to the son of her sister's killer, on the word of the man hired to serve the interests of the killer, no less.

Clement, a man of law and experience, trusted his instinct and called Luca.

"I didn't think I'd be hearing from *you* again. You don't trust me, you don't believe me, so why do you want to talk with me?"

"Luca, I know where Cristin McClaren is. I...."

"Where?"

"South Carolina. At her sister's home."

Luca shook the steering wheel, then hit it with a fist.

"Good. I left Virginia hours ago, headed for South Carolina. Is Cristin safe? What has she been told? Does she know to stay away from Damien?" He raked his hand though his hair, feeling his nails graze his scalp.

"I don't know. That's why I'm calling. I've called her mother. She's aware that you are not the villain in this macabre ring of revenge. We believe Damien to be the threat."

"I hope we're not too late. I went to the police in Virginia this morning and told them my story. They couldn't help me, because I don't even know where either one of them is. I left for Carolina because I didn't know what else to do and thought she might be with her sister. I just couldn't bear waiting any longer. Do you have Cristin's new number? Has she been notified?"

"Yes, I just spoke to her mother and she's making the calls to her daughters now. They're both at Lizzie's home. They will notify the local police to pick Damien up for questioning if he shows up."

"I'll be there in less than an hour. I need to talk to Cristin. Can I speak to her mother? Do you have a number for her?"

"I'll text Cristin's number to you. Best not talk to the mother. I'll ask Mrs. McClaren to alert the police that if they find him first, to hold him so you can speak with him. You know him best. Call me when you've either talked Damien down or diffused the situation. Be careful, Luca."

"Thank you, Clement."

****

Luca called Cristin's cell number, but there was no answer. She wasn't picking up. Surely her family had been in touch with her. His mind wandered to how compelled Damien might be. He recalled when Damien had first told him about what his uncle had done to him. Although they hadn't talked about it in depth, Damien too had been abandoned in a sense. His parents hadn't believed him. Damien had balked at school counseling. After all, why would he open himself to be vulnerable, showing his soft underbelly, becoming exposed and defenseless to anyone? Luca had always admired Damien for protecting himself with an armor of silence on that count. A person couldn't be too careful, even with counselors and friends, prodding to "understand." Damien and he never spoke of his abuse again. Just that once. It had been a tacit bond between them.

His cell phone rang.

"Luke, this is Lizzie McClaren. I've talked to my mother. That man in Switzerland called her, and we need your help."

"I know. I'm on my way. Less than an hour out. Where is Cristin?"

"I don't know. We arrived earlier today and Dane was here. He'd parked outside the property line and climbed the fence. He was waiting for us on the dock. We thought he was our friend."

"Where is he?"

"That's just it. I went up to the big house to talk to Cristin, to get her away from Dane, and they weren't there. She just left a note saying they had gone for a drive and would be home within the hour. That was over two hours ago, Luke. I'm scared."

"Have you called the police?"

"Yes. We told them the make and color of the car. But as urgent as it is to us, I have the feeling it's not pressing to them."

"Is there anything he said that could give you a clue as to where they are?"

"No. We didn't speak. He just appeared, they talked up at the big house and took off. Maybe they're just on a long drive."

"I doubt it."

"Why? Why would he want to harm her? *His* mother didn't write that fucking letter."

"I'm so sorry, Lizzie, believe me. If I'd seen this coming, I would have tried to stop him earlier."

"I know. I mean, I don't know. I don't know so much. I only know bits and pieces. Someday, when this crisis is over, I'll need to know the whole story. For the first time in my life, I don't want to be Cristin. I'm terrified for her, Luke."

"I don't know if it will do any good, but please believe me, I am not the danger. I am not my mother's son."

"I know. I think. Just get here. If we can find them, maybe you can talk to him. Talk him off the ledge. Please, hurry."

Luca tried Cristin's phone again but there was no response. He left a text message.

Cristin, I'm on my way. If you are with Damien, do whatever it takes to stay safe until I can get there. Agree with him. Talk to him. Tell him he's right. Tell him you don't love me. Submit. Whatever it takes. If you read this, contact me, somehow. I need to know where you are. I love you.

He knew Damien had probably taken her phone or it was turned to vibrate. Or maybe it was still at the big house. She probably wouldn't see the text, but he had to try.

His phone buzzed. He looked down and read a text that said, *I have her. Honor thy mother.*

Luca felt a shiver that took its time undulating through his upper torso down through his legs. He picked up his phone again and talked into the microphone.

Damien, I love you. I should never have turned you away. I'm coming to you. Tell me where you are, and let me deal with the McClaren girl. You were right all along. Let me honor my mother. It was her only request of me. If you're with Cristin, keep her alive until I'm there.

He felt the chill of his most heinous lie settle in his solar plexus like a granite boulder. His phone buzzed again. He picked it up to read a message from Damien. *Nevermore. His shame was reproved within a beacon of light. Now it's her turn.*

Luca knew where they were.

CHAPTER FORTY-FOUR

"Even in the terrors of the night, there is a tendency toward grace that does not fail us."—Robert Goolrick

"It's a beautiful day," he said. "Let's park the car here in the shade so it stays cool, and we can hike to the lighthouse. We won't be long, but since we're trespassing, it's better to keep the car out of sight, don't you think?"

Cristin concurred. It was a beautiful day, a bit on the warm side. They lowered the windows to let the car fill with a breeze before their return. They walked through the tall weeds that were the perfect hiding place for insects and palmetto bugs.

"I hope we don't step on a snake," Cristin said.

"I have a first-aid kit in the car, just in case," Damien replied.

She shot him a frightened look and he laughed. "We'll be fine. Here, hold my hand."

As they approached the door that had at one time been sealed, she noticed the lock was gone.

"I thought you said he replaced the lock."

"No, I said he bought a lock but he must have forgotten to replace it."

Damien pushed in the door. There in the middle of the cool vacant floor of the lighthouse were a rope and a stool, just as he'd planted them hours before.

Cristin shuddered.

Damien shut the heavy door behind him and slammed a weighty metal bar in place. It was chilly inside. He reached into his pocket and entered a text, then moved the stool to the farthest point from the door against the cold stone wall. His time felt restricted.

"As you can see, I was telling the truth. There is a rope, a noose, if you will, and a stool. Just as I said."

She nodded. "I've seen enough. I want to go."

"Sit down for a minute, please." He smiled and invitingly motioned with his hands. "There's more to the story, and since we're alone and I don't want to share it with anyone else, we'll stay just a while longer, if that's all right with you."

She backed away from him and took a seat, as tentatively as a first-class passenger being demoted to coach, but not having a choice. Her eyes skittered from wall to wall.

"Did Luca ever tell you that my uncle molested me as a child?" he asked.

Blood drained from her face. She shook her head slowly, almost indecipherably.

"Luca is a good friend in that respect. Honorable. He guarded my secrets well. My uncle molested me, many times, actually. I told my parents, but they didn't believe me. I finally found my way to a police station when I was nine years old and told my tale of terror to the *polizia.* They brought me home and told my parents, who were forced to confront my uncle. They found him three days later. He'd hanged himself … in a lighthouse. You see, Cristin, since then, I've been fascinated by lighthouses. Not for their stately beauty, their utility, the light that guides seaworthy vessels, or the phallic symbol they suggest. I am fascinated with them, because it was within the walls of this architectural wonder that my uncle's shame was rebuked. Shame must be punished before it can be absolved. Shame must have an end. Shame must have its just death."

"Dane, you're scaring me. I want to go home." She reflected on the fearful feeling in her prescient dream. Why hadn't she listened to herself?

"It's not time yet. There are more things I need to share with you." He moved toward her and blocked her path to the door.

"You see, Cristin, the only thing worse than everyone knowing your story is no one knowing your story. I've told you my truth, but I haven't yet shared the whole truth and nothing but the truth to anyone, so help me God. The truth is that the whole lighthouse idea was mine. Luca has never been inside this lighthouse, although he was with me when I thought of it."

Cristin's eyes darted skittishly around the room. The door was barred and the stairs to the top were barricaded. There were no windows on the ground level.

He continued. "One more truth. He and I *did* play the rope game in school. He watched. I played. But that's where the truth as you know it, ends. The only reason I'm telling you this is that I think it's fitting that one person on this planet know to what extent I have gone to make my dream come true. And although my dream took an unfortunate detour, you are the lucky recipient of my story."

"Dane...."

"Shh...." He put his right index finger to his pursed lips, and then he licked and sucked it, pulling it out of his mouth with a popping sound.

"You see, I found the coveted letter last year in my home in Italy, beneath a large Persian rug in my father's office. I had been alerted by my mother that someone was looking for it—Clement Germond, that man from Switzerland who told you to beware of Luca? And in case you don't know, Clement is Gabriel's father, Luca's attorney, and Luca's father's dear longtime friend, God rest his soul. Anyway, Clement was looking for an important envelope regarding Luca's inheritance, which caught my attention. I was in love with Luca. I bet you didn't know that juicy bit of the story either. I decided to intercept it on his behalf. To help him. He was still in school, so I borrowed his passport and flew to Vancouver, where his mother had left instructions for him in a safe deposit box. It was a great inconvenience to myself, I might add. But I would do anything to help Luca.

"When I was in Vancouver, I actually masqueraded as Luca, and it was quite appealing. It was there that I created a backup plan to have another identity, if I ever needed one. You should have seen me. I changed my hair color, styled it like Luca's, and bought brown-tinted contacts. It was a lark. When I finally fooled the guard and had the safe deposit box in front of me, well, what to my surprise...I found the names and addresses of your dear family members who had made Luca's mother Sofia's life a living hell. The instructions were specific and unequivocal. You were the target of her revenge, and it was the only thing she ever asked of her son, albeit posthumously. Also in the safe deposit box was in excess of a million dollars, which Luca doesn't know about. It's now waiting for me in a box at the Bank of America in Charlottetown. God bless America." He dangled the key that hung around his neck. "I planned to lavish it on him in our life together, but he's destroyed that dream. Now, I will enjoy it alone."

Cristin started to cough, as if she were choking, writhing, struggling to breathe. He stared at her as she convulsed.

"Please," he said. "You can't manipulate me. This is fucking amusing. If you choke to death on your own, it makes my job so much easier. I'd rather enjoy the poetic justice, actually."

Cristin stopped coughing, paralyzed at his last statement.

Damien continued, as if he hadn't missed a beat. "Discovering that you, Cristin McClaren, were the namesake of a woman named Cristin Shanihan, I went to Nebraska, and using a different name and creatively contriving a circumstance, I met your mother who told me where to find you."

"My mother? Dane, please let me go. I don't want to hear any more. You're really scaring me. I want to go back."

"Not yet!" he barked. He lowered his voice. "There's more to the story." He took a deep breath and shook his head at her.

"You and I both know that Luca never met you online and had never heard of you until I introduced you. I thought that if he met you, it would be easier for him to get close to you. After all, a high percentage of people are killed by people they know, not by strangers. I always found that fact fascinating. All was going reasonably well until the night we returned from South Carolina. When I disclosed what I'd done for him because I loved him, he turned on me. He was in love with you, not me, and had no intention of harming you, despite the fact that his mother demanded it. *Honor thy Mother.* That's what my mother taught me."

He turned sideways to check a message on his phone. "Oh, look, Luca sent me a text. Excuse me. I need to reply."

This was her only chance. While his eyes were momentarily averted to his phone, she bolted to the door and dislodged the bar that locked them in. He grabbed her before she could open the door. The strength of his grasp clamped into her arms like an eagle's talon. She screamed.

"Shut up! And don't do that again! Do you want me to end this right now? I *will.* But I'd rather tell you my story."

He dragged her back to the stool as she whimpered.

"Let's go back to our dilemma. You see, Cristin. I love Luca but Luca loves you. That presents a problem. So he must now be punished. *And all the king's horses and all the king's men couldn't put Luca together again.* All Luca had to do was dispose of you to right the wrong done to his mother. Justice was required. Anyone could see that. Oh, but imagine my surprise when it came out that your dearly departed grandmother was the one who snuffed out Sofia. Full circle. Tit for tat. *An eye for an eye...*for an eye."

Damien walked toward her, circled her chair, all the while watching Cristin's expression that fed his greedy appetite to terrorize her. This is what dreams were made of.

"Now we're going to play a little game. *Fe, fi, fo, fum.* Just like Luca and I did. Except fair Cristin, you're not going to revive. And that's how this chain of events will resolve. Luca will lose the love of his life, as I did. You will lose your right to live, as your grandmother set in motion, and voila! Sofia Gherardini's life will be avenged."

"And you think you'll get away with this?" Cristin yelled. She needed to stall, to distract him somehow, so she had one more shot at the door. He hadn't resecured the bar.

"Of course I'll get *away* with it. Like I said, no one will think to look inside an isolated, abandoned, inaccessible building like this.

I bought the replacement lock, not Luca. It's really quite a find—rusty, antique, if you will, looks like the original. After I'm done with you, I will merely lock the heavy door behind me and drive away with all that money and leaving no clues. No one will ever hear of Damien Scardina again."

Cristin started to cry but through her terror, she spoke.

"Dane, Damien, please listen to me. I'm truly sorry about what happened to you as a child. I'm sorry Luca couldn't return your love. But you will love again, I promise. If it makes you feel any better, you should know that I can't be with Luca now. There's too much bad blood. I couldn't live with the history of his mother. I couldn't sentence my family to a lifetime of having to face him. Now that all of this has come out, we could never truly love each other. Now you and I have something in common, Dane...we've both lost Luca."

Damien turned his back and slammed his fist against the barred door.

Cristin continued. "I could never marry Sofia Gherardini's son. And now that he knows what my grandmother did, he won't want me either. He may think he does, but he won't be able to look at me. I agree with you. We shouldn't be together, and I promise we will not. So don't punish Luca by killing me. Don't punish him for anything. He can't help how he is any more than you or I can. Just let me go. I won't ever bother you again. You could live your life with a clear conscience. Start your life over. He doesn't need the money you took. As long as no one is hurt."

Damien interrupted. "You're living in a dream world, bitch. We may both have lost Luca, but Sofia didn't deserve to die."

"But she did. And I bet you don't know this part. Let me tell you what his mother did to our family."

"I don't need to know."

"I think you do. I owe you the truth, just like you owed me. Luca's mother killed my Aunt Cristin and her own parents in a fire, and assumed my aunt's identity. She killed my Aunt Tia's best friend Yvette to assume her identity. She killed my mother's nephew Shep and his pilot for money. She married Luca's father to escape her past. And then, she killed Luca's father and Luca's brother, Nico."

Damien hit his head with his fists in frustration. "No, she didn't kill Rudolpho. His father was a good friend of my father. Why are you saying this?"

"Because it's true. My mother shared the whole story in the hospital. I knew none of it before then, I swear. And when my family hunted Sofia down in Vancouver, she knew they were on to her. She had taken Luca's father's fortune and was on the run. She knew she was in trouble, she wrote that letter and put it in the bank box in case she was caught. It makes perfect sense. But when Sofia felt trapped and started to stalk and terrorize my family, we stopped. Someone else was going to die. My grandmother was wrong to kill, but she was right to protect her family. Sofia Gherardini was evil, Damien. You don't have to avenge an evil person's death. God would not want you to do this."

"It's too late. Vengeance is mine," yelled Damien.

"That's not what the Bible says. It says, *Vengeance is mine, sayeth the Lord.* It's not your right to take another life. We are not the final judge, Damien. Your God, my God is. And our God is giving you an opportunity to do the right thing. Please, Damien, let me go. Go live your life. Find someone who loves you. Luca and I will go our separate ways, I promise you."

"*Blessed are those who act justly, who always do what is right.* Stand up!" he shouted.

She didn't move.

"Stand up!" He lunged at her with fury in his eyes and gripped her arm, pulling her off the stool. With his other hand, he grabbed the stool and scraped it across the floor, positioning it under the noose.

She screamed and struggled to free herself from his hold.

A blast of air filled the room. There, standing at the door, was Luca.

"Damien, please," he shouted. "Let her go. I will stay. You and I will talk this through. But you must let her go."

"You wouldn't believe what she said about your mother, Luca. She has blasphemed your mother and her memory. She has to be stopped." His intensity had morphed into a suppliant voice, pleading for understanding.

"Let her go, my love, and I will listen to everything you say. I won't leave you here. And if you are right, she is mine to contend with, not yours. Remember, that's the way you wanted it to be. I should have listened to you. I was wrong. I am here, and this is where I want to be."

"No, Luca, you can end this right here, right now. This is your chance. She's standing right here. I will help you."

"Damien. I don't care about her. I care about you, and I'm not willing to start our lives together with this on my conscience. Let her go."

Damien released his grip on Cristin. She ran out the door like a released prisoner, afraid of being shot in the back.

Luca walked up to his friend and held him. They both heard the car drive away. Damien began to sob and held Luca like he'd always wanted to hold him. For the first time in his life, he felt safe. When they broke the embrace, Luca kissed him.

"This is all I wanted. All I ever wanted," Damien said. His eyes welled with tears, and his face softened with gratitude. "But Luca, she said some horrible things. She said your mother killed Rudolpho and Nico, murdered your father and brother, all for money."

Damien watched his friend swallow hard. A tear ran down Luca's cheek.

"I'm afraid it's true. I just learned the story from Clement. My mother was not a good person. May she rest in peace. But my mother's life was not worth avenging, Damien. We must both accept that."

"Cristin said she can never be with you because of the damage your families have done to each other. She could never ask her family to accept you. She says it's over."

"It is, Damien. She's right. We haven't talked, but we're not reckless people. First, I need to prove to you how much I love and trust you. Damien. We are right together. I trust you with my life. I'll prove it to you."

He put his hands on the stool.

"Remember how I was afraid to play the game? Well, here we are. Just the two of us. Let's play our game to prove our trust, our love. I'll go first."

Luca picked up the stool and placed it under the noose. "After we prove our trust to each other, we'll leave together. All right?"

Damien took a deep breath and frantically nodded, "Yes, yes. I'm so happy. I didn't think you loved me." His eyes were wide with incredulous joy and relief.

"I do."

Luca climbed on the stool, put the noose around his neck and kicked the stool from beneath him. He hung without resistance until he motioned that he needed Damien's help. Damien responded and replaced the stool, helping him down.

"So that's how it feels," Luca said euphorically. "I love you." In tears, Luca embraced him, not letting go.

The world was good after all, Damien thought. Maybe Cristin had been right. He was not the judge. He was a simple man who wanted to be loved, to feel safe, and to know that his life was valued. Luca was his partner, and now, it was his turn to prove to Luca that he trusted him, as Luca had just done for him.

He stood on the stool, put the rope around his neck and kicked away his lifeline. Before he lost his breath, he smiled at Luca and said, "I love you."

CHAPTER FORTY-FIVE

"Do not go...But if you must, take my soul with you."—Rumi

The sun had set by the time Cristin returned with the police. A line of squad cars with sirens and lights, loud and imposing, indicated to people for miles, that something big was going down. Luca watched their approach from outside the lighthouse with his hands in the air. The lights were blinding. As soon as the first car stopped, he was ordered through a megaphone to lie down on the ground, on his stomach, with arms and legs outstretched. He complied.

An officer asked what happened. All Luca could say was, "He's in there. He hanged himself."

There were headlights and flashlights and floodlights everywhere. He heard Cristin in the background wailing his name. He looked up and saw an officer restraining her from coming forward.

"I'm all right Cristin!" he yelled. "Do what they tell you."

One of the officers, who had gone into the lighthouse came out and asked Luca to stand. He frisked him and pulled a pocketknife from Luca's jeans.

"I always carry a pocketknife. It is my bottle opener and nail file, too."

"Show us some identification, sir."

Luca pulled out his driver's license.

"This is an international license, Mr. Gherardini."

"Yes, sir," he replied, and corrected the mispronunciation of his surname. "Don't you want to ask me what happened here tonight?"

"I think you should have an attorney present, Mr. Gherardini." The officer mispronounced it yet again.

"I don't need an attorney. My friend hanged himself!"

"Hung himself?"

"No, hanged himself."

"And you watched him hang himself?" the officer asked.

"No, of course not. If I'd known he would do it, I would have stopped him. He was my friend."

Luca clenched his teeth and fought back his tears, panting like a caged lion.

"So where were you when this happened?"

Luca took a breath to compose himself.

"After we talked, he asked for time to himself and asked me to step outside which I did. I didn't think he was going to kill himself!"

"Why was there a rope, a noose, in the lighthouse?"

"My girlfriend will corroborate everything. Can I see her?"

"Not right now. Why didn't you call the police?"

"Because I thought I could talk him down from hurting my girlfriend. Maybe I was wrong. I thought I was doing the right thing. Can you cut me some slack?"

"You should have called the police. You were trespassing, by the way."

"I was trying to save the woman I love! I didn't fucking care whether I was trespassing. Don't you get it? My friend just killed himself!"

"Come with me," said the officer. "I'm going to cuff you and we're taking you to the station."

Luca watched Cristin watch him be handcuffed. She sat in a separate police car with her hands over her heart. She'd been crying, enraged not to be able to talk to him.

It suddenly occurred to him that she didn't know about Damien yet. He sat in the back in the police car, in the dark, lights still rotating on top of the vehicle. He watched a gurney carried into the lighthouse. Then he broke down and cried.

****

Luca crossed the border from South to North Carolina, and his mouth no longer watered for red beans and rice, catfish chowder and fried okra. He no longer longed for a breeze filled with the intoxicating scents of magnolias and shellfish. He didn't ever want to hear docks on the water moaning like cellos again. Or see a grove of eucalyptus swaying under the celestial conductor's baton. Pat Conroy was an author who had fed him with beauty, but now he'd rather starve. The chapter of South Carolina was closed.

It had been a grueling interrogation. Before he could see Cristin, he'd answered exhaustive questions for two days straight. The police had taken as evidence, a safe deposit key from around Damien's neck. It led them to a box with an excess of a million dollars which validated Damien's confession to Cristin, concerning his manic obsession with Luca and the misguided degree to which he was willing to go to impress the man he loved. Also found in the box were the passports of both Sofia Gherardini and Madison Thomas, proving that they were indeed the same person. And a small Bible, in which Damien had highlighted the words that supported his manic Biblical mantra of honoring thy mother. The safe deposit box was damning, and with Cristin's confirmation of facts, Luca was released. It was ruled as death by hanging. A tragic end to a brilliant young mind, damaged by life, deprived of love, and ultimately, depraved by some form of insanity.

When Luca briefly talked to Cristin at the police station, they agreed to meet at a restaurant in Charleston. She would drive with her sister, and her mother was flying in from Nebraska.

He used the drive time to his benefit, to decompress and think about his next move. The person who had expedited his finding of Cristin was Clement Germond. Clement deserved a call.

"Clement, this is Luca. I'm calling to tell you that Cristin McClaren is safe."

"Thank God. Fiona, the girl is safe!" he yelled to his wife. "Luca, thank you. Fiona and I have been fraught. What about Damien? Is he all right?"

"No. He is not. Damien took his life three days ago."

"Oh."

Luca listened to a protracted silence and surveyed a litany of things he could say; explanations, a schedule of happenings, memories. He decided to remain silent.

"How and where did it happen?" Clement asked.

"He hanged himself in a lighthouse in Beaufort, South Carolina." The words bit him.

"Just like his uncle. But far away from home. Lost souls, they were." Clement's voice faded as he spoke. "How did you know where to find them, son?"

"Through a text from Damien with a remark he once made concerning his uncle and a reference to Edgar Allan Poe. It's complicated. Clement, when I found him, he had Cristin, and I am certain that if you'd not trusted me with his whereabouts, I would not have made it in time. Thank you. You saved her life, and I promise you, it is a life worth saving."

"So you do truly love the girl, Luca?"

"I do. But I'm afraid it won't have a happy ending. I think it's now a forbidden love. Too much bad blood. We're meeting in Charleston tonight, in the presence of her mother and sister, to make plans for the future. Most likely separate plans."

"I'm sorry to hear that, son."

For the second time, the word son sounded comforting, and he felt love for Gabriel's father. Love and gratitude and indebtedness.

"Has anyone notified Mariana?" Clement asked.

"Not to my knowledge. Would you mind?"

"I'll take care of it. Does Gabriel know?"

"No. Will...?"

"Done."

Luca felt relief wash over him like a magic wand. It was over. Cristin was safe. Damien was no longer a threat. Clement respected him.

"We'll talk soon, Thank you Clement." He hung up, and once again, he was alone.

By the time he hit the outskirts of Charleston, Luca had heard from Cristin three times. Twice, just to hear his voice; and once, to let him know that she had been pregnant, but had lost the baby in the hospital. It was not something she wished to talk about in front of her family, and she hadn't had the chance to speak with him since her hospitalization. She kept thanking him for saving her life, over and over again.

They agreed to meet at seven p.m., but in a public place of her choosing—a small, quiet Italian restaurant, where they would have little interruption and relative privacy. Her mother did not want her to be alone with him. He was Sofia Gherardini's son, and nothing, not even saving her life, would change that fact.

He arrived early and asked to be seated at a table for four. Cristin, Lizzie, and Trina would join him. The air smelled of garlic and tomatoes and sadness. At the appointed hour, the family walked in together, Cristin first. She ran to him and hugged him. He kissed her neck and filled his soul with what would soon be the memory of her smell, her embrace, her love. When she pulled away, he could see the gratitude and sorrow in her beautiful eyes, the color of jade. Lizzie followed Cristin. She whispered in his ear, "Thank you. Thank you. Thank you." When she pulled away, he could see the gratitude and sorrow in her beautiful eyes, the color of coffee.

Cristin then made the introduction.

"Luca, this is my mother, Trina."

Trina nodded and stared through cold, unaccepting eyes, the color of steel. When they took their seats, Luca was flanked by the sisters, while Trina sat across from him. The camps were divided.

Luca began speaking. "Mrs. McClaren, I am sorry to meet you under these circumstances. I imagine this is difficult for you. You have hated my mother for longer than I've been alive, and I understand why. After her death, I don't think you ever imagined that you would meet me, or that I would have caused you more suffering. Let me say, that from what Mr. Vingiano, Cristin, and Clement have told me, I think I have pieced together the puzzle of your nightmare. I want to break it into pieces and set it on fire. I assure you that although I am Sofia's son, I am also my father's son, and he was a good man. I will never do your daughter or anyone in your family harm. On the contrary, if I can ever help you, I will."

Trina composed herself. She leaned forward and clasped her hands on the table.

"Luca Gherardini, the only reason I'm here is to thank you for coming to Cristin's rescue. That's all. I hope that you have the decency to go back to Europe, far away, without incident."

Cristin squeezed his hand under the table, and Lizzie pressed against him in silent support, without openly defying their mother.

"I understand," said Luca. "Cristin and I haven't had time to talk, but I think we both see the situation clearly enough to know that it's the right thing to do. The bad blood between these families ends here."

"That's all I need to hear," said Trina. "Lizzie, there is another table by the window. I'll sit there for dinner. I suggest you join me so Cristin and Luca can talk privately."

Lizzie shot a glance at Cristin who tearfully nodded in compliance. The duo stood and tacitly excused themselves.

"Mom," Cristin said, "thank you. And Mom, please ask the waiter to leave us alone. We won't be eating but we'll tip him well."

She turned to Luca when her mother was out of hearing range. "She's right, you know. As much as it breaks my heart, she's right."

"I know. I love you, Cristin McClaren. I want you to always know that. The thought of losing you, due to a family vendetta about which neither of us even knew until recently, is so wrong. We never had a chance."

"I know. Maybe with time, we can find each other again. Time is healing. You told me that once."

"Not for your mother. I can see it in her eyes, the way her mouth is rigid and set, her body language. She will never forgive my mother or me by association. And I understand. Life isn't fair. I've had time to process what your grandmother did, and I understand that too. When you fiercely love someone, you will bend the rules to protect them; you will do whatever it takes to protect her."

Cristin's eyes welled with tears. "Luca, I have to ask you something." She stopped speaking to compose herself. "How did Damien die?"

He looked at her directly and said, "He hanged. He was a tormented soul, unable to free himself from his own demons. He was also a dangerous man. But you will never have to be afraid of him again, my darling." He choked back the lump in this throat. "Damien truly loved me, you know. I loved him, too, in a different way. He was my faithful friend, as damaged and warped as he was. What he did came from loyalty. The universe works in mysterious ways. You heard what I told the police, and that's all I have to say. Damien Scardina hanged himself."

Cristin shook her head, paused, and then nodded. With tears burning her cheeks, she leaned herself against his strong shoulder. He put his arm around her to comfort her, to feel his Cristin next to him one last time, and whispered, "I will always love you."

They sat quietly...for an imagined eternity.

Trisha St. Andrews

CHAPTER FORTY-SIX

"An unexamined life is not worth living."—Socrates

THREE YEARS LATER

In dead of winter, Clement Germond sat in his study, overlooking Lake Lucerne. The ice was gray and thick. A winter storm seemed to be brooding in the northwest, providing a backdrop of foreboding. Fiona had stoked the fire in the stone fireplace. The wood blend of orange and eucalyptus crackled, and its primeval scent and radiant heat warmed the room. She'd brought him a pastrami sandwich on rye and a hot cup of Mandarin green tea. He was blessed.

He opened the Gherardini file. There was much work to do.

He thought about Luca. The boy's abandonment by his wretched mother and callous, self-centered half-brother. Luca's father Rudolpho had died too young, and his death set off a sequence of events that had proven tragic. Clement recalled the day of Rudolpho's funeral and his own part in triggering Sofia's flight from Italy. He had told her that some American women were looking for her, naively thinking that Sofia would have wanted to see them. He remembered the look on her face, the panic that he translated as anxiety of the day, but which had actually been terror that she was about to be exposed. Her sudden departure from the reception was a precursor of her permanent disappearance the following morning, never to return. Now he understood that she'd thought she was safe from discovery by marrying Rudolpho and changing her name. But Clement had alerted her to the fact that the Americans knew she was alive and were on the hunt. If only he hadn't shared that information, the Americans would have found her, and Rudolpho's death could have been proven a murder. The precipitating cycle of death could have ended there. If only he had said nothing.

He thought about Luca as a student at the conservatory, how he had acted out and even been a suspect in the death of young Harold Brockmeyer. By that time, Clement had opened the threatening letter that indicated that Sofia wanted revenge on the Americans. But the second letter explicitly naming them and their locations, had been at large for years. In good conscience, Clement had figured that if he never told Luca about the first letter on his eighteenth birthday, Luca wouldn't know that the second letter existed. Only Fiona and Mariana Scardina knew about the missing letter. Now, years later, Clement knew that Damien had found it and acted on it. How was Clement to know that this bright young son of his friend and associate Santino, was bi-polar, abused, and in love with Luca? If he'd known those facts, he would have told no one. If he hadn't alerted Mariana about the missing letter, Damien would never have searched for it. If only he had said nothing.

Hardest to face, however, was his response when Luca had turned to him in despair. When Damien had presented his demented assembly of untruths to Gabriel, the story appeared seamless and believable. Clement had let Luca down, reverting to his original belief that Luca was damaged. Because despite the privilege and fortune, Luca was still his mother's son. Where was the sense of justice in that judgment? That was the judgment that disgraced him the most. If only he had given Luca the benefit of a doubt.

Since that time, he'd learned so much more that had transpired. According to Cristin's account of Damien's confession which correlated to Gabriel's conviction that Damien had been in

Vancouver, it became clear that Damien had stolen Luca's passport to set the stage for his personal agenda.

In recent years, Clement had the chance to piece together the complex puzzle. Fragments with jagged edges from Vingiano, Gabriel, the psychiatrist, the professor, Trina, and Luca. Everything he learned, he shared with Luca until there was nothing else to give him but love and support.

He knew that Luca had promised Trina McClaren to not have contact with her daughter. But Luca loved her so, he and Cristin had been in touch. Gabriel and Cristin's friend Flora had facilitated two secret meetings, to which Clement was privy. Clement didn't have it in his heart to judge them.

And now he needed to make the call.

Fiona entered the room with a pot of tea to refresh his cup.

"There's a storm approaching. I'm glad we aren't going out tonight," she said.

"Fiona, would you mind staying for a few minutes?" he asked. "I need to make the call, and I'd feel better if I were not alone."

"Of course, dear." She poured a cup of freshly steeped tea and took a place on the settee across from his desk.

He picked up his cell phone, dialed a number, and waited for the connection.

"Hello, is this Trina McClaren?"

"Yes. Who is this, please?"

"This is Clement Germond, calling from Switzerland. Do you have a moment?" He glanced at Fiona and took a deep and strenuous breath.

"Clement. It's been a long time."

"I have tried a few times to reach your daughter Cristin directly but haven't connected with her so I'm resorting to call you. Can you relay a message for me?"

"What is it?"

"I am calling to inform you of Luca Gherardini's death."

There was no comment.

"Luca will never be a threat to you, even in your minds, and that fact might give you comfort. I grew to love the boy as a son, and I know he loved your daughter." Clement's voice cracked. "How is Cristin?"

"She's had a tough time, Clement. I think she truly loved Luca, but it wasn't meant to be. She told me that she wrote to him. Not knowing where he was, she sent a letter to your son in Spain, I believe. She wanted Luca to know that she was ill, that her kidney was failing her, and they wouldn't have had a long life together, as it was. She never heard back from him, to my knowledge."

Clement swallowed hard. So that was the storyline. The McClarens didn't know that Luca and Cristin had been in contact.

"How is she now?" Clement asked.

"She'll be fine. She's recovering from a transplant that, if successful, will have saved her life."

"A transplant?" he reiterated, glancing at Fiona.

"Yes, from an anonymous donor, God bless his or her soul."

Clement hesitated before continuing. He looked at Fiona with distress and placed his elbow on the desk. His suddenly heavy head fell into his hand to brace himself while he attempted to swallow his emotion.

"I'm happy to hear that she is fine." He continued, but his voice trembled. "Please give her our regards. I regret we never met, and probably never will, but I know that you are a good woman with a good family, and I am sorry for the heartache you have endured over the past twenty years. May your lives from this day forward be blessed with good fortune. Quite literally, Mrs. McClaren. Your daughter Cristin is named as Luca's primary beneficiary. He has left the bulk of his fortune to her. She is a very wealthy woman."

"Pardon me? What did you say?"

"You heard correctly. Please give her my number. I'll be in touch with her when the estate is settled. He truly loved her, Mrs. McClaren."

Clement began to quietly cry. He surrendered to the tenderness of his spirit that melted his strength

"I will tell Cristin the news. Clement, I can hear in your voice that you loved the boy. May I ask one more question?"

"Of course," he said, covering his mouth to disguise the sound of his sadness.

"How did he die?"

"Complications from a surgery," he answered tearfully through a mere yarn of his voice.

With that said, he hung up.

That night, as he lay in their bed, Clement held Fiona closely and thought not about the evil of Sofia, or the damaged soul of Damien, but about the goodness of one man. He'd thought that Luca, at one point, was on a path of retribution. It turned out to be one of redemption.

Then once again, in the privacy of his heart, mind, and soul, he acknowledged his unwitting accountability in a series of events that had spun out of control and resulted in the deaths of two young men. It would haunt him for the rest of his life. As he drifted to sleep, he heard an owl in the distance and whispered to himself,

"If only I hadn't opened the letter."

ACKNOWLEDGEMENTS

A special thanks to my editor, Scott Morgan, who reined me in to teach me more than I could have learned by earning another college degree; to Amber Jerome-Norrgard for formatting my manuscript with patience and conscientious expertise; to the artistic talent of JT Lindroos who has designed each of my covers in this trilogy; and to John Mayben and Ben Andy Hein for their guidance.

Thank you to each person whose support has created a readership base that I'm truly grateful to have. There are too many of you to name, but a special thanks to my husband Rich, Beverly Wallace, Brigitte Archer, Donna Moore, Heather Haith, Heidi Wiessner, Jackie Harman, Jane Grivna, Janine Mazenc, Joan Halvajian, Kathy Newman, Liz Weatherhead, Phyllis Amdurer, Phyllis Anderson, Sandy Hames, Shari Rotherham, Tera Freese, Terese Walton, Tracey Reimann, Val Scardina, and my wonderful Minnesota family. A shout out for the support from my three book clubs—The Classics Book Club of Coto de Caza, Diane's Book Club (in honor of our friend Diane Bettencourt who died from breast cancer in 2001,) and the Bad Ass PV Book Club On The Hill.

I hope you've enjoyed reading *The Soul of an Owl* as much as I've enjoyed writing it, and rewriting it, and rewriting it (that was for my editor's benefit.) Please share my stories with your friends and your book clubs, and visit me at www.trishastandrews.com where you'll find reading guide questions and an opportunity to give me your feedback which I value.

I hope my words provide you with pleasure, entertainment, memorable characters, compelling stories, evocative descriptions and ideas. That is my mission. You are a reader and I write for you. Now that the trilogy is finished, on to the next story!

Namaste.

Trisha

ABOUT THE AUTHOR

Born in Canada, raised in Minnesota, Trisha currently lives in southern California, with her husband, near her three married sons and families. She graduated with honors from the University of Minnesota with a degree in the humanities and history.

This is the final book of her Heart/Mind/Soul trilogy which completes a story that spans over twenty years in the lives of her characters.

WHERE TO FIND TRISHA ST. ANDREWS:

www.trishastandrews.com

www.facebook.com/trishastandrews

www.twitter.com/trishastandrews

trishastandrews912@gmail.com

BOOKS BY TRISHA ST. ANDREWS

The Heart of a Lynx
The Mind of a Spider
The Soul of an Owl

Made in the USA
Middletown, DE
21 August 2018